Butterfly on Bangla

Anthony Cameron was born in Melbourne, Australia. He escaped in his early twenties to central Victoria years before the big 'tree change'. He designed and built a sustainable house, and raised two sustainable children.

Anthony worked for twenty years in the performing arts world as a sound engineer, lighting tech, tour manager and head tech. He recently relocated to Thailand where he spends his time scouring the beaches for treasures.

Other Novels by Anthony S Cameron:

Driftwood (2014)

www.amazon.com/author/anthonyscameron

Butterfly on Bangla

by

Anthony S Cameron

This is a work of fiction. Names, characters, businesses, places, events and incidents are either the products of the author's imagination or used in a fictitious manner. Any resemblance to actual persons, either living or dead, or actual events is purely coincidental.

For Johnnie Barker, for your wisdom and madness.
And to all the others who have shone and flickered in my life.
You know who you are.

PROLOGUE

Castlemaine, Australia
1979

Jake was the first one to make the jump. His new BMX glistened briefly in the sun, catching the bike in mid-air before he landed heavily in the powdery dirt of the mullock heap and skidded expertly to a stop. He flicked his long hair off his handsome face and waited for the sound of Tyson's nobbies sliding through the loose stones and then the silence that meant he, too, had launched himself off the edge. Tyson didn't manage to pull off any mid air moves with his converted dragster, opting instead to stare with an expression caught between exhilaration and fear at the rapidly approaching earth beneath him.

Jake laughed as Tyson's landing threw him over the front of his handlebars and sprayed him across the dirt floor of the gully. The sound of his bell coming apart and spinning to a stop against a pile of slate rocks resonated longer than it took for the dust to settle around them. Jake was still laughing as Tyson wiped the dust from his eyes.

"Good one, mate, shoulda seen the look on your face just before you hit. Priceless, mate, bloody priceless!"

Suthers was next, launching himself off the edge of the heap with careless abandon, the combination of his weight and the amount of shit he had adorned his bike with contributing to him barely leaving the ground at all. The open bag of chips shoved quickly into his pocket did fly up in the air though, landing at the boys' feet as he cruised to a stop in front of them. He looked sadly at the dirty, inedible chips for a moment, then looked at his best mate Tyson with the embarassed grin they both knew so well, a grin seen way too often in his eleven years on the planet. He rearranged the long springs with the plastic eyeballs attached to them that dangled off his handlebars and waited for the inevitable smart arse remark to leave Jake's mouth.

"I like you Suthers," Jake announced, "even though you know you're gonna fuck it all up, you still have a go, mate. Gotta give him points for that, hey Tys?"

Suthers fiddled with the fake gear stick taped to his centre bar, and toyed with the idea of cleaning off the spilt chips and eating them in a last attempt to save his failing bravado, when he heard Doug's bike skid to a stop on top of the mullock heap.

They all looked up at Doug as his large bulk blocked out most of the available sunlight. Tyson could hear Doug's bike frame groaning under the weight of his bloated twelve year old body.

"Well c'mon Dougy," Jake goaded, "have a fuckin go, then!"

Doug's eyes narrowed as he took in Jake's swaggering form, then opened wide when he saw just how far down he had to go.

"I've got a better idea," he countered, whilst easing his groaning bike down the rocky, slippery slope. "Let's go check out the old Thompson mine, it's just over there," pointing with his chin to the thick bush surrounding them. He skidded the last metre as if that would make up for chickening out of the jump, almost losing the bike under him as he did so.

"Last one there's a rotten egg!' Jake yelled as he tore off towards the nearest mullock heap and began powering up its face. Tyson raised an eyebrow at Suthers, sighed deeply, retrieved his bike and followed Suthers and Dougy into the dust left by Jake.

Down in the bottom of the gully it was damp and cold despite the midday sun boring holes through the thick canopy. A huge black wattle sat directly above the entrance to the mineshaft and Tyson couldn't help but wonder if that was in fact the largest black wattle he had ever seen. Doug saw him looking.

"Fuckin tree hugger!" Doug said, growling just like his old man did when he watched the evening news on TV.

"That tree's gonna get more hugs than you ever will, Dougy!" Tyson replied, feeling a sudden wave of self-satisfaction rising in him. All three of them laughed.

"Whatever, fuck -face. Anyway, this mine here still has gold in it, boys, so whatd'ya reckon, should we go down there and get rich?" Doug's eyes shining almost maniacally on the word 'rich'.

"Anyone got any chips?" Suthers asked.

"Only the one on my shoulder. C'mon boys, let's go! Or are you shitting yourselves?" Doug shouted, his confidence now fully restored.

"Would've been handy if one of us had a torch," Tyson said matter-of-factly.

"You mean like this one?"

Suthers handed Jake the sturdy little torch his Dad had given him for his birthday. They all followed Jake under the rotting timber supports, dodging the drips of water slowly making their way through the soft rock above their heads, and entered the mine shaft proper.

All except Doug.

Doug stood in the entrance, again blocking all the natural light, and peered down as the boys descended into the bowels of the hillside, a curious pleasurable feeling coming over him, like a warm face washer on a winter's day. He looked around at the darkness, felt the damp, musty air on his skin and was struck by how good it made him feel. There was something about this place that made him feel, well, like he was home. Finally home.

He grinned to himself and walked on in.

Chapter 1

Castlemaine, Australia
2004

Tyson watched a movie in his head.

The movie opened with a long shot of the local pig factory at night. The place was lit up like a Christmas tree and through the many windows he could see people moving around inside, lit as they were by hundreds of fluorescent tubes, the odd one flickering to create a mild strobe effect. He could faintly hear music being played by an orchestra.

In the middle he could see smoke stacks spewing black smoke into the night and off to the right a ramp that connected the third level with the loading dock on the other side of the street. He started moving slowly towards the building.

The squeals of the pigs were just audible above the hum and hiss of the factory and the classical music rose up above it all, a slow fade that seduced his attentions, like a lone spotlight on an otherwise dim stage, and then faded down just as slowly. The early morning light was beating up against the east wall and the ramp, illuminating both in an almost accusing way.

Tyson focussed on the illuminated ramp and next thing he knew he was in mid-air, floating smoothly towards it. The closer he got to it, the more audible the squeals became until he could barely distinguish between the shrieks of fear coming from the killing floor and those coming from the pigs being unloaded from the trucks. The squeals from the killing floor rose up full of fear and panic, sending a ripple effect down the ramp to the truck, infecting each pig in its path. The music in his head surged, the strings started to swell, and he could almost hear the horn section's collective intake of air as they dug in, adding a pregnancy to the bizarre visual spectacle before him.

All he could see now was the concrete wall of the ramp and the clouds of cold air capturing the terrified squeals and giving them shape. He hovered momentarily, then very slowly began moving to the left, following the pigs as they were herded through barriers, then stand waiting their turn to die, the fear so thick it resembled a haze; a surreal layer of panic hanging above it all.

Tyson continued moving around the outside of the building, a slow, languid feel to his movement. He reached the corner of the east wall, executing the turn in an almost seductive way, then continued the slow movement, about six feet off the wall of the factory. The first window came along, entering from his left and exiting to his right and he could see the pigs being hung up and slaughtered, one at a time. He could see the ocean of blood running down drains and a conveyer belt in the centre of the room running off to the left.

For a few seconds more he saw the brick wall between the windows until the next one appeared. A couple of employees stood next to the conveyer belt with their arms crossed staring back towards the killing floor. They were wearing white coveralls, white gumboots, white gloves, white hairnets, white masks and clear safety glasses. One of them seemed to be telling a joke as the pair gazed emptily at the murdering going on in front of them. The other threw his head back and laughed, then moved off to the left, returning shortly after with a broom just as Tyson was moving towards the next window.

The pigs were now being dismembered by men wielding hatchets and knives. The conveyer belt was being filled up with pig parts, the men's arms moving fast as legs and heads were thrown roughly onto the belt, and there was something almost theatrical about their movements. The music he could hear edged towards playfulness.

The pig parts were now being run through band-saws, and many people were standing either side of the belt, tagging the parts with green or red or yellow tags, the tags wobbling as the pig parts hit a join in the belt. He could hear the low whir of the conveyer belt motor struggling under the weight. A man in a short-sleeved shirt with a clipboard stood there, pen poised above the page as Tyson tracked past, the music ducking down as his vision was bathed in bricks again.

Cellos competed with violins; flutes blew over the top of clarinets as he passed another window. This time the scene was some kind of lunchroom; a TV was blasting a soap opera into the empty space, the light a subdued blue. Just as Tyson was leaving the window a group of employees entered from left to right, most looking blankly ahead, some with their eyes already fixed on the TV screen as they formed a queue in front of the Bain-Marie.

Tyson then dropped down swiftly yet gently to the second floor as if on a cushion of air, and continued tracking along the wall, this time from left to right. Through the first window he could see the smaller pig parts being packaged in foam and plastic, a brain-dead looking bunch of employees manning the belt.

The next window revealed the belt now full of boxed pig parts as they headed towards a large square machine perched over the end of the conveyer run. The music swelled in an almost comical way as each window approached, sliding into a sustained blast from a dozen flutes as he watched a pallet machine spinning a pallet of boxes around in front of a plastic spool. To him it looked like some kind of dance, some sort of twisted, industrial ballet.

And through the last window he could see the pallets of boxes wrapped in their tight film of plastic sitting in lines. There were large, open, pallet sized bins piled on top of each other in the corner.

Tyson slinked across and down the wall to the first floor, where the pallets came down on the huge moving platform from the second floor and forklifts busied themselves loading the pallets onto waiting trucks. They manoeuvred back and forth like they had rehearsed it for weeks, dancing around each other deftly.

The music rose to a crescendo. Tyson pulled back and hovered above the loading bay directly above an open truck full of loose bones and skin, and as it pulled out Tyson moved backward, away from the factory walls, the open belly of the truck in his foreground. The truck picked up speed and moved off to the right as the music faded and he was left looking at the empty road in front of him. He felt himself dropping down smoothly until he was just off the ground, still backing away from the pig factory in the wake of the truck. He entered a drain and the last thing he saw was the pig factory fading in the distance.

Everything went to black and all he could hear now was water rushing past and the strange hollow sound it made as it resonated up and down the pipe. Just as suddenly, light rushed up the walls of the pipe and he was flying out the other end and hovering ten feet above a toxic looking creek. He looked across at the creek bank, which was covered in all sorts of rubbish illuminated by the waning moon. There were shopping trolleys, car tyres, plastic bags, discarded shampoo bottles, dog food cans, forgotten shoes and bashed-in and rusted 44-gallon drums. Just as his eyes began to focus, the truck he was hovering above earlier drove noisily over a bridge not far from him. He zoomed in on a strange looking object at the water's edge.

As he got closer, he could make out the shape of a woman's leg with a tattoo on the thigh, and an anklet, wet and shining in the harsh early light like a beacon amongst the industrial debris.

***

It was the trucks horn that snapped Tyson out of his movie with the deafening conviction of a late night infomercial. He opened his eyes and tried to get his bearings when the ground started to shake and the truck passed doing a hundred kilometres an hour a few feet from him. He saw it at the last moment, didn't even get time to brace himself. Gusts of wind tearing along behind the truck attempted to suck Tyson along the gravel onto the road. He made a fairly pathetic attempt at rolling away but gave up quickly, dug his fingers into the rough stones and just waited for the wind to subside. He heard a muffled ringing, blinked, opened his eyes, and fumbled through his clothes for his phone. It was caught up in leads of some sort at the bottom of one of the cavernous pockets of his oversized, second-hand pants. He struggled with it until the entire contents of the pocket fly out onto the ground around him: a small movie camera; a charger; the black 'leads of death' that had caused the tangled mess; and in amongst it all, the source of the ringing, his phone, flashing and vibrating demandingly. He mustered the resolve to sit up, reached over and clasped his bony hand around it. The sitting up and the blinking was followed by a dull black throb at the base of his skull that quickly spread across his head like an empty highway at night and he could feel himself falling over slowly, like an action replay, over and over.

He jolted himself out of it, opened his eyes again and focused on the phone until it was in his hand and he was pushing the talk button. He attempted to speak, but couldn't. He pushed his lank, long hair off his face and after a few seconds he heard Suthers' voice on the other end.

"It's Suthers, Tys. Where the fuck are ya, mate?"

Tyson dredged for a face to put to the name, eventually unearthing the image of his longhaired, chubby, bespectacled housemate and sound-engineer friend of many years. He looked around at his surroundings: A standard stretch of Australian country road, bush around its edges, guardrails, and a slight curve to the right.

He managed to clear some phlegm and spat it onto the roadside next to him.

"That's just it, I dunno!"

"Well, what does the girl look like that you're laying next to?" Suthers inquired, ending with a chuckle.

"I'm on the side of a road, Suthers, alone, and I haven't a fucking clue how I got here."

"What mate, did ya get a few drinks in ya last night?"

Tyson thought for a moment, rolling his tongue around in his mouth, searching for some tell tale residue. His mouth tasted like cardboard.

"Uh, don't think so, unless you can get drunk eating cardboard!"

"Huh?"

"Never mind. D'ya reckon you could come and get me?" Tyson asked, already forgetting he didn't know where he was.

"Yeah sure mate, but don't you think it will be a lot easier if I knew where to look?" He sighed heavily.

"Oh yeah... right. I'll see if I can spot anything else," he said as he made the slow transition from sitting to standing which was accompanied by a thumping head and images of his girlfriend Suzie bending over him and laughing, her mischievous sideways grin splitting her face in two. He lurched forward and to his relief his legs remembered what their gig was – to propel him forward, or in this case, from side to side as well. He staggered along, muttering into the phone.

"Let's see, we got ourselves some scrubby bush on the left, a train line that runs parallel to the road and I can see a cutting in a hill for the train about a kilometre away," his head starting to rid itself of the fuzz surrounding it. Suthers was breathing heavily over the line, a slightly laboured sound to it as he scanned his pre-Google Maps brain for the location.

"Is there a bridge over the cutting, like an old one?"

"Yeah..."

"And is there 'CONSUME, BE SILENT, DIE' sprayed in black across it, and the words kind of follow the curve of the bridge?" Suthers was chewing now as he talked, shoving chunks of his bacon and egg roll into his mouth between words. Tyson had trouble hearing him through the squelchy chewing.

"Huh?" then, realising what Suthers was asking, "Let me get a bit closer."

Tyson stumbled off the shoulder of the road and headed towards the bridge until he could faintly make out the graffiti scrawled across it.

"Yeah mate, how'd you know?"

Suthers' mind wandered back to the drunken evening that had him hanging off a rope with a can of spraypaint in his hand.

"Long story, Tys. You're in Barkers Creek, not far from DF Bacon. I'll be there in fifteen; stay put dude, OK?"

Tyson hung up and returned to his strewn possessions. He picked up the camera and unravelled the relentlessly evil cables, turning the little camera over and over in his hand whilst wondering if he had used it last night. And whether there might be something on it to remind him of how the fuck he blacked out and ended up five kilometres out of town, on the side of the road, with a 40-tonne semi bearing down on him.

Chapter 2

Phuket, Thailand
2014

Tyson woke to the sound and smell of a distant long-tail boat. He could also taste sand on his tongue. The sun was hot and beating down on him, producing a layer of sweat all over his body, he could feel it running down his temples in small streams. He could hear the gentle lap of tiny waves hissing apologetically as they hit the sand and spread out like so many memories arriving all at once, like relatives to Christmas lunch; when before you know it, every surface, every table and bench is full of cling-wrapped bowls, impossible cakes, huge legs of ham, seafood platters.

An orgy of food.

He had come to almost enjoy the moment his eyes opened and gave shape to all the other sensations – a face, if you like. It was when his frown turned to slight wonder for a short time, as he shifted from one reality to another. One nightmare to another. It was the small moment of hope, the glimpse of happiness before he was delivered back into the numbed, lost state of his existence.

Faint images ran through his head, but never lasted long enough to be relished: a glimpse of the woman he loved walking towards him in an early morning moment; a glimpse of a long past gig; a glimpse of a factory belching smoke. Always variations on the same themes. Tyson grabbed at these moments like an obsessed shopper at the ever-dwindling lingerie pile on Boxing Day. But he could never get a firm grip on any of them. They slipped through the loose, frail fingers of his memory and then his mind would go blank again.

And he would wake up.

Tyson opened his eyes and looked around, hoping Suzie was here lying next to him, hoping he wouldn't be stuck in the same shit again, alone and lost. The disappointment welling up in his body burst out in the form of a guttural howl.

The howl of a lost man.

Torturous images came out of nowhere, pinning him to the spot, mesmerising him with their ominous intent, like a threat without the follow through, like a taste without being able to swallow and let it linger.

Why me?

The beach was empty at first glance and Tyson calmed himself with the realisation that the waking could've been, and often was, much worse than this. At the far end of the beach he could see someone moving, although from where he lay, it was no more than a blur of shifting colour.

Another human being at least, better than a pack of angry beach dogs with territory issues. Much better.

He rolled up into a sitting position, rubbed his eyes and tried to ascertain which beach in Phuket he had passed out on this time. The area looked kind of familiar to him, especially after ten years of waking up at various places at random and wondering where the fuck he was. After ten years he had gotten used to it, but that didn't stop the fear rising up in his gut every time he felt consciousness returning.

The beach was long with not even a breath of wind as Tyson made his way towards the blurred human movement. The tide was low and the exposed sand had a silvery flat sheen, making walking easy. He looked back to where he had woken up, on the odd chance he had left a bag or something behind. But of course there wasn't any bag.

There never was.

He reached into his pocket and pulled out his little video camera, turned it on to check out the footage from last nights blackout, but the battery was dead.

Fucking great.

Suddenly, images were flooding his brain from the first blackout ten long years ago. He remembered waking up on a lonely stretch of Australian country road, the camera in his pocket as a truck thundered past, completely unaware at the time that what was on that camera would change his whole universe...

This time it was a beach in Phuket and a dead battery.

He tried to move his thoughts back into the now by watching the blurry figure moving back and forth along the beach. It looked like he or she was carrying things and putting them in piles. As Tyson moved closer, he could make out a squat foreigner, in a perpetual half-bend, as if he was always about to pick something off the ground. He noticed how the man seemed impervious to his surroundings, buffered from the elements in some way. He could make out a long beard and long silvery grey hair and piles of what looked like rubbish.

As he walked through the early morning haze the sweat poured off him. It was always this way after a blackout; it felt like the rivers of perspiration were his memories leeching out of his body and landing on the sand. It was a toxic evacuation; a way his body could keep motoring on, and he often thought that, if he didn't sweat, maybe he would go mad.

Instead, he was a sweating man with amnesia.

Great. Just great.

He rolled his eyes.

Tyson was about twenty metres away from the longhaired man when he stopped to take it all in. The man had separated all the debris he had been collecting and put it into distinct piles, and he was crouched in the middle of it all tracing a shape in the sand with a long stick. Tyson crouched also, intrigued by what he was seeing. The old man didn't even seem aware that he was there. He finished with the stick and flung it into a waiting stack, then stood upright for a moment to survey the other piles. A smile crept up behind his beard for an instant, then was replaced by something half-way between a grimace and a frown, his eyes the only part of him still smiling. He started whistling as he selected the first piece.

Tyson watched him intently.

Before long he could see a shape forming. The man had lashed four beaten-up bamboo poles together to create a spire shape and had begun wrapping the tangled fishing ropes and nets around it, hiding the bamboo slowly in a gentle swirl that corkscrewed the length of it on all four sides.

The old man whistled to himself and to each piece he picked up and wedged into the structure. Now he was back on the ground, winding sticks and plastic bags through each other to form a rough circle. A few minutes later Tyson watched him clamber up the side of the spire with the circle of sticks and, with his shoulder, heave them into place on the top of the spire.

He climbed down and took a few steps backwards.

The frown was still there, but the kind eyes joined it to create a thoughtful look, like he had encountered a puzzle to be solved. He stopped whistling and suddenly his eyes flashed wide. He looked over his shoulder, scanned the immediate horizon and scurried off towards the water's edge, whistling again, where a cluster of circular fishing floats the size of footballs lay, almost like they were waiting for him. He threw them over his shoulder and half trotted back to his creation, not even breaking his stride as he climbed the structure and hurled the balls into the circle of sticks.

Tyson stared in awe at the strange old man and his sculpture. The man continued whistling as he headed over to a pile of industrial debris. An old plastic chemical drum, a large plastic cog, a broken circuit board, an old desk lamp and masses of electrical cable slowly transformed into a metallic bird, which he placed gently next to the eggs. One leg of the bird was straddling one of the eggs, Tyson guessed, in a show of protection.

Tyson wondered what the baby chicks would look like, hatched from an industrial nightmare such as this.

The sculptor paused in front of his creation. The whistling had stopped. The job was done.

Tyson stood up, having decided to approach the man and thank him for the peculiar performance he had witnessed. The old man finally looked over at him with a blank look on his face, almost like Tyson wasn't there. He then promptly headed off in the other direction. Tyson slowed his pace when he saw this, his shoulders slumping almost imperceptibly as he recognised another failure to connect, another good thing slipping through his fingers.

Now he was standing where the sculptor had been, looking up at the bird's nest, noticing that the metallic bird had a stomach filled with plastic bags and flip flops bulging out on all sides. Tears made out of bottle caps ran down over its beak and down onto the plastic eggs...

Chapter 3

Castlemaine, Australia
2004

Mayor Jake McCardle strode down Barker Street, Castlemaine, like the world was his oyster. And of course, it was. The TV crew were filming him from behind as he walked down the main street of his town. He paused for a shot of himself with a constituent, shaking hands, pulling the guy in close to tell a dirty joke, pulling back and laughing just as the sunlight glanced off his smooth, tanned forehead

Jake then turned to the TV crew to check they got the shot, but of course they had. Jake was a pro at this stuff and the camera loved his handsome face. He strutted down the street with his entourage, stopping momentarily in front of a shop window that had one of his election posters staring out at them. He glanced at the film crew before arranging his face with an expression of mock surprise as he pointed at the photo staring back at him. The shot captured, Jake continued his cocky swagger and, although we see his creased, weather beaten neck making contact with the stiff collar of his business shirt, we do not see his face. Only the dazed constituents receive that honour today.

And today Jake was on fire.

A mother with a child approached and Jake leaned over to one of his entourage and mumbled under his breath,

"Couldn't be better if we scripted it ourselves!"

A jazz bass riff came up out of nowhere sounding like something from Herbie Hancock just before the LSD, or Miles before *Nefertiti*.

The child was thrust into Jake's outstretched arms and he immediately held him above his head and slowly brought him down into shot for the kiss. The child screwed its face up upon receiving a cheek full of bristle from the great man. He quickly handed the baby back because, as every politician knows, a good publicity shot can quickly go pear-shaped with a baby as the prop.

Jake and his entourage continued on, taking a left into Mostyn Street. The TV crew rush to get in front of him as he neared the rotary club sausage sizzle stand, sensing another Mayoral Moment about to happen. The light from the camera blasted Jake as he sauntered proprietarily up his main street, and from behind it created a halo around his carefully prepared hair.

Jake had his hand out, used-car salesman style, ready to grasp the hand of the old man behind the BBQ a good three steps before he was there. The old man fumbled with his BBQ tongs, managed to eventually put them in his left hand, freeing up the right to receive the crushingly firm handshake coming his way. He knew it well. Jake and the old man went way back. Everyone went way back with Jake.

"How ya goin' Fred? Selling a few snags mate?"

"Oh, you know Jake, it's a bit slow really," Fred drawled, stretching out the word 'slow' and looking at the TV camera crew.

"And what's this caper then, Jake?" he asked, pointing to the media circus that surrounded them.

From behind you could see Jake's ears go up and back down, like he was smiling.

"Oh y'know mate, you gotta do what you gotta do, gotta grease the wheels of the publicity machine. Can I have that snag there, mate?" pointing to the least-burnt one to the side and giving the TV crew a wink.

"For you Jake, m'boy, it's on the house!"

The old man handed him the snag, which was wrapped in white bread with some limp onion and tomato sauce on top. Jake put the snag to his mouth, then opened wide as he turned towards the camera and took a massive bite, somehow maintaining the smile throughout. Mayoral Moment captured. Jake wiped the sauce and fat off his face with a napkin, hands both the soiled napkin and the half eaten snag to one of his entourage and continued walking on up the street.

His street.

His town.

Jake then jumped the temporary barrier and entered the area blocked off for the Arts Festival. He stood amongst the scaffolding, lighting rigs and speaker stacks holding his arms over his head, as if to say, 'check this out!' as the camera clicked and the TV crew hovered. From this distance it looked almost surreal, all this showbiz in this sleepy little town. Jake jumped athletically back over the barricade and headed for the film crew, hand outstretched, the winning smile turned down to five. As he was thanking them his phone went off. He flipped it open mid shake: the caller ID said 'Doug'. Still smiling he answered,

"G'day mate, what's up?" as he moved off from his entourage, giving them the 'stay there' hand signal.

"Jake, I'll make it quick." Doug's voice was gruff and low and surrounded by heavy breathing. "They found her Jake, in the creek. The cops, that is," he grunted.

"Uh huh." Jake replied. The smile that had seemed plastered to his face was now completely gone. He turned around, put his head down and started scurrying up Frederick Street towards the council chambers, a shortcut with not as many people to appease along the way.

Stuttering, Jake asked,

"W... Well, what do we do now, Dougy?" his voice tentative, unsure.

He made it to the steps of the Town Hall and from behind we see him taking the steps two at a time and glancing furtively over his shoulder, his left hand pressing his phone to his ear.

"Well Jake, what we do is keep our FUCKING mouths shut and let this thing play itself out!"

A pause, then, "I'll be seein' you soon, Jake," Doug grunted, with an added layer of gravel.

Jake's hand reached out for the stairway bannister. The bounce in his step had gone and as we follow from behind and see him half pull himself up the ornate winding staircase to his office, we notice that he doesn't even glance at his hot little secretary, doesn't even stop to stare vacantly at her cleavage like he normally would. He walked into his office, made his way around the huge leather-inlaid antique desk and plopped himself down in his reupholstered antique desk chair. Even the familiar squeaks of the springs can't comfort him as he peered nervously out of the Mayoral window, his face now haggard, riddled with worry, his reddened eyes bulging out of their sockets like garish lights at a circus he should never had gone to in the first place.

Chapter 4

Phuket, Thailand
2014

Tyson couldn't remember the walk back to Patong. He rarely did. If he remembered anything it came in snatches, disconnected snatches: sometimes it was a section of road, or a restaurant, or an expression on someone's face, or a dog. Sometimes it was just a smell or a sound. Fragments he couldn't put together. That's why he carried a small camera around most of the time. It was a way of remembering. That is, of course, if he thought to turn the fucker on.

He came out of a soi surrounded by jungle onto Wiset Road just near 'Simon Cabaret'. The first thing he noticed was the faded lavender paint peeling off the entrance façade. And then he remembered 'Simon' the last time he saw him. The last night anyone saw him, as it turned out. Did a runner with the month's takings three years ago, leaving a trail of debt behind him, not to mention a few angry local mafia chiefs wondering how a transsexual cabaret performer had managed to do them out of so much money. Tyson smirked to himself as he walked past, silently tipping his hat to someone who had got out before the inevitable catastrophe of doing business in Patong finally crashed down on him. And ever since, Simon's 'creation', a gaudy purple cabaret venue with bus parking, had slowly fallen into disarray, and now looked wonderfully decrepit. Tyson liked it better this way. It fitted.

He took the right into Nanai alley instinctively, avoiding the centre of Patong. No one should see Patong that early in the day, especially Bangla Road. Patong at that time was the worn out bar girl walking back home, her cheap stilettos in one hand and a smartphone in the other, the make-up skewed, the harsh morning light revealing stuff that nightclub lighting doesn't.

He shuddered.

Not far from Gaew's place now, as his thoughts turned to the old man on the beach and the defiantly sad bird, and the way the old man darted about furtively between the piles. He cut through a couple of small interconnected sois that spat him out a block away from Gaew's, a block away from finding some small solace and a place to rest his weary body.

Fuck, how far did I venture last night? Tyson wondered, as he dragged his tired body past a tuk-tuk taxi stand. Even at this early hour he could smell the Hong Tong whisky from five feet away. From inside the makeshift shelter, which was leaning against an electricity pole and had old banners as a roof, five bleary-eyed faces stared out at him.

"Taxi, mister? You want taxi?" they slurred at him.

Tyson stopped in front of them, grinned back in a slightly deranged way, and said,

"No thanks, better you don't get behind the wheel, hey?" all in English, knowing they wouldn't understand him, due mainly to his rapid fire Australian accent.

"You want girl? Massage? You want two girls? Three?"

Tyson was used to this shit after ten years. This was Patong for fuck's sake, where everything was for sale, where every word was spoken through a forked tongue, every promise broken, every moment a proposition that could go either way.

And Tyson was never buying. They knew it. He knew it. It had been reduced to a pantomime now for him. On every corner, in every bar it went on. The hustle. It was Patong. It couldn't be any other way. And Tyson liked it; there was an almost insane edge to every day here.

The three flights of stairs to Gaew's place nearly did him in, and he found himself struggling for breath as he knocked on the door. He leaned against it for a moment, resting his forehead on the number 96 until he could hear the soft pad of Gaew's feet on the tiled floor. At the last moment he rolled across the doorjamb, using its edge to bounce him back upright.

Gaew opened the door with a scowl on her face, looked at him for a second, then turned on her heels and padded back into the bedroom, letting little disgusted sighs leave her lips as she went. Tyson had arranged his face into a distorted version of a 'surprise darling, how ya doin?' expression which he quickly changed back to his usual dead stare. He shuffled apologetically into the room, closing the door behind him.

It was often like this between them. It was a little game they played.

For a while he just stood there, staring out of the window at the street below, watching his neighbourhood wake up. Patong woke up late with a vague cheated feeling and a scowl just like Gaew's. Shopkeepers swept their entrances whilst dreaming of the wealth that drove past them in BMW's everyday. Old Thai men sat on front porches and watched the able-bodied going about the business of making a living. Tyson could hear the rolling clang as the security doors were flung open up and down the street, a staccato rattle than resonated in him much longer than it actually lasted, sucking him slowly down into the belly of his past. He saw Lulu sitting at the kitchen table with him as he played a tune on his flute for her. He could see her little legs kicking playfully back and forth. He could see her head rocking in time with the music as she shovelled cornflakes haphazardly into her mouth, hitting the mark as much as missing it, giving her a milk beard and making both of them laugh.

He closed his eyes, trying to shut the emotion down before the tears came, before the fragments of images flew in and out, plunging him into another blackout, another chunk of time lost.

He opened his eyes and Lulu was gone, replaced by the awareness of Gaew moving behind him. He turned slowly to see her leaning against the bedroom doorjamb in her pyjama shorts and singlet, rubbing her eyes sleepily, the scowl a distant memory.

"Where you go? I not see you for two day?"

He smiled at her. This was part of the game. He watched her play with her long black hair like a bullfighter backstage, warming up with the cape.

"Oh, you know, here and there," he replied, playing it low key.

"You not remember again, huh?" she snorted at him in disgust, like he was a little boy who got lost on his way home from school.

But he had zoned out already, his gaze wandering across the room, past Gaew to his shakuhachi flute lying up against the bedroom wall. He imagined he was picking it up, examining all the details, cradling it in his arms, running his hand up and down its worn surface.

How long is it since I've played it? Played anything?

The shakuhachi was the only instrument he had left, the only one he thought he might need to have around. The rest of them – his trumpet, saxophone and clarinet, various guitars and an old Farfisa organ– had been left behind, along with the memories of the person he used to be. The person that disappeared that horrible night, ten years ago.

"HEY TYSON!" Gaew screeched abruptly, snapping him out of his daze. She gave him a satisfied smile of white teeth.

The cat had started purring.

"What, love? What?" he implored softly.

She twirled her long hair around and around in the fingers of her left hand and looked straight at him. The smile became a pout as she purred,

"I very tired. I wait for you, very tired. I go back my bed now," raising her eyebrow suggestively.

Tyson was fumbling through his pockets looking for his camera as he replied,

"OK, love, sleep well!"

He came across his camera at last. He pulled it out, looking up just in time to see the hair being flung aside and the pout becoming a snarl.

"I'll be there soon Gaew, just gonna have a quick look."

Her cue to unleash on him.

"Yes, I know before what that mean. Fuck you, Tyson!"

Part of the game.

She turned her tattooed back on him and gave him the black hair running down to her arse as she stormed back to bed, slamming the door on the way.

He could hear her cursing him in Thai through the door, the shrill ugly sound of the Thai repertoire for 'asshole' seeping through the cracks. He smiled to himself and plugged his camera into the computer and prepared to see snatches of where he had just been.

It's same old routine, every time. And we never seem to tire of it.

As the images were being copied he thought again about the old man on the beach: the utter strangeness of it, and the vague feeling that there was something oddly familiar about him too.

The first images that came up were of him walking in the darkness on the side of the road, the road the only thing vaguely visible amongst the blackness of the night, enveloping the sound of his solitary footsteps. The camera was mounted on his forehead. Tyson fast-forwarded through a full two hours of the same sort of footage. There were no other images recorded, just footsteps in darkness.

Nothing to go on. Fucking great.

He shut the lid of the computer dejectedly, stood up, and headed for the bedroom where a hot-tempered cat lay in wait...

***

A little while later Tyson found himself staring at his reflection in the mirror. He studied the worn features that stared back at him: the shoulder length, dirty, brown hair was peppered liberally with grey and he was pretty sure it wasn't that 'cool' grey hair; the tortured bloodshot brown eyes were surrounded by crow's feet and had two heavy lines running off them heading south, gouging a crevice in his cheeks that hadn't seen the light of day in years; his formerly angular, vaguely handsome face had been distorted by grief into some sick parody of what it once was, being perpetually frozen in one expression – that of a broken man. He closed his eyes.

When he opened them, Tyson was there again, staring back at him. This time it was a very happy Tyson, a Tyson that didn't have lines or grey hair. Instead he had a sparkle in his eyes that made him look like he would stay young forever. Two pirate earrings caught the light and drew his attention there, just as Suzie appeared from behind him wearing nothing more than a cheeky grin. He could feel her soft skin on his naked back as she leaned in, and with her slender hand swept his long hair off his neck and buried her teeth in the soft flesh she found there. He closed his eyes, threw his head back and drowned in her touch.

"Tyson? TYSON?"

It was Gaew.

He opened his eyes and looked again at the sad figure in front of him. Now the face wore a grimace on top of the defeat, and beneath that a glimmer of a smile; a smile tinged with the regret that comes from a life half-lived. He smiled back at the tortured face in the mirror, turned and walked back into the arena where Gaew lay, feigning contempt.

Chapter 5

Castlemaine, Australia
2004

It was well after dark, and Mostyn Street was virtually deserted. Tyson could hear a band playing in the distance and see the half-built rigs of the festival stage lying around on dollies where cars normally would have parked. From where he hovered, about ten feet off the ground at the western end, the scene looked reminiscent of an abandoned, half-built theme park. He started floating down the street fluidly, noticing how the shops at either edge of his focus seemed to bulge and then shrink again as he floated past. One shop after another swelled past him: the jewellers, the bank, the fruit shop, the hardware store, the mini-mart, the credit union, the haberdashery, the army disposals store, the picture framers, the butchers and the fish'n'chips shop all became larger than life for a brief moment.

The music rose in level as Tyson approached the Royal Theatre. He became suddenly aware of his breathing, hearing it easily above the muffled tones of the band. In the background he could hear himself 'blowing' through his trumpet, checking that it was clear of any foreign matter that might colour the sound. The hundreds of old incandescent light bulbs that surrounded the entrance blink off and on as Tyson floated down to street level and crossed Hargreaves Street. The music was even louder now and more of the top end was audible. Cymbal crashes and guitar riffs forced their way through the thick walls and bounced into the gutter as he passed over it. Tyson looked down momentarily, sure he could see all the used notes blowing away down the street. Then he continued floating through the front doors of the venue, just like a regular customer.

The band was cooking now, a funk bass line underpinning the melody that was being carried by the guitar, as Tyson floated through the second door and entered the venue proper. The barman looked up instinctively, put a drink on a coaster for his invisible customer, then stared off at the band going nuts on the stage. Tyson could still hear his own measured breathing even though music filled the room. To his left, he could see Suthers in front of the huge mixing console, riding levels and bringing reverbs and delays into and out of the mix, his lank, dirty, prematurely grey hair hanging down and getting in his way. He had an unlit cigarette dangling limply out of the corner of his mouth. His eyes have a slightly insane look to them.

Tyson floated through the crowd, tracking towards the band, and it is then that he saw himself up on stage, holding his trumpet and staring at the floor, his right leg tapping out the strange time signature.

How could this be?

The crowd was bouncing around in front of him as he moved towards himself and he couldn't help but notice that they mostly looked like festival crew; lots of black T-shirts, piercings, tattoos and dreads, either drunk, or just plain happy of their own accord. And how could they not be? The band had everyone moving and smiling, carrying them away on an addictive layer of swampy jazz/ funk fusion.

Tyson made his final approach toward his musical self standing up on stage feeling himself merge just as he lifted his trumpet up towards his lips.

Suddenly all he could hear again was his own measured breathing. He could feel his lips on the mouthpiece just as, the band dipped down, leaving that little space for him to launch into his solo.

He began tentatively, leaving spaces empty rather than filling them. Then he built a dazzling array of jazz licks out of nothing and explored each one, leaving the audience with their mouths agape and gaining the full attention of Dave, the guitarist, as he leaned almost forlornly on his silent guitar to watch a master at work. Tyson's playing was superb, his technique faultless as he elevated a great tune into a brilliant one. Bass and drums laid down a spacious beat that gave him even more room to move.

In his head he pictured Suzie walking towards him sexily, saw her running down a hallway, laughing. The image then melted until all he could see was a swirling vortex of screaming, blurry human shapes. And he was in the centre of them all. He could see the notes coming out of his trumpet, squeezing past the mute he held over the bell and hitting the swirl of blurry shapes. Every time the notes hit, a sub-sonic rumble came back at him, wrapping itself around him like a warm blanket. As the blurry human souls whizzed past him they all whisper something different in his ear: cries for help, sighs of gratitude, stabs of anger, declarations of love, admissions of hatred. They came at him jealous, affable, comical, until he couldn't take it anymore.

Most of the crowd were staring up at him and had stopped dancing. He attempted to regain some composure in the sea of faces being blasted at him in his dream He blew his last riff, a bunch of long high notes with upper order harmonics laced through them.

It was fucking beautiful.

He pulled the trumpet away from his mouth, and with that the crowd went crazy, whistling and whooping, stabbing their arms in the air in a kind of collective triumph.

It was then that Tyson opened his eyes. He blinked a few times, his eyes adjusting to the stage lights as he scanned the room for the familiar shape and movement of Suzie. In a sea of adulation he floated there, almost oblivious to the commotion, breathing slow and deep as Tim, the drummer, put the icing on the cake with a flourish across his cymbals loaded with loose rivets, his brushes elucidating the ring and sending it out into the room where it sat for a moment, before fading into the padded walls and disappearing.

At the back of the room, in uncharacteristically low lighting, Jake McCardle stood nursing a scotch and staring at the spectacle before him. There were no pretty young things bobbing around him: he was alone.

Very alone.

Chapter 6

Phuket, Thailand
2014

Tyson was slumped on a stool at the end of the bar when the two men walk in, one of them staggering, the other knocking over a chair as they attempted to get themselves nearer to the alcohol.

"Aaah, fuck mate, get ya shit together!" he heard one of them say to the other.

Aussies, a couple of drunken Aussies in Patong.

"Here we go," he muttered to himself.

He took a sip of beer and readied himself for the floorshow that had just walked into his local. He stared at the mirror behind the bar so he could see their distorted faces without turning around and risking having to talk to them. That's the last thing he wanted. He generally avoided Aussies, even though he was one. Especially Aussies that were overseas. Did all he could to evade them. He often saw them wandering around the streets during the day with longneck beers in large stubby-holders in their hands. If they were shopping, they had a beer. If they were at the beach, they had a beer. Aussies assumed that being on holiday in Thailand meant getting pissed day in and day out until you landed back at Tullamarine airport with a tongue like 80-grit sandpaper and a pounding skull.

Tyson nursed his beer and listened to the two boys whilst letting his mind wander.

"Dead set, Gazza, this is the best fuckin' place in the whole world, Patong beach. All those hot little Thai chicks for us to bang, all this cheap beer, mate, I think I'm gonna jizz if I keep talking!" the one with the shaved head and tattoos said.

Tyson watched the reflection in the mirror and noticed more people coming into what ten minutes earlier had been his quiet little local.

Dead set... Someone I used to know said that a lot...

He watched the three new customers make their way to a table near the bar. One of them was holding his hand in the air and looking at Nid, the bargirl.

"YO!" he yelled, "Three Tigers over here!"

"Americans," Tyson murmured into his beer.

This'll be fun.

He watched as Nid delivered the three Tiger beers to the American boys. The one who ordered them held his up in the air. The others followed.

"Cheers!" they all said, following up with a round of high-fives.

Tyson sighed to himself. Americans were almost as unbearable as Aussies to him, and then he realised, when it came down to it, ANY more than two men together gave him the shits. There was just so little intelligence there.

The two Aussies noticed the high-fives, prompting the tattooed one to say loudly to his mate,

"Shane! Looks like we've got ourselves three septic tanks here, mate!" as he stumbled over to the Americans' table.

"G'day fellas, couldn't help but hearing your accents, are you wankers from America by any chance?" he asked belligerently, whilst using their table to steady himself.

"Hey man," one of them replied, "we don't want any trouble. We just wanna have our beer, y'know?"

"OK, sure, but answer me a question first, can ya? Can you tell me how the stupidest, most brain-dead zombies on the planet, such as yourselves, end up proclaiming yourselves the leaders of the fucking world? 'Cause, you know, me mate and I were wonderin' about that?"

There was silence from the table. The loudest of the three made a big show of smiling whilst he drained his beer in three gulps. Next thing his bottle was in the air and connecting with the tattooed guy's temple. Shane, the other Aussie, slowly took his phone out of his pocket and placed it gently down on the bar, sighing as he did so. He turned around, picking up a bar stool on the way through, and proceeded to ram it into the loud American's ribcage, then pulled it back and slammed it over his head, encouraging him to sit down and have a little rest on the table. Which he did.

Gazza had only just registered that he had been hit in the head when the other two Americans jump him and tackled him to the ground, punching and pounding as they went.

"That's it... Suthers!" Tyson said to the mirror.

Shit, haven't thought about him in years.

He wondered if Suthers was still doing gigs, still doing sound. He remembered the gig at the Royal all those years ago. A lifetime ago. Then he thought about his daughter, Lulu. He could see her running down the steps of her Mum's place and into his arms. He saw himself swinging her around and around at arms length, then pulling her in for a squeeze hug. He saw Lulu laughing hysterically...

A chill ran through him despite the heat.

A crashing sound snapped him out of his daydream as the boys went at it, just like boys the world over. Part of a table slid along the floor and stopped next to Tyson's stool. His cue to get the fuck out, which he did, going through the bar to the kitchen and then out into the alley, a route he had taken many times. The last thing he saw was Nid getting the shotgun out from under the bar.

Another night in Patong, he mused whilst checking that he had put his little camera back in his pocket. He rolled it around in his hand as he walked, still dazed from his flashback and torn between the need to shut it out as usual, and the desire to dwell there for a while.

It was all he had left.

When Tyson remembered stuff from the first blackouts, the walls quickly caved in on him. He would become catatonic and would stare for hours at his neglected flute, as if the answer could be found there. But his desire to play had died that night ten years ago, along with all his other desires, except for the desire to get lost. And he was in a perfect place to do just that.

Patong had done its hair and set its makeup on 'whore' by the time he made it onto Nanai Road. Restaurants were pumping and the bars were full of rowdy men watching football. The massage girls had begun to line the streets in their short shorts and some kind of miracle bra that pushed their small breasts up and under their heavily made up chins, holding flyers and smiling that 'Thai smile'. He took a left just as a Ute covered in posters cruised past with a couple of Muai Thai fighters standing up on a platform, whacking leather pads together and making shadow moves as the driver yelled into the microphone.

"TONIGHT! TONIGHT! AT PATONG BOXING STADIUM! KIT THE KID AND KNOCKOUT NICK FIGHT TO THE FINISH... TOOOONIGHT! SUPA FIGHT!!!"

Tyson never ceased to be fascinated by this shit. He particularly liked the old style Chinese theatre music they used as background, which gave it all a kitsch, surreal, Bollywood feel. He watched the truck go past and continue down the street towards Bangla Road, circus central, the cheesy sound fading slowly as it went.

He didn't know where he was going, and he didn't really care...

***

When Tyson came to, he found himself in the middle of an open truck packed tight with Myanmar construction workers. The truck was lurching around a tight bend and everyone was leaning with it. He noticed a glum look on the faces packed in around him, faces caked in coloured powder swirls, like some kind of war paint.

No one was talking. They were all staring at him. He could feel a glimmer of curiosity swelling up around him as he woke, producing furrowed brows in some and childlike, quizzical looks in others. He broke into a smile and aimed it at those closest. Some returned the smile and others kept looking blankly at him from under their straw hats. Some of the younger kids had white earphones in their ears and smartphones in their hands: tapping out a status update, he guessed. He wondered what they would say...

> Being packed into this truck sucks!

or

> Only 14 hours of work today, sooo love short days!

Even 21st century slave labour had smartphones now, Tyson reflected. They didn't have ID cards, passports or any right to own anything in the land of smiles, and they lived in slums, but they had smartphones.

Tyson derived some sort of perverse humour when he thought about how messy things had become. Sometimes it even made him break into a hopeless kind of a laugh, so amazed was he at the human gullibility displayed and the voracious greed that had created it.

It was a sick laughter.

The women were all wearing loose, shapeless work pants tucked into gumboots, long T-shirts with the construction company logo on the front, and cheap straw hats to protect their long black hair. Woollen gloves could be seen poking out of pants pockets. The men looked pretty much the same, except most weren't wearing hats. Some wore beanies, or T-shirts expertly wrapped into mean looking bandanas, and dark wrap around sunglasses. Tyson couldn't tell whether they were relaxed or angry. He noticed a scattering of Red Bull bottles rolling around on the floor of the truck between the hundred pairs of legs that were bracing themselves for the approaching hill, and assumed the latter.

The driver geared down noisily, crunching through the gears and rapidly losing speed until he was down to his lowest gear and the truck was barely moving forward. Everyone in the back leaned forward slightly and Tyson felt a hand brush across his pocket. Without looking he casually put his hand in his pocket and retrieved his camera, sensing that his move had served its purpose, that the wandering hand was gone. He turned the camera on, keen to see what he filmed last night, keen to avoid the steady gaze of the bandana men in front of him.

Images of flowing water filled the little LCD screen, close-ups of a fountain or something similar, the sound just audible through the tiny in-built speaker in the camera. Suddenly there were shots of a ladyboy walking theatrically away from the camera and looking over her shoulder whilst rubbing her long right leg, wearing ridiculous heels and too much make up. He watched numerous shots of the same thing, like seeing all the takes of a movie, all the times it takes to get it right, to bring all the elements together in a fluid way. He could feel those behind him watching now and upon seeing the ladyboy, they let forth a shriek of something bordering on delight, and started talking and laughing with each other. These were the first words spoken since Tyson had woken up, and he struggled to understand any of the words, so vastly different in sound to Thai. Every now and then a shared word jumped out at him, a Myanmar version of a Thai term.

Now there were two ladyboys on screen, giving an impromptu street performance of *I Want To Break Free* by Queen, right down to the Freddy Mercury pout between lyrics. Tyson turned around to see a few rows of the Myanmar all peering at the little camera, laughing and talking, some of the girls bouncing their hips off each other and giggling with embarrassment. He moved the camera up higher so they could get a better view. Tyson was enjoying himself now. He started singing along with the ladyboys and soon enough a few of the braver ones around him joined in on the chorus.

Here I am, on a slow truck with a bunch of Myanmar slaves singing 'I want to break free', accompanied by a couple of miming ladyboys...

Tyson smiled to himself. This was part of what he loved about Phuket, the absolute randomness as western culture smashed up against the third world and whatever shards were left, such as songs like this, seemed to resonate in every human.

Soon enough they were all bumping and grinding and holding pretend microphones and nailing the lyrics in their own way. Some were humming vaguely in tune and looking shyly at their friends, others had opted for the fist-raised-in-the-air style, whilst some, especially the bandana men, had gone for the head-nodding-repressed-man style, though for a moment Tyson thought he had seen one of them smile.

After the song came to an end an eerie silence descended on the truck. No one seemed sure what to do next. Tyson looked around at his fellow travellers and was humbled by their hard faces, stained as they were with concrete dust and years of hard labour, and he suddenly became acutely aware of how different his journey was to theirs, how easy it was for him to jump off the treadmill and just wander. They had families depending on them for food and shelter.

Tyson had no-one.

It paralysed and freed him at the same time.

He looked distractedly at a patch of coastline not far from the road, and was suddenly overtaken by an urge to get to the beach, so he made his way through the dense pack of humanity, climbed up the tailgate of the truck and down the other side until he was inches from the road surface. The truck was moving so slowly that the dismount was easy.

He waved to the powdered mass of faces being pulled up the hill.

A few of them waved back. And more than a few of them were smiling.

Chapter 7

Castlemaine, Australia
2004

Mayor Jake McCardle walked towards the council chamber's stairs, attempting to make his way through the crowd of protesters. Upon seeing him smiling that famous winning smile they closed ranks around him and raised the level of furore. Placards were being shaken angrily up and down, the 'no freeway' anthem they were chanting going up several notches, wiping the smile off of Jake's face and replacing it with wide-eyed fear. He kept his head down and shuffled through the throng, aware that the TV camera cannot get a good shot if he does this. He reflected for a brief moment on how natural this had become for him, how he almost had an intimate sense of the 'money shot', and the way he had manufactured his image so brilliantly. A smirk appeared briefly at the corners of his mouth, but disappeared just as fast. One irate protester shoved a placard in his face and was shouting right at him when suddenly Jake's legs go out from under him, the great man having tripped over one of the protestor's children. Again he reflected on how quickly one's fortunes can change and how wrong one can be, as the TV crew go in for the kill and capture him falling.

Got the money shot after all.

He stood back up, brushed himself off good-naturedly, and willed his smile back into existence. It now had a strained aspect, like it was being stretched unwillingly across his tanned face.

Eventually he made it to the steps, not stopping at the top to survey his town, as he normally would have done. This time he scurried through the front doors.

Doug was waiting for him in his office, staring out of the window at the scene on the street, not even grunting in acknowledgement of Jake's presence. Jake was the first to speak as he positioned himself on the wrong side of his huge leather inlaid antique table and consequently looked a little lost. He shuffled uncomfortably and adjusted his Zegna suit as if all of a sudden it no longer fitted – an impossibility, of course.

"Morning, Dougy," he started, the words kind of falling out of his mouth and landing at Doug's feet.

Doug grunted and snorted air into his huge lungs, still looking out at the crowd below them. Jake's shoulders slumped.

"Fuckin' hippy drug addict losers," Doug declared, "Sittin' 'round on their fat arses waiting for another dole cheque so they can go and buy cardboard and wood and marker pens and fuckin' go out and protest!" he rasped, slowly turning his massive frame around to face Jake, a task that produced even more grunts and groans.

Jake brought out what he thought was a confident smile but Doug's beady eyes bored into him, extinguishing it like a match in the wind.

"So Jake, what's the fuckin' story mate? Everything right to go for tonight?" he growled, referring to the Council vote on the freeway route scheduled for that evening. Jake pursed his lips, an uncharacteristic thing for him to do as it hid his full lips that were such a large part of his trademark handsomeness.

'W... Well Doug," his stutter reappearing, "The boys will vote for Route 5 as directed and, outside of the raucous hippies, it should all be sweet, mate..."

Even he could hear the tentative tone pervading his words.

Doug's eyes were like guided missiles that had found their target and there was an almost perfunctory air to his tone now, as if he knew he had the upper hand. How could he not? Owner of the largest business in town, 'DF Bacon'; extensive real estate holdings throughout the district, including land around the proposed freeway route; president of the rotary club; he owned half of the main street and the bus company. Honour boards in various pubs throughout the town attested to his remarkable ability to out drink anyone. In short, Dougy owned the town, but like most megalomaniacs, it was never enough.

"You better be right Jake, that's all I can say. For your sake. Oh, by the way, I've formed a new company, here's my card!" handing it to Jake as if dealing out cards at a poker game, something they had done many times over the years.

Jake looked at the card. There was a huge bulldozer clearing a path through a hill with 'Farris's Earthmoving' emblazoned across the top of the hill in gold letters. Jake could hear his antique chair groaning and creaking as Doug dropped his morbidly obese frame into it. Jake broke out in a sweat as

Doug's massive bulk spilled out the sides of the chair. Doug snorted aggressively as he said,

"Do I need to say anymore, mate?"

"Preferred contractor for the freeway I take it?"

"Not just a pretty face, are you Jake?"

Jake put the card on the table in front of him and stared at it as he asks,

"And what about Suzie, Dougy, what the fuck happened there?"

Doug stared out at the town.

"Better you don't know mate. All I can say is that she got in the way and it got messy."

"Messy is right, mate. I mean, I thought you were gonna dispose of the body in the standard way?" Jake continued, picturing the huge meat grinder at Doug's factory.

"Yeah mate, so did I. The boys fucked up, what can I say? Don't worry about it. I'll make that little bitch work for me now even if she wouldn't when she was alive. Funny how things work out, isn't it?" Doug says, his voice like crushed metal.

Jake stared at the man who had just had his daughter executed.

"Yeah mate, real funny."

Chapter 8

Phuket, Thailand
2014

Tyson could hear the water running over Gaew's body and the large splashes from the bucket falling onto the hard tiles around her. He stared at the computer screen. Images of a white curtain blowing gently back and forth stared back at him, followed by close ups of a tidal lagoon emptying itself into a brooding ocean, the water forming soft waves that made it appear to be moving in the opposite direction than it really was. It reminded him of Suzie's long blonde hair lying across his pillow, her soft blond waves moving up and down with her breathing, like a river running through him.

He looked across at his shakuhachi flute lying up against the wall in the corner near the bed and pushed his hair off his face, just as Gaew opened the bathroom door so he could see her dousing her supple copper flesh in soapy water. He caught a glimpse of soap suds running over her breasts and coming together just above her hips, then running down her inner thighs before pooling at her delicate feet. He felt nothing.

He returned his gaze to the images on the screen, clicked an icon and soon enough he was looking at the ladyboys miming the Queen song, which he expertly spliced into the previously edited footage of the curtains and the lagoon, suddenly hit by a wave of inspiration.

For the first time in years he heard a melody in his head; a minor-chord melancholic tune, and he found himself reaching for the flute with a strong sense of foreboding. He felt for its familiar leather case whilst fixated on the images in front of him, and now he could see the music forming as clearly as he could see these dreamy images before him. Sensing his distraction building, Gaew cleared her throat loudly and bent over to 'retrieve' the sponge that she had 'dropped' a moment ago. She snorted in disgust upon realising that he was once again miles away. She could've danced naked in front of him for all that it mattered. Tyson heard the bathroom door slam shut, but it was as if he was at the other end of the street, at the other end of the world.

Which in some way, he was.

He took the flute from its soft felt covering and held it nervously in his hands whilst watching the images of the lagoon shoot from left to right across the screen. His foot searched for the pulse in them and found it, laying the bed that his flute would curl up into. He sat cross-legged on the floor in front of the screen, listening to the sounds around him; the almost spiteful splashing of water on flesh, the gentle sound of the wind blowing against the microphone and the chaotic sounds of the street below him. His breathing became deep and meditative as his grasp on the bamboo flute tightened. He stared at it for a long time before putting it to his lips.

His grip loosened and the first notes were tentative, almost apologetic and for him, strangely amateurish, and he almost put it back down, down into the messy recesses of his past. Then a thought hit him: *in order to see, you have to stop looking...* so he focussed instead on the fluid movement of the camera as it enveloped the cavorting ladyboys and then he heard himself playing at last... and it was as if he was outside of the experience somehow, like a spectator craning his neck to catch a glimpse of the show that everyone else could already see.

The notes were breathy, airy and uncommitted at first, but transformed quickly, becoming a flowing, seductive thing. He was almost startled as each riff searched out the sublime, and found it.

He paused momentarily to frantically search for pen and paper so he could jot down the music that was flooding his head for the first time in more years than he could remember. He hit repeat on the edited footage and continued to blow, rushing through chords to get to the next, in a gorgeous interplay between the ideas and the music, a dance he thought was a thing of the past for him, so glued down with the grief that had become his life ever since those fateful final days in Castlemaine.

He was desperate to stay in this moment, this rare moment. He dared not look away from the repetitive images lest he lose the vibe, yet he was also overcome with the urge to record it, get it down on tape, because no matter how carefully he wrote the music, he may not ever be able to reproduce this unique feeling.

With evangelical zeal he put the flute down on the floor and scrambled across to the bed and, with one arm resting on the sheets, searched frantically under the bed with the other until he found the box behind a pile of forgotten clothes. Inside was a Neumann U87 condenser studio microphone, a thing of beauty in itself. He smiled to himself, remembering how he ended up owning it. He pictured the gaunt, pale, heroin-addled face of the producer forced to sell it to support his massive smack habit, the way he scratched absentmindedly at his nose as his sweaty, feminine hand took the few hundred dollars that Tyson held out to him.

He plugged into the phantom power supply/interface and almost immediately a small icon bounced up and down on his desktop. He clicked it and then found himself looking at an audio mixing window. He tapped the mic with a finger and watched the green LED meters on the screen turn to yellow. He was ready.

He placed the mic in its suspension clip and wedged it between piles of dusty books as a makeshift mic stand. He clicked record and hit play on the now frozen images, and he was off, not even glancing at the sheet music on the floor next to him. And this time he closed his eyes.

He hadn't felt this clear in years.

The earthy, wooden tones of the shakuhachi filled the room and Tyson glimpsed the freedom he once felt, the pure hot bliss that was at one time like a drug to him, a place of solace and inspiration, a place he would relish with an intensity bordering on madness. He could hear the air being pushed out of the way and the music taking its place and inside he was alive again, truly alive.

Down on the street below, the old sculptor sat at a cheap plastic table on a cheap plastic chair at a *som tam* restaurant, trying not to let the chilli cascading down his throat prevent him from smiling broadly to himself. Tyson was finally playing again and, even though he found Patong disgusting beyond belief, the trip was worth it. He listened to the faint sounds of the shakuhachi compete with the rhythmic pounding of the pestle and mortar as the lady from *Isaan* worked another papaya salad into shape right next to him. And yet the pounding seemed to duck in volume for him as the woody tone of the shakuhachi made its way to his ears. It was a sound he had waited for over ten years to hear again. His wild hair had been tied back into a ponytail as his gesture to the city of lost souls he spent most of his time avoiding. Less stares that way, a few less scowls and more smiles, even though they were hard to come by here if you didn't at least look like you had money.

And the sculptor certainly didn't look like he had more than a few meals worth of coins in his worn pockets. The wealth he had, however, was immeasurable. He looked up at the apartment where his friend was finally coming alive.

He wondered how long it would be now before Tyson started to remember.

Tyson was jamming now, jamming with the chaos of the street, the hum of motorbikes like bees around honey, the splashing of water over Gaew's body and the pregnant moment of silence before the water hit the floor. He opened his eyes and stared into space for a moment, suddenly seeing Lulu's smiling face and his younger, happier self watching her dance around his broken down lounge room in Castlemaine. His fingers froze and his breath shortened, becoming shallow and desperate, like a pack-a-day smoker climbing a set of stairs. Then he heard the bathroom door open and Gaew padding across the room, the sound of her wet feet like a dull slap in the face, snapping him out of his bliss and back into his daily nightmare.

She was standing in front of him with a towel wrapped around her when he stopped the recording. He let the flute slip from his grasp and land in his lap, his gaze following it down and it was from there that he saw the towel fall off Gaew's body and pile up on the floor next to him.

He didn't look up.

***

Tyson climbed quietly out of bed whilst Gaew slept, stepped into his Thai fisherman's pants and T-shirt, and took one last look at her as he slipped silently out the door. She stirred and rolled over onto her back, her tiny breasts jutting straight out. He heard her asking,

"Bpai nai?" *Where you go?*

He answered by clicking the door shut behind him. He heard a book hit the door as he reached the top of the stairs, and as he descended, the hungry growl of another Patong night surged up to engulf him in its strangly hollow, listless ferocity.

Chapter 9

Castlemaine, Australia
2004

It was late morning by the time Suthers, newspaper in hand, ran up the steps of their dilipidated house. He burst hurriedly through the front door, his long, grey, Dero's coat ballooning out behind him in his wake. He trotted down the hallway that a real estate agent might describe as 'chic squalor', but to the eye uncoloured by the need to make money, it was just another worn out share house. Torn posters for forgotten gigs on the wall, a hat stand with scarves and jackets piled up all over it and a naked mannequin jammed into the umbrella space with her hand pointing up into the air expectantly. Shoes were strewn across the floor, one of which Suthers kicked out of the way as he entered Tyson's bedroom.

The space was dark except for a thin shaft of light coming through a crack in the curtains, which partially illuminated the room's decrepit state. Suthers pulled open the curtains quickly and flooded the room with piercing morning sunlight. Tyson was passed out on the bed; his clothes and shoes still on, not even stirring as Suthers kicked him several times with his unlaced, second-hand army boot.

"TYS, hey Tyson, wake up, man!" No response.

"Hey Tys, wanna bong?" No response.

"Hey, TYSON! You're on, the crowd is waiting!"

Finally Tyson opened his eyes and sat bolt upright, squinting repeatedly against the alien sunlight.

"Suthers, what the fuck, man? What's the time?"

"It's early, I'll get coffee."

Suthers disappeared out of the room, still clutching the newspaper in his chubby hand.

Tyson stretched and fell back down on the bed, head throbbing like a free-jazz drum solo. He blinked again and again until the blinding light of the day ceased to be a searing white laser burning his retinas. His mouth was dry, his ears still ringing from last night's gig, this rawness being the last residue of the experience for him. He trawled his memory for details but at this early stage of the waking moment they were sketchy and vague.

He scanned the bed for the familiar shape of Suzie but he was alone. No gently rising mound to reassure him, no sexy sighs, no womanly scent to taunt his libido, no toes curling unconsciously off the end of the bed. He searched the floor for some respite from the dryness in his mouth but all he could find were discarded magazines, an overflowing ashtray and a dirty bong made out of garden hose and a plastic water bottle, the cone a makeshift wrap of aluminium foil. He groaned as a wave of nausea flooded his body and joined the sense of foreboding he had carried for two days now.

His senses returned to him briefly, so he celebrated by attempting a thought, which made his head spin and the rhythmic throbbing go up a notch, resonating into the sweat-soaked pillow and down through the worn mattress to the floor, with all the other refuge of his life.

He looked across at his bedside table at the photo of Lulu smiling at him. A wave of love and regret hit him and he smiled back at her image, focussing on the light dancing in her young eyes.

How long has it been since I've seen my little girl?

Suthers blundered back into the room, a steaming mug in one hand and the newspaper in the other.

"Here mate, drink this," handing him the coffee, "and then this..." pulling a flask out of his old man's pants. "Something tells me you're gonna need it, bro..."

Tyson looked up quizzically as he sipped the coffee.

"What's goin' on Suthers, you're acting really strange."

Suthers tossed the flask and then the newspaper onto the bed next to Tyson.

"I just want you to know that you're me best mate, and I'm here for you," backing out of the room as he spoke.

Tyson looked down at the folded paper and the flask where he saw a partial headline with the word 'bacon' in it. He flicked the flask out of the way and opened the newspaper, the Mt Alexander Mail, to reveal the front-page story.

BACON BOSS'S DAUGHTER FOUND
DEAD IN BARKERS CREEK

It seemed to take forever for Tyson to make the connection, his coffee cup caught mid-way to his mouth, the stillness of the room pressing down on him with the force of a thousand bass drums struck in unison, the wave pushing him back against the wall and causing his coffee to fall from his failing grasp. He stared at the photo of Suzie's stiff body embedded in the creek bank, at her tattooed thigh poking out of the rotting rubbish all around her as the first of many tears cascades down his cheeks. He gazed at the newspaper, willing it to transform into the usual banal banter it was well known for, but the local rag was having none of it.

Tyson looked out of the window at the day pouring in and hoped like hell that he was dreaming, that he was having another blackout, that this was some kind of twisted take on his reality and that soon he would wake up, that his girl would be lying next to him in peaceful slumber. That they would greet the day with their usual sense of awe and wonder for the world they had created for themselves: one where the heart-racing sense of adventure at the fleeting nature of it all would still exist, as tangible as his tears hitting the page.

He reluctantly dragged his gaze back to the paper and began to read...

TUESDAY MARCH 9

The body of Suzanna Farris was found early yesterday morning by a jogger. Farris, 23, was the daughter of Doug Farris, prominent businessman and owner of the largest business in the district, DF Bacon. She was well known to locals as a cheerful and intelligent girl, active in the arts community, and a frequent patron of the Royal Theatre, becoming as much a fixture as the building itself. An only child, she was expected to take over the reins from her father in the near future.

'It's a terrible loss. Words cannot express how I feel right now,' a tearful Doug Farris was quoted as saying upon hearing the terrible news that his daughter was dead, possibly murdered.

'I can't understand how anyone could do this to my little girl... you can rest assured that, if foul play resulted in her death, I will hunt down the perpetrator and make sure they feel the full brunt of the law and, failing that, I will personally ensure that retribution is felt,' the visibly emotional father added.

Detective Superintendent Brown, at the crime scene yesterday, responded similarly:

'The police are investigating the circumstances of this terrible crime and are waiting for forensic reports before launching our investigation proper. At this stage we don't have much to go on.'

Farris was found embedded in the creek bank downstream of DF Bacon's outfall pipe. At this stage, police believe there is no connection between her death and the well known 'pig factory'.

Our heartfelt condolences go out to her parents, and to all who knew Suzanna.

Tyson was frozen now, as if a week's worth of psych drugs had just kicked in, leaving him with a deadened, slack-jawed expression. But inside he was howling, feeling the first pain of a wound he knew would never heal.

***

Doug Farris leaned back in his office chair, allowing the springs to take the full load of his ample bulk as he set fire to a large cigar and blew smoke out of his lungs, savouring the way the smoke billowed out above his head like a benign storm cloud. He stared down at the newspaper on his desk.

"Let the games begin," he grunted to himself, and watched as his words echoed across the empty room, punching holes through the discarded layer of smoke.

Chapter 10

Phuket, Thailand
2014

The lone sculptor was working at a feverish pace, muttering to himself and scanning the beach around him. The tide was coming up and he didn't have much time. The wind was buffeting him – a gale strong enough to bend the palm trees, the massive pieces of junk the ocean was throwing up onto the shore testimony to its malevolent force. Huge logs, car tyres, massive cable reels, lumps of concrete and masses of tangled rope surrounded the old guy as he worked.

He worked briskly at untangling the blue, yellow and white rope and rolling them into neat piles separated by colour and diameter, a preparation that gave him an odd sense of satisfaction. Normally he wouldn't bother; he would simply throw himself at the task with a frenzy bordering on insanity, and revel in the chaos of the moment. But there was just so much material here that even he found it difficult to see the potential in it all.

Meanwhile, two kilometres inland, Tyson slowly became conscious of a heavy, rhythmical knocking against his leg. He could hear the wind howling through the trees and the occasional snuffling and snorting as he struggled to open his eyes. Suddenly he was being picked up and turned over onto his back, and it was then that his willpower won the battle with his fatigue and his eyes opened wide. Wide enough to see an elephant's trunk inches from his face. Wide enough to see the huge ears flapping and the skin on a massive leg squashing down into a mass of wrinkles under the tonnes of weight it was being asked to carry. He tensed his body for the inevitable moment where one of the mammoth legs would also explore this curious lump of human. He heard the sound of a chain dragging, running his eyes along its length to where it was tethered to one of the beast's rear legs. The chain was thicker than his arm and yet he sensed the complicity of the beast in its incarceration, given the enormous power his wrinkly friend had in his possession.

Suddenly Tyson was being lifted up in the air and carried towards the huge head.

But I thought elephants were vegetarians, he mused distractedly, as he passed the huge saliva encrusted mouth. The elephant seemed to know just how much pressure to apply to hold him securely without crushing his torso. And then he was looking into the eye and he was lost again, this time lost in the depth of emotion he found there. The elephant held him in this position for quite some time, partly, Tyson imagined, out of curiosity, and partly out of indecision.

Tyson relaxed his gaze and looked deeply into that soulful eye and in that moment reconciled himself to whatever fate may come his way. He smiled, the smile so deep that his eyes shone with the momentary wisdom that his life had come down to this: locked in an embrace with a captive elephant, caught in the vortex between disbelief and calm understanding, between fear and capitulation.

The elephant considered him for a while longer, almost as if allowing Tyson the opportunity to communicate. Then the eye shut slowly and Tyson could hear something large and wet hitting the ground, and a moment later, the stench hit him. The eye opened again and now there was a distracted glaze over it as the elephant completed his task. Moments passed, he blinked again, and the glaze was gone.

Suddenly Tyson heard someone yelling loudly in the distance. The elephant's eyes went wide with alarm and, without as much as a 'good to hang out with you', it dropped him, Tyson rolling and coming to rest a foot away from the steaming mountain of shit. The yelling increased in volume, enough for Tyson to hear the slurred, guttural tones of a Southern Thai man barking at the elephant as he approached. He looked up and saw the slight, dark figure with a hooked stick in his hand, and within seconds the steel hook was making contact with the wrinkled, leathery skin and the elephant was cowering before his 'owner'.

The man looked down at Tyson and the steaming pile of shit and said,

"Chok dee, mai?" *Good luck, yes?*

He smiled, showing Tyson a mouthful of betel-nut stained teeth, the red juice dripping out of the sides of his mouth, his eyes bloodshot and opaque, making him look more mysterious than he actually was. He hooked the elephant behind the ear and tugged him to the side, giving Tyson the opportunity to crawl to safety. He got to his feet and took one last look at his new friend, and as he turned to leave, the wasted man called out,

"Tham arai?" *What are you doing?*

Tyson paused, then replied with,

"Mai luu..." *I don't know...*

He gave them both the closest thing to a smile he could muster.

***

The tide was retreating now as the old man began constructing the day's sculpture. He had sat amongst the piles of debris for over an hour, staring out to sea as the wind blasted his being. Now he busied himself coiling the smallest rope around the base of a long twisted log that had embedded itself in the sand, the waning tide starting to reveal its smooth worn surface. The ocean roared away in front of him, humbling him as waves thundered up and down the beach.

A figure appeared in the distance and started making its way in his direction. The sculptor drew his attention back to his work as his idea slowly took shape before him, his hands moving frenetically in front of his calm, immovable face.

Ahead of him Tyson could see the sculptor moving about hurriedly and with some effort he quickened his pace, not wanting to miss him this time. He took in his surroundings as he walked. The beach was about two kilometres long and curved sharply, making the sculptor look closer to him than he actually was. He made his way through the tonnes of debris that had found their way, through some unique combination of wind and currents, to this beach. Jagged lumps of concrete, endless lengths of tangled rope, plastic bottles, flip flops and rusty nails sticking out broken timber and to Tyson they all looked like they had been through some kind of hell to get here. He grinned to himself as the irony sunk in. Everything landed in Phuket a little worse for wear.

He wiped his mouth and tried to clear his thought pattern and start a new one. He fixed his gaze on the wild grey hair of the mad sculptor flying about in the gusts of wind.

Why doesn't he tie it back? Why not get that stuff out of the way? Tyson wondered. He glanced up at the sculpture taking shape under the deft hands of the old man.

Tyson slowed his pace as he approached, partly out of deference to the creative process taking place, and partly out of a desire not to scare the sculptor off. He sat on a broken tree branch ten feet away and pulled out his camera, keen to record, surreptitiously if he had to, the creation as it grew. The sculptor continued wrapping rope around the log seemingly oblivious to Tyson's presence.

He started recording, then stopped immediately, realising it might go better for him if he asked permission first. He stood up and walked tentatively over to the old man, clearing his throat nervously along the way. He was only a few feet from him now and still the sculptor didn't look up.

"U... Um, excuse me?" holding his camera up so the old man could see it.

If he was looking, that is.

"Do you mind if I film what you're doing there? Looks pretty fascinating... um... do you think it'd be OK?"

Without looking up the sculptor replied,

"Up to you, mate."

"OK, thanks."

Tyson stood there expecting the sculptor to look up and fix him with a withering stare, but nothing. He opted for the non-invasive approach and wedged the camera roughly in the bough of a low hanging tree, set it on record, and stepped back in order to view what the camera would capture.

"Make yourself useful and pass me that roll of blue rope," the old man said gruffly, raising a hand for an instant to indicate which blue rope he was referring to, surrounded as they were by the many tangled, angry lumps the volatile ocean had created.

Tyson quickly retrieved the rope from the pile and stood in front of the sculptor, holding it out to him.

"OK, just drop it there," and then, "Thanks."

Still no eye contact.

Tyson could not make out his accent, it hung somewhere in the mid-pacific, part American, part English, part Australian, part nowhere in particular. He looked at what the old man was making. A bulge of carefully wound rope wrapping itself around what appeared to be a whale's tail that he had fashioned out of an array of flip flops, fanning them out, using the smallest ones to make the required V-shaped curve.

"Gees," Tyson began optimistically, "looks like a whale lashed to a log, am I right?"

"What are you, a fucking art critic now?" the old man inquired, the same way a fist inquires as to the softness of the flesh it hits.

Tyson was taken aback again.

"Um, sorry mate, didn't mean to upset you. I was just curious."

"Smartest thing you've said all day. Pass me the red one now, would ya, buddy?"

It was almost as if the old man's accent traversed the globe with every sentence and Tyson sensed something calculatedly mercurial about it.

He did as he was told, then settled back and watched him wind it tightly around the base of the tail, pulling it tighter with each turn, the rope digging deeply into the layer of flip flops, strangling them. The sculptor's frenzied activity produced the mangled shape of a sperm whale's head now, this time constructed out of thick flaps of rubber constrained by fishing nets. He used fisherman's round plastic floats shaped like doughnuts for the eyes, and small white bottle caps for the teeth. And with a knife he carved chunks out of the rubber and stuffed more red rope into the holes so that the head now looked like it has been hacked at with machetes.

Next he got to work on more rubber, this time attaching a smaller 'whale' to opposing sides of a car tyre so that it resembled a whale calf with a car tyre for a stomach. His arms were a blur of movement as he filled the stomach with all manner of battered plastic remnants; flip flops, small plastic toys, the torsos of dismembered dolls, drinking straws, cigarette lighters, tangled fishing line, bottle caps and lumps of polystyrene, until it was overflowing from the sides of the tyre.

Tyson stared at the bleak depiction the lone sculptor had made, and wondered if his previous pieces were as full on as the two he had seen.

"Well, spit it out, son!" the sculptor challenged, sensing that Tyson was about to ask something.

Tyson cleared his throat and stared at the ground.

"I was just wondering if all your sculptures are this bleak."

The old guy stopped what he was doing and finally looked square on at Tyson, his calm smiling blue eyes belying his gruff response.

"Don't know what you're talking about buddy. I just have these thoughts and then the next thing I know they've taken a physical form. You going all art critic on me again? Because if you are, you can go fuck yourself! Always looking for some thread, some deeper sub-text that enables you to talk about themes the artist explores and shit like that. Sometimes there is no fucking reason. No reason at all, got it?"

Tyson blinked nervously and looked past the old man, incapable of maintaining the constant stare.

"Yeah, got it... Sorry, I just thought..."

"Well that'd be where it all went bad for you... Thinking!" the old man interrupted, crushing what was left of Tyson's confidence.

"And besides, how can you be having a go at thinking when you're not even awake?"

And at that the old man returned to his work and to his silence, as if Tyson wasn't even there.

Chapter 11

Castlemaine, Australia
2004

The crime scene was deserted when Tyson got there, the morning light having just begun to illuminate the multi-coloured plastic ugliness. He took a deep breath and ducked down under the 'POLICE LINE: DO NOT CROSS' tape that distinguished the scene of woe from the general state of decay. He thought of Dave's guitar strap, which is a strengthened version of the same thing, a yellow slash around his shoulder that the stage lights bounce off. Except there is no crowd to fuel his ego here, no pretty girls bouncing around on the dance floor, no stage lights directing his focus, telling him where to look. Tyson made his way, grim faced, to the place Suzie had been found. He paused next to a rusted upturned shopping trolley to spin one of the wheels around on its swivel whilst listening to the crunching ball bearings attempting to do their job. He loses himself for a moment in their grating reluctance. He reached over to the opposite wheel and attempted to spin it as well, but of course it had seized. There was always one, on every trolley, that meant you could never steer it straight down an aisle, instead you had to put your back out correcting the sideways pull, and even here in the creek it was the same.

He made his way past a broken TV wedged in an old car tyre to the place where his love had lain. Still paralysed by disbelief, he struggled to connect with the moment he was in and what it meant to him. He could see the marks her body had made when it landed, the plastic bags crushed and shaped in to a mirror of her contorted body.

A wall of denial stood between him and the moment, a paralysis that was cheating him, robbing him of the experience, denying him some truth that he tried to embrace but failed. He felt for the tears that should be on his cheeks, leaving a trail of grease from the trolley wheel, rendering his face a surreal version of the clown's eyes that secretly traumatise every child that sees them. He sunk to his knees, hearing the crunch of broken glass before he felt it. He placed his hand over the depression Suzie's body had made and looked up past the police tape to the top of the bank where he imagined she had been thrown from. A shudder went through him, taking his breath away and he struggled to pull himself together as he felt the warm trickle of blood run down his leg. He watched as it dripped onto his hand.

He put more weight on his bleeding knee until he could feel the glass digging further into his flesh, pleading with the inert waste of a forgotten drinking session to help deliver him here, naked and raw, into the grief that evaded him.

He could hear the echo of the bacon factory outfall pipe as another batch of liquid murder made its way to the edge and fell unceremoniously into the toxic creek, creating a deep sound that resonated towards the bridge where it hung stagnantly, almost flagrantly tugging at his heart strings. He got up, stumbled over to the bridge and sat down at the base of one of the pillars. For a while he just stared at the graffiti covered concrete wall and listened to the sound of the water echoing under the bridge around him.

Tyson dragged his sluggish thoughts away from the moment and into happier times. He saw Suzie laughing and skipping away from him playfully, and looking at him suggestively. He saw himself with his camera filming her escape. She disappeared through a white doorway in the distance, her laugh echoing through the dark, empty spaces. The sound of his feet landing on hollow metal and the clicking of his boot heels was all he could hear, until her squeal of excitement cut through his soul. He made it to the doorway, the camera peered into the blackness and he craned his neck so he could hear her wild shrieks.

Then he was back at the creek again, the sound of a truck passing overhead breaking his trance and equalising his slack jawed, lost expression. Suddenly he felt his pocket vibrating, eventually registering it as the throb of an incoming call. He let it buzz for a few seconds whilst he decided whether or not he can be bothered answering. He retrieved it, glancing at the caller ID as it rang for the last time. It was Maggie; Tyson's ex, Lulu's mum.

He hit the green button and listened to the silence at the other end. Eventually he answered, his voice cracked and broken by the phlegm building up in his throat.

"Yep... Hello?"

"Hi, Daddy! When are you coming to pick me up?"

Tyson's face transformed when he heard the voice of his little girl.

"Lulu!" he exclaimed, pushing as much positive feeling into the words that he could muster, but even to him it sounded hollow.

"So Daddy, guess what? I did a drawing for you and the teacher put a gold koala sticker on it!"

"That's great darling, that's great," his voice trailing off at the end; his eyes fixed on the graffiti in front of him.

"So Daddy, I was thinking, you should take me to the park so I can show you how I swing upside down on the monkey bars, then we should go get some fish'n'chips and sit up at the monument and eat them!"

"OK darling, sounds good. What's the time, sweetie?" Tyson asked, using all his failing energy to stay focussed on the call. He could hear Lulu shouting to her Mum, asking her the time.

"Mum says it's late o'clock, you were supposed to be here an hour ago! Come quick, Dad!"

He loved the sense of urgency she applied to everything when she was excited. What he didn't like was that he hadn't remembered that today was his access day with her, being so lost in the grief of Suzie's death, in the stinking toxic creek and the rotting plastic.

"OK sweetheart, I'll be there in a jiff," he said and signed off, staring down at the outfall pipe for a moment as the last trickle of toxic water dripped into the creek, the spaces between getting bigger and bigger until all that was left was the hollowness of their potential.

Chapter 12

Phuket, Thailand
2014

Tyson was sitting in his usual spot at the end of the bar staring into the large dirty mirror and sipping his beer, thankful that the place had reverted to the quiet, forgettable little place he liked so much. Nid had cleaned up the broken tables and bent chairs from the brawl and he could see her at the other end of the bar, wiping it with a cloth absentmindedly, her weathered face reflected back up at her. He watched her zone out as she stared at her bloated face, her eyes narrowed into slits and the rest of her features forming the sullen, grim expression you could see on every second face here in Patong.

Tyson liked Nid. She had a way of accepting all kinds of bad shit, of dealing with every calamity that walked through her door wearing board shorts and a Chang beer T-shirt. There was something, some core part of her that couldn't be broken, couldn't be fazed. And it wasn't from not giving a shit; it was something immovable, a resilience in her DNA that kept her going, kept her sweeping the sidewalk and wiping her bar with a sodden cloth, and staring at the door with a vague sense of hope that maybe one day the right person would walk through it and she would let her heart race again.

Tyson stared at the door with his own set of expectations, and falling in love didn't make the list. He thought of a T-shirt that men could wear that would sum up their experiences: he imagined a large ATM card with legs running away from a cluster of Thai girls in the Patong uniform; short shorts, a skin-tight brightly coloured singlet, and enough red lipstick to smear on a dozen pale faces, screaming 'helllooo... welcome, sexy man' whilst clawing at each other to get to the front. He was staring back toward the mirror when he heard the squeaky hinges of the front door.

Lulu was standing there in her pyjamas, clutching Rufus, her favourite teddy bear, and rubbing her eyes.

"Daddy, I can't sleep. Bad dreams, can you play for me?"

He blinked several times but she was still there, silhouetted by the pounding midday sun pouring into the room around her.

"Daddy, can you hear me? Can you play for me?"

He choked back tears, and looked at his long lost daughter.

"If only I could, sweetheart," he heard himself replying.

"But why, Daddy? You always play for me. There's a bad man in my dreams, Daddy, and he tries to steal me every night!" she was sobbing now as she turned to leave.

"Wait, sweetheart!" he pleaded, but he was too late. Next thing he knew he was looking at a young Thai woman in denim shorts and ridiculous heels and she was snarling at him. He could see her mouth moving, making word shapes.

"Alai, na?" *What?* Her full red lips an eerie counterpoint to the pissed off expression on her face.

"Pood mai, krub?" *Say again please*, Tyson asked, confused.

She looked disgustedly at him, then spat,

"Khun baa maak!" *You very crazy!*

She turned on her cheap heels and gave him the tight arse as she stormed out of the bar, leaving a trail of sickly sweet perfume as a parting gesture.

***

This time it was the sound of fists pounding leather and the smell of sweat that woke him. His eyes struggled to focus on the blurry shapes moving in front of him. He was lying at the foot of a boxing ring and all the moving shapes were side–on and moving back and forth, over and over, a demented, angry dance that ended with the leather pounding slaps that woke him. He could make out the smattering of tattoos on white skin, legs and arms covered in variations on the same theme: bad ass, 'fuck you world' declarations and bloody-minded belief systems that only a combination of youth and the stupidity of the mob could create. Some even had 'job-stoppers', Tyson's term for neck or facial tattoos, and in Patong there were heaps of them, often plastered on the most unlikely of men, on the most unlikely of faces.

Muai Thai boxing camps had sprung up all over the island, rivalling prostitution as the biggest drawcard that brought the masses of tourists to

Phuket, and, after so many years of blackouts, Tyson had finally woken up in one. He felt a wet sensation on his leg and looked up just in time to see a mangy white dog take a step back, a snarl mid-way to forming, the hair on his back raised in anticipation of a wayward leg finding its way to his scarred torso, which wasn't much more than a patchwork of lost fur and battle scars.

Tyson smiled at the dog the way De Niro smiles, nothing friendly in it at all. The dog sensed this and didn't seem to mind – he continued on with the business of finding a food source as if this altercation was a normal thing. Tyson groaned as he sat up, his back and neck stiff from his latest choice of bed – a cold concrete floor caked in layers of sweat – and watched the slaves to aggression get their morning fix.

The last thing he remembered was Lulu walking into the bar and turning into a snarling bar girl before his eyes. He willed the images to go away, willed the memory of his daughter to slip back into the morass of brain cells from which they came so that he could function now, punch through another day without the gnawing, empty feeling that betrayed the turmoil within.

A Thai man wearing boxing shorts bounced over and asked,

"Tham arai?" *What are you doing?*

Tyson looked up helplessly and smiled at him, holding the empty hands up that illustrate his standard reply.

"Mai luu." *Don't know.*

"Maow laew, mai?" *Drunk already?*

"Mai, sap-son diaw." *No, just confused.*

The Thai boxer looked at him for a good ten seconds, as if deciding whether or not to make an example of him in front of the Red Bull riddled eyes of his students, and finally muttered,

"Bpai loei!" *Go away now!*

Tyson stood up slowly, nodding to the man, grateful for his apparent leniency. He shuffled out onto the street; his eyes wide, as if taking in all available light would make his location less of a mystery.

After a few minutes of walking he realised he was at Rawai beach on the southeast side of Phuket, twenty kilometres from Patong and a long walk to the relative safety of Gaew's bed. He looked down at the high tide lapping gently on the sand and the empty speed boats waiting for the first busload of Korean or Chinese tourists to arrive, often dismounting the bus with their lifejackets already on and iPads thrust out in front of them like a blind man's cane. He nodded at the speedboat owners languishing under their makeshift offices of old banners and a broken-down bamboo sala, all wrap-around sunglasses and missing teeth and Buddha tattoos assuaging their guilt. He couldn't help but grin at them. They replied with the toothless version, and with the wrap around sunnies, Tyson thought, it was perfect.

From the foreshore he made his way down to the small amount of sand not yet relinquished to the incoming tide, and skirted between it and the succulent ground cover that marked the crossover. Up ahead in the distance he could see a wrecked fishing boat half buried in the sand and listing drastically to one side. As he approached he could make out the familiar grey hair of the lone sculptor moving about inside it.

Tyson smiled widely, overcome by the strange synchronicity of it all. He was intrigued by the old man's gruff persona and the fluid moves that sprang out of him to create the beauty that was so at odds with its maker.The old man was throwing pieces of the boat out onto the foreshore; large pieces of coloured wood that were part of the cabin. Tyson watched him clamber up onto the cabin roof and start wrenching and tugging at the wooden handrail that skirted its edges. Tyson yelled out to him, holding his hand up to shield his eyes from the sun. The old man stopped abruptly, as if woken from a trance, and glared in Tyson's direction, then returned his attention to the task at hand: the resistant handrail. Tyson moved closer and, looking around him for something with which to create leverage, found a long piece of hardwood plank. He passed it silently to the old man, whose frustration with the handrail was turning to fury, and for the first time Tyson saw a dark edge to the calm, peaceful blue eyed stare that was only ever partly visible beneath the grey swirl.

The old sculptor took the timber from Tyson without any acknowledgement, without even a glance towards him. Instead he looked away when eyes could've met, as if unable to climb down from the frustration that had possessed him. Tyson retreated slightly and started stacking the rapidly growing pile whilst keeping an eye out for fresh pieces thrown by the sculptor that might threaten to knock him off his feet. There was a loud cracking noise and he looked up just in time to see a section of the handrail spring off the roof and land on the sand next to him.

The old man laughed to himself as the last two pieces of the handrail landed on either side of Tyson, one grazing his ankle on the way through.

Tyson looked up at the old, obviously mad sculptor.

"Bit off your game today, old fella?"

There was silence for a full minute as the sculptor straightened up and stared at Tyson with a gaze so penetrating he had to resist the urge to turn away. Tyson could feel the wind blowing between them. The sculptor was holding a small piece of wood in his hands, turning it over, tossing it in the air and catching it, all whilst maintaining the piercing stare. Finally he spoke.

"It's better when you don't talk," flinging the wood underarm, low and flat, at Tyson's stomach. Tyson caught it in both hands and looked up challengingly at the old cool blue stare and caught a glimpse of it turning to a smile.

Suddenly the old man leapt off the boat and landed next to Tyson with that menacing grin spreading across his face. Again he stared long and hard at Tyson, then said,

"Well, pick up all that wood and follow me!" as he moved off away from the beach, towards the surrounding hills.

Chapter 13

Castlemaine, Australia
2004

Tyson and Lulu sat silently eating their fish'n'chips and looking out at Castlemaine spread out below them. They sat beneath the monument to two largely inept explorers who died 'opening up' a stock route from the south to the north end of Australia, expiring in the harsh desert heat that had cooked what was left of their addled brains. Dying of starvation, surrounded by bush tucker and local wisdom and yet ignoring it in their colonialist way, to their peril. Of course they became heroes.

Tyson looked blankly out at the rolling hills dotted with the Bunya pines that marked the old sandstone mansions; Neo-gothic, Victorian and Georgian relics from another time. Tyson watched as dusk fell early on the little valley, the scattered, brightly coloured rooves catching the last of the light.

He was struggling to keep it together enough to connect with his daughter, who had until now been consumed with a mouthful of chips. He was immersed in a thick layer of grief and shock, a seemingly impenetrable barrier to the moment he was in. And yet, he couldn't think of anyone he'd rather be with, the only person in the world that would let him be with his misery and still love him unconditionally. How Tyson longed for the innocence of a child, for the intuitive acceptance of things as you found them, for the ability to forgive and forget, as he could do neither.

"So Dad," Lulu began, "how come you and Mum don't love each other anymore?"

Normally he loved her directness, the way she could condense a difficult thing and make it seem simple, but his usual buoyancy evaded him and all he could picture was the sad face of Maggie, imbued with the perpetual disappointment of a muso's spouse.

"Dunno love, we just couldn't keep it together, he said vaguely, searching the horizon for something to distract her.

"I wish you and Mum could get back together…"

Tyson wished he could say 'me too' but he knew it was a lie. He had barely given Maggie a second thought after Suzie came into his life.

"Lulu, you know that isn't going to happen," attempting to disguise his defeated tone, and failing.

"But Dad, imagine the fun we could have! You could take me to the park everyday if you wanted to!" her tone of optimism breaking the wall he had built between them.

He turned to look at her at last.

"We can still have fun can't we?"

"Of course Dad, but imagine if everyday was like this, instead of once a week?"

"Yeah it'd be great," he said flatly, feeling himself drifting again into the puddle of heartache lying at his feet.

Lulu's legs swung playfully under the bench seat as she carefully chose another chip. Tyson turned back to the view, noticing the festival crew rehearsing the opening ceremony off in the distance, a blaze of stage lights fading in and out, changing colour and moving about, throwing light in several directions.

"Wow, look at that sweetie! Look at those coloured lights!"

"Oh WOW," her angelic deep brown eyes widening so much that Tyson could see the lights bouncing off them.

"Let's go take a closer look, what d'you say?"

"Yes Daddy, but first I think we should finish these chips!" and she proceeded to thrust another chip in her mouth whilst pulling faces, like she was going to burst. And laughing. Tyson watched the light dance in her eyes.

***

Later, in his room, Tyson looked at the computer screen and watched the light dancing in Suzie's eyes as they raced through the bacon factory at night. At times he had held the camera behind them, so Tyson could see both of them running through the large expanses of the killing floor, their giggling filling the space with an incongruous levity.

He had forgotten he had shot this footage, had forgotten about that night, the night that had ended up being their last one together. He had dredged his mind for details in the past, but there were none.

And now here that night was, right in front of his eyes.

He saw himself staggering after Suzie, who kept pausing in doorways so he could almost catch up, then racing off in that little black skirt, with that sly giggle which resonated now and hung in his empty room. He was inches away from losing it as he watched the love of his life in the last moments of hers, and the reality of it all hit him like a drunk football player on a Saturday night, all heavy intention and blundering steps. He felt the blow before it hit him, but kept watching helplessly as he slumped to the floor, a perpetual spectator in his own nightmare.

The images rolled across the screen: he saw himself running down a dark corridor and it reminded him of 'Blair Witch Project'; the panicked, jerky camera; the heavy, laboured breathing. And then he saw Suzie again, right in front of the camera, and she was pouting, then licking her lips and making her eyes flash somehow and, for Tyson, this was the moment that tore it. He was gone, his head in his hands, wailing huge guttural sobs with large intakes of air, like a whale coming to the surface. Large, desperate breaths that fuelled more tears and delivered him squarely into the heart of a grief that knew no end.

"You wanna fuck me right now, don't you baby?" he heard her asking the camera, and so he dragged his head up, wiped the snot out of his nose with his sleeve and looked at the image of her once again. There was nothing but darkness, the click of her heels on the polished concrete floor fading out with her. Then he saw her leaning in a doorway twenty metres away, and as the camera moved in, the near darkness was slowly replaced with the image of Suzie in the lit doorway. She was holding her finger to her lips to quieten him as muffled sounds reach them through the door, the muffled sounds of someone screaming in pain.

Tyson's eyes cut a line through his tears to the computer screen. He stared hypnotically at the images, willing the muffled screams to transform into something else, but they only get louder. On the screen, both Tyson and Suzie were moving towards the source of the sound, and this time there was nothing hurried about it. They snuck up to it slowly, apprehensively, and Suzie turned to Tyson and the camera, and whispered,

"What the fuck?" as they approached the only lit room in the building.

Suzie was the first to peek through the glass door into the room and the camera saw her face drain of colour and her mouth drop open, slackened by the horror of what she was looking at. The screams of a man echo out of the room and envelop them both, prompting Tyson to stand up and point the camera through the glass.

What Tyson saw on the screen was a surreal image of torture. A man was being fed live into an industrial meat grinder, the torturers stopping and starting the machine as another question went unanswered. He was nearly half way through the machine and still hanging on, shaking and screaming and crying and bleeding and it was then that he saw Doug Farris walk into the room, the perpetual cigar in his mouth, the morbidly obese frame a thing of strange fluidity. He could see Doug walk across to the grinder and switch it on again whilst blowing cigar smoke into the tortured man's face.

Tyson looked away from the screen, put his head in his hands and let forth a howl from the depths of his being.

Chapter 14

Phuket, Thailand
2014

Tyson's arms were aching from the load of boat timber and his legs strained trying to keep up with the sculptor. The old guy walked with the briskness of a young man and if it wasn't for the stoop, the long grey hair and beard, and the driftwood walking stick, you could be easily mistaken. He strode ahead of Tyson with the vigour of someone discovering new frontiers. And Tyson was his packhorse. They had left the road and had been making their way through thick tropical jungle for some time when they reached the top of a hill and the old man stopped to take in the view, which gave Tyson a chance to catch his breath.

"So, you're haven't been completely stupified then," the sculptor stated matter-of-factly, "See how well we get on when you don't talk?"

Tyson could see the faintest smile in the old man's blue eyes. He let the wood go and it made a loud clatter when it hit the ground. He straightened up and stood next to the sculptor and they both looked out. Beyond the tall trees he could see the ocean, dotted with islands and old Thai fishing boats. At the foot of the hill there was a tiny beach, mostly worn granite boulders with sand between them. There was a large house perched on the right hand edge and Tyson could see some rough steps cut out of the rock leading from the house to the beach.

"C'mon, not much further now, let's go!" the old man said, with an upward inflection on the last word.

Soon enough, they were heading down into a small ravine that Tyson couldn't even see until they were in it. It was so steep that he slipped several times and almost dropped his precious load. The old man was silent the whole way, except for the odd knowing grunt when he heard Tyson about to fall. The old man crouched down and disappeared into the undergrowth and Tyson followed clumsily. When they came back out into a clear patch Tyson could not believe what he was looking at.

It was one of the most beautiful structures he had ever seen: a series of organic shapes that wound around and up into the trees. The lowest roof was shaped like a large field mushroom and had a spiral staircase made from vines and pieces of fishing boat winding out of it, up and around a large adjacent tree. The second level was smaller and didn't have walls, just a wooden floor and palm leaf roof, which again was wrapped around the boughs of the trees in a totally fluid manner. The downstairs walls were made from earth, curved and rendered by hand, with soft, rounded corners going to window frames of bent driftwood that betrayed the builder's inherent love of the tactile. Figurative sculptures lined the track leading to the mushroom; each one constructed out of recycled paraphernalia from the beach, each one an exquisite expression of the beauty of the found object. Tyson was speechless.

"Just put that wood over there, Tyson, and come on up to the platform," the old man said, in an almost conciliatory way.

They both sat on the platform and stared out at the Andaman Sea.

"How'd you know my name?" Tyson asked cautiously. The old man's eyes went wide for a moment, and then returned to their half squint as he whispered,

"Maybe it's time I told you a little story."

He cleared his throat.

"There's this guy I used to know..." he began, pushing the hair off his face for the first time Tyson could recall as he continued staring out at the Andaman sea, as if he was searching for the words, the right words, to appear on the horizon. He turned around to face Tyson and smiled for the briefest of moments whilst tying his hair back with a reclaimed elastic band that had washed up on the beach.

"He was generally a good guy but he never seemed to fit in anywhere. He had been like that since he was a boy, and by the time adolescence had come and gone and left its mark on his face, he had become comfortable with it. The same way one becomes comfortable in hand-me-down clothes. But this feeling wasn't handed down to him. His brothers slotted into the world around them as if it was a perfectly natural thing, and to them it was. They weren't plagued with the gnawing feeling that there was something else out there for them, something the shape and form of which was constantly changing. And he was never really sure what he was searching for. He just had this sense of waiting..."

Tyson sat silently as the old man continued to stare somehow through him at the mercurial ocean beyond. It was a strange sensation, being looked at in this way. There was nothing intense about it at all, if anything it was the opposite, like being in the eye of a tornado..

"As soon as he could this guy left the small town that raised him and hit the city. He was eighteen years old, and what he owned he carried on his back, mostly books and a few clothes. The books were his treasured allies; they had carried him through the tempestuous years of his youth. The clothes on his back were his brother's cast-offs..."

The beginnings of a grin teased the corners of the sculptor's mouth beneath the mass of grey beard that covered his face.

"He sensed something was terribly wrong with the world, or at least the way people behaved towards each other and towards their mother earth. Something was askew, both in him and the chaotic city that threatened to swallow him up like he wasn't even there. He just couldn't put his finger on it. He found a job on a big construction site in the heart of the city and everyday he watched the commuters get on and off trams and trundle towards the towering edifices that swallowed all of them up until the last light had faded from the sky, after which they were released onto the streets again. He looked at the blank faces, the defeated walks, the uniforms they either felt compelled or were forced to wear. The emptiness tore at him and after six months he was furious about it. How could they do this to themselves? What had made them like this, so... so lifeless?

"At night he would pore through his books and others he borrowed from the library, looking for clues. He read Joyce, Kant, Shakespeare, Byron, Austen, Nin, Miller, Hemingway, Camus, Hesse, Sartre, Grass, Ghandi, Greer... anything, in short, where he felt someone tugging at the taut chain attached to their collar. Often it was the mad who would nail it just before they were lobotomised or locked in a dark cell for a very long time. Why was it at the end of things that we finally got it? Why not now, in the middle of it all? It ate away at him like sea lice on a floating corpse..."

They both looked out at the ocean. Tyson wondered where the old man's story was going, but was thoroughly enjoying it nevertheless.

Johnny took a sip of water, cleared his throat and continued.

"And then one day one of his co-workers fell to his death from the 30th floor not more than ten metres from where he stood tying steel re-bar together. The impact of that guy hitting made the ground shake under his feet and seemed to strengthen his resolve to go deeper, find a way to make a difference before *he* was the one falling and wondering, in his last moments, why his life added up to not much more than a bunch of numbers in red on a page and a family weeping at your graveside. In the aftermath of the accident the union rep ran around talking about safe work practises and ridiculously tight deadlines that sent that man into an area before the safety nets and rails had been installed. He was handing out flyers for some kind of meeting and when he handed one to our man and he saw the Industrial Workers of the World Unite slogan, he felt as if he had finally found the reason he was looking for, the thing that he could throw his formidable mind at. Was this the answer to what had plagued him in his youth? Don't get me wrong, Tys, he was still an outsider, it's just that he had found a way he could belong to something that mattered, for however long it lasted.

"You still haven't told me...."

"And last it did," the old guy continued, "And it changed him. Now he was reading political literature, Marx and Engels, Mao, Trotsky and when he got to Lenin's *'What is to be done?'* he felt that he had found his calling at last. He could see how capitalism had turned humans into slaves, how employers rarely gave a flying fuck about their workers and that profit was their only desire. And they didn't seem to care how many people were crushed under the bulldozer tracks as it searched out more resources to plunder. They didn't care at all. And our guy realised he had found something he could believe in at last. It was the most alive he had ever felt..."

Tyson sat there in rapt attention and looked at the old guy with a feeling approaching awe, but he also had butterflies dancing in his gut, as if he had just woken up with his toes gripping the edge of the high diving board. And the water looked a long way away.

"So he immersed himself in it. He drank in pubs with union officials, he sat in smoke filled rooms with the radical student left and argued over how to re-distribute the wealth that they were the recipients of. He went to various workplaces and attempted to incite dissent, and if he was lucky, give it a focus, a target, a reason. He demonstrated, he marched, wrote press releases and 'shouted' the bar at the journo's watering holes. And all the while reading more and more until he was full of quotable phrases, and the best part of it all, he believed in his cause. This guy was on fire, Tys!"

He paused for more water, spilling most of it in his excitement.

"And then it slowly went sour on him. He discovered that the leader of the Union movement was in bed with one of the biggest developers in the city. They had struck some kind of a deal to propel the union leader into politics, and suddenly he could see the writing on the wall. The ideals of fair and equal distribution of wealth, of state funded free hospitals and schools, of free tertiary education for all, were just words used to enamour the people, and as it turned out, actually served to disempower them. Chasing a carrot held above their heads by the man who had already sold them down the river. This man he'd put on a pedestal used political slogans as devices to numb the electorate, so that the rich and powerful could continue to be rich and powerful. His youthful idealism was being beaten to a pulp in a dark laneway behind the Albion hotel in Brunswick, right in front of his eyes. It nearly broke him..."

The old sculptor narrowed his gaze and looked squarely at Tyson, who was looking, it was fair to say, a little bewildered. Suddenly a chill went through him. *Could it be?*

"So this guy saw no other option but to retreat away from people again. He found himself an old hut in the bush not far from the town he grew up in and started reading books on mythology, spirituality. He was still looking for a reason even though his years in the city had tarnished his spirit..."

Tyson looked up at him, tears forming in the corners of his eyes, a look of utter confusion on his face.

"Johnny?" was all he could get out.

The old man turned finally and looked at him with those calm blue eyes bursting out of the grey mass around them

"It's good to see you again, mate."

Chapter 15

Castlemaine, Australia
2004

It was nearly midnight when Suthers stepped out of the OB van and lit a much-needed cigarette. He leaned his large frame against the wall of the council chambers and blew a plume of smoke up into the air towards the flickering street light and resumed the coughing fit he had been working on since the last smoke. He stared vacantly at the '3CCC Community Radio' sign peeling off the side of the truck when he felt a rumble of indignation coming through the wall. He reached through the van window and retrieved his headphones just as the shouts and stamping of feet rose in level. He threw his cigarette down on the ground, stamped on it and immediately lit another as he listened to the councillors discussing Item 42 on their agenda – the proposed route for the freeway.

The raucous public gallery were creating a deafening sound of dissent, consisting almost entirely of Suthers' friends and acquaintances, the rare few that could sense an injustice occurring and got off their well-fed arses to do something about it. Little did they know that the meeting was just a bit of theatre, the decision having been made months ago.

The veil of democracy was working well tonight.

Inside, Jake sat at the head of the table and stared at his clasped hands as the public gallery gave him all they had, the shouts of 'corruption' and 'murderers' going over Jake's head like low flying wasps.

Harmless, as long as you don't swat at them.

He stared vacantly at the map in front of him, depicting the freeway route that will tear a path through one of the last remaining forests in the area. The thought of the millions he would soon be making from the land deal made his cock twitch under the table and he quickly checked his expression, lest it betray his true feelings.

Making money always turned Jake on and before he knew it he was thinking of his last big land deal and the three girls on ecstasy that followed. He squirmed slightly in his chair and cleared his throat, looked sideways at the member for Coliban and winked confidently at him. Everyone around the table was making money tonight, thanks to Doug and Jake at the helm. A look of pity crept across Jake's face as he stared out at the crowd.

If only they knew how it all worked, he thought. But of course he knew they didn't, and they never would, not if all the boys around the table played their cards right.

Through the headphones, Suthers heard the gavel come down. The meeting was over and already his thoughts were piling up on top of each other with the urgency of a man who had spent his life trying to 'keep the bastards honest': Public meetings, media blitzes, invitations to state politicians, public marches, demonstrations and – one of the last on the pile – industrial sabotage in the form of sand in the fuel tanks of the bulldozers already lined up and waiting to tear through a swathe of forest. He took the headphones off and looked up again at the flickering streetlight when a side door opened and Jake slipped through it. Suthers watched as Jake pulled a phone out of his Zegna suit pocket and started talking.

Suthers shuffled closer so he could make out what Jake was saying and thanked himself for the darkness of his second hand clothes.

"Yeah Dougy, all went as expected, although there were heaps more protestors there than anyone expected. It was standing room only up there."

Suthers watched Jake pull the phone away from his ear as Doug started yelling at him so loud even Suthers could hear the odd word, mainly the words 'fuck' and 'fucking' and of course the word 'hippy' until Doug ran out of steam and Jake could finally return the phone to his ear.

Jake made it to his black 5 series BMW just as Suthers had crept, as much as a man with a lot of bulk and a lot of crap hanging off him can creep, behind a car nearby.

"Are you done yet?" Jake asked.

"Done?" Doug screamed incredulously, "Mate, I haven't even started yet!"

Suthers stuck his head up above the car just as Jake was opening his door and leaning against it, the arm holding the phone a good two feet from his ear as Doug launched into his next tirade.

"Jake, I don't have to remind you what's at stake here, do I? How easy it would be for me to put a fuckin' match under your career and watch it burn?

Keep your eye on the fuckin' ball, mate, and get me that contract, OK?"

Suthers heard bits and pieces, enough for him to smell something big and dirty going down.

"Look Dougy, gotta go, talk later." Jake hung up and hopped into the soft leather interior of his black cocoon as Suthers slid slowly down the door of the car he was leaning on, his mind in overdrive now. He retrieved a tattered note pad from his coat pocket and started writing.

Meanwhile, in an abandoned woollen mill cellar close by, Doug put his phone back in his pocket and watched his boys 'initiate' a new girl into their club. The dank, damp smell of the cellar reminded him of his childhood; the empty, reverberant space transporting him back to the sound of three boys' fearful laughter echoing up the mineshaft. He let the echo of his past spread itself across his present. He worked his face into a grin.

The girl was chained to a post and being repeatedly slapped and taunted, her eyes blindfolded, while a man in a gimp mask and a leather G-string brought a leather whip down hard across the top of her young shoulders, ripping more soft flesh off with each strike. Blood was trickling down between her legs, running past a shiny black baton to a nearby drain, a drain she wished she could slip down into, and float far, far away.

Doug lit another cigar, savouring the first puffs through a cold grin as he dragged his grotesquely fat body towards the sobbing and barely conscious girl.

Chapter 16

Thailand 2014

Tyson's past was smashing up against his present. Images reared up out of the haze full of torment, dragging him through a montage of repressed pain, of a loss his mind had hidden from him in an act of pure survival. Then he remembered what Johnny had done for him that night. Incredulity and disbelief soon turned to the pure simple joy of finding an old friend. Tyson beamed.

"Fuck, it's good to see you, Johnny."

"Long time, my friend."

The moment grabbed a hold of them, pulled them in tight so all they could do for quite some time was grin at each other. Tyson had a million questions but they congealed before he could get to them.

Tears ran down his cheeks and fell into the ravines widened by his smile.

"Been a long road, hey mate?"

"Yep..." was all Tyson got out before he started sobbing and choking on phlegm? Johnny reached over and put his arm around him and stared out at the Andaman stretching itself over the horizon like melted butter over bread.

"But, how did you…"

"Find you? Well mate, it wasn't easy I can tell you!"

"I've been lost for a long time, Johnny. Since that night. Been running ever since"

"I know, mate. Figured you had some kind of amnesia. Do you remember anything, anything at all?"

"Not much. Just flashes."

"UH Huh."

Johnny stared off into the jungle. This was going to be harder than he thought.

When Tyson made it back to Gaew's, he headed straight for the bedroom. Luckily for him, she wasn't there, so he had the place to himself, a rare thing. Normally, this room was full of the pouty, sullen energy of Gaew, and would've smelt of baby powder and cheap perfume. He picked up his shakuhachi, got a Tiger beer out of the fridge and headed out onto the tiny balcony overlooking the street.

His mind was racing again. A part of him couldn't believe he had found his old friend Johnny. Then when he thought about it, the fact that Johnny had searched for him for over ten years sent a warm rush through him, humbling him in an instant. He could hardly wait to see him again tomorrow.

He smiled in gratitude as he sat down on the child sized plastic chair, cracked his beer, placed the wrapped shakuhachi on his lap, and then stared down at the chaotic street. Thai food smells wafted up into his nostrils, reminding him that he hadn't eaten since yesterday afternoon.

He unwrapped the flute and held it gently for quite a while before bringing it to his lips. He pictured Johnny on the platform in the jungle and a long low note echoed out across the street. The note continued resonating and he placed another on top of it, sympathetic in tone to the first, opening the floodgates of potential places he could go. Before too long he was lost inside his music again, the long pensive notes like a soft bed after sleeping rough, and he surrendered to them, letting the pulse go through him until he could feel the tightness between his shoulder blades relaxing. He opened his eyes and let in the visual madness of the street and transformed it with his flute, making the endless chatter of the street sound like a symphony. Each motorbike, each girl yelling 'massage!', each clang of spoon against frying pan came together through his mad improvisation to become an escape from the daily soul massacre, from the endless mad scramble that was Patong coming through his window.

Chapter 17

Castlemaine, Australia
2004

Suthers darted through the rowdy gathering of protestors on his way to the OB van. He nodded and grunted at a few friends who were patting him on the back, thanking him for getting the word out, whilst he wondered whether he switched on all the panel mics on the Town Hall stage. Jake was amongst the members of the panel, talking nervously with them, their hands over the mics, trying to look like a bunch of old friends sharing road stories. And in a way, they were just that.

Suthers exited via a side door, looked back, and noticed that no one in the crowd was sitting on the chairs provided – the only ones seated being the powerful few on stage.

Jake nodded at the member for Coliban and the Minister for Roads, took his hand off his mic and cleared his throat loudly, the sudden amplification startling the noisy crowd and stifling all but the most committed of any thought of being noisy.

"Let's bring this meeting to order." Jake suggested, fidgeting uncomfortably in his seat, the first of many beads of sweat appearing on his smooth, tanned forehead.

"OK, thanks everyone. The first to speak will be the honourable Jack Marriot, Minister for Roads. Bit of shoosh please!"

The honourable member thanked Jake and launched into his well -rehearsed speech, outlining the government's lengthy and comprehensive selection process regarding the proposed freeway routes, making reference to environmental impact studies, economic growth corridors and the big picture of linking Melbourne with its outlying satellite cities. He was about to hand over to the crowd when a placard was thrown at him, narrowly missing his carefully prepared hair.

"FUCKIN' WANKER!" one of the protestors yelled,

"What about the black wallabies you will drive to extinction, you FUCKIN' LIAR!"

And with that the crowd erupted. In the OB van Suthers chuckled and checked his levels, double checked that he was in fact going to air, settled back in the tattered chair and rolled a cigarette, pre-empting the moment with a couple of deep, liquid coughs that made the old chair squeak.

"If you refer to subsection 17, paragraph 27 of the impact study...." the Minister began, but the crowd were on a mission, and listening to a politician muddy the waters was not a part of it.

If only the people realise there is nothing they can do about it, Jake mused, whilst maintaining what he hoped was a composed and thoughtful expression.

If only they knew how his game worked, that this was just an elaborate piece of theatre. Stupid fuckers, the decision was made weeks ago. Go back to your TV's, go back to your dull lives and be fucking thankful for the financial injection five hundred construction workers are going to make to your town. To my town...

Jake's thoughts suddenly turned to taking a long lunch with Bernadette, the new young hottie he has stuck behind the counter at the council offices. He suppressed the sexual tingle heading to his groin just before it turned his thoughtful expression into one of intense personal satisfaction. He looked at his watch absentmindedly.

Hopefully we can knock this over in less than an hour. More time than the democratic process deserves. After all, didn't they vote me in so I could make decisions for them?

***

A few blocks away, the funeral procession pulled slowly away from Farris and Makin Funeral parlour (owned by Doug's half-wit of a cousin) and made its way down Mostyn Street. Doug was in the lead car of course, black sunglasses hiding the glint in his eye from his long-suffering wife, Gladys. He tapped the armrest, the jingle of gold rings on his fingers almost giving him away as he drummed the rhythm of one of his favourite swing tunes. He reminded himself that he was supposed to be playing the bereaved father, not the anxious capitalist pig resenting even more time being stolen from him by his ungrateful daughter. If only she had behaved as he had dictated, then she would still be alive. A broken wreck of a girl, tortured beyond repair, but alive, nevertheless.

Doug was not one to dwell on things so he focused on the road ahead, which was passing under them excruciatingly slowly. Ahead of them the road was closed due to the festival and this meant a more convoluted route to the cemetery. *Even more time lost,* he bemoaned quietly to himself. An army of black clad festival crew were putting the finishing touches to Stage 1, festival central, phones jammed in their ears as they rigged lights and hung banners, lost in their own little worlds. He could sense their urgency and frenetic energy from the comfort of the plush leather seat his ample bulk has distorted almost beyond recognition.

The opening ceremony was tonight; the streets would be full of townspeople, crew and performers. Doug could see the festival artistic director mincing around, pointing at things, and hoping that any last minute hurdles wouldn't hamper his 'vision'. Doug suppressed a guffaw, satisfying himself with his standard 'fuckin' poofta', uttered under his breath in case it broke through Gladys's relentless sobbing.

A few blocks further away, Tyson was lurking on the bridge overlooking the creek where Suzie had been found, still grappling with her death, still frozen in a state of disbelief, still numb to the point that he could barely recognise himself anymore. Happiness seemed like some kind of dream he would never realise, a lost lotto ticket on the road to his personal hell.

Fear overtook him like a runaway train and a chill ran down his spine, paralysing him where he stood. Through his haze, he was finally making the connection between his last night with her at the pig factory, and her gruesome death. A growing sense of foreboding swamped him and turned his legs to jelly as the funeral procession made the left turn that will take them past Tyson. He turned his head instinctively as the long black hearse entered the street, his legs began functioning again and he turned his whole body around to watch it pass, a man with his heart in his hands and his spirit scattered to the wind.

In the lead car, Doug had relaxed his bereaved father expression and was resisting the urge to get out his phone and start barking orders at anyone he could think of when he noticed a long-haired man standing on the bridge, his head bowed with his back to the street, right above where Suzie was found. He slid his sunnies down his bulbous nose and stared out of the window at the man, curiosity overtaking the myriad of entrepreneurial thoughts running through his bloated brain.

Was that fucken Tyson?

Chapter 18

Phuket, Thailand
2014

Tyson walked through the blazing Patong afternoon, heading north for no apparent reason. There wasn't the usual accompanying feeling of emptiness though; rather, he was feeling more buoyant than he had in years. He was making his way to the coast road, filled with an eerie lightness, and feeling, on the surface anyway, strangely unburdened. He was on his way to meet Johnny.

How did I end up here? He pondered, having no recollection of what made him decide that this was the place to disappear to. Patong was full of people like him, escaping their previous lives and looking for the 'reset' button. Most ended up drowning in cheap beer in grungy bars with cheap whores attached to their bulging appendages and of course, Tyson was thinking about their wallets here. He laughed out loud; it had been so long since he had made himself laugh.

He strode down street after street filled with a thousand different ways to lose your soul on the instalment plan – a little piece at a time. And the twisted irony of it was that those who indulged in the seedy Patong menu actually thought it was empowering them, as they drained another beer or emptied the contents of their semi-hard cocks into a waiting disenchanted mouth, more often than not a ladyboy's. He had lost count of how many times he had heard some loser's story of 'accidentally' waking up in the morning next to one or two ladyboys sleeping soundly, or how many times he had heard some guy boasting about the hot Thai chick he had just nailed all night, without having to pay of course, given he was such a stud.

But as Tyson was acutely aware, nothing in Patong was free. Nothing at all. One way or the other, you always had to pay...

As he turns left onto Soi Ratchapathanuson, a man steps out in front of him.

"Hello sir, where you from?" he asks before Tyson has even registered he is there.

"Zimbabwe, what's it to ya?" Tyson replies.

"You wanna suit sir, very nice suit, very cheap?" the Indian tailor asks him, grabbing him by the arm and attempting to lead him towards his over-lit shop with a life-size photo of Brad Pitt in the window, presumably wearing one of this man's suits.

Tyson resisted the arm hold with a smile, saying,

"No thanks, save it for a tourist, mate," the last word slipping out before he had time to check himself.

"Aah, an Aussie, hey? AUSSIE AUSSIE AUSSIE!" he leads off, expecting Tyson to 'OI OI OI!' him, but this was actually Tyson's cue to move away as quickly as possible, so repugnant this repartee was to him. He hadn't identified himself as Australian for years. He hadn't identified himself as anything. He didn't have a home and he liked it that way. There was something to be said for getting lost.

Before he knew it he was in Kalim on the outskirts of Patong, the neon lights and the plastic speakers that spat out the dance tunes fading as he climbed the hill towards Kamala, and with each step a little more grime came off him, and Tyson felt like he could breathe again.

***

It took Tyson a while before he realised the ground was moving under him and for more than an instant he convinced himself that he was dreaming; that the rocking was some kind of a trick his mind was playing on him. He resisted opening his eyes as usual; relying on his hearing to feed him the clues as to where the hell he had woken up this time. He could hear waves lapping at the shore in the distance and, closer to him, the sound of ropes landing on wood, large lumps of rope. He could smell the stale stench of the ocean where he lay, and the familiar scent of Cat brand tobacco, coming to him in wafts.

The staccato lung rattle of a heavy smoker finally urged him to force his eyes open into tiny slits: just enough to show him the inside of a long tail boat; just enough to reveal a pile of multi-coloured fishing nets; and just enough to see the toothless smile of an old Thai man, complete with a hand rolled cigarette dangling from his lips.

He worked on a return smile until he had it, then held it there whilst taking in the scene in the periphery of his vision. It seemed that he had made it as far north as Kamala: the familiar curve of the beach and the concrete wall that ran for a few hundred metres on the southern tip confirmed this for him. The small creek they were bobbing up and down in was full of long tail boats and the all too familiar stink of rotting garbage, the water being choked with it, as was every watercourse on the island. The old man was easing the boat out of the creek and into the ocean with a long oar, pushing against other boats or the sandy bottom, propelling them slowly away from land. Tyson looked at the converted car engine balanced expertly on its pivot and the long shaft and propeller tied to the inside of the boat right next to him.

It looked like he was in for a spot of fishing.

Once they had cleared the shallow inlet the old man untied the shaft and propeller and effortlessly swung it 180 degrees until it was perched just above the water line. He wrapped a piece of rope around the flywheel and tugged at it until the engine roared to life. Neither of them had said a word yet, and now with the deafening roar of the engine there was even less chance, which suited Tyson anyway. The old fisherman also seemed happy with the silence and fixed his eyes on the horizon. Tyson watched a calmness overtake the old man, he was clearly in his element, gunning the motor and staring out to sea.

Tyson found himself staring out with the old man. There was some kind of camaraderie to be found there that was better than language, and at times he snuck glances at the old man and wondered what he thought of this strange, bedraggled 'farang' sharing the moment with him. His face was indecipherable, he had a glazed look to his eyes and his frail looking, yet deceptively strong body, leaned instinctively forward, countering the thrust of the motor. Tyson looked at the calm turquoise water being gently pushed past the bow and got lost in its mesmerising rhythm. Within half a minute his camera was in his hands and capturing another moment to be spliced into his little movie. He had music running through his brain and he wished he had his flute with him. He could've played it for the old man, given him something back, something that might transform the blank face into a smile. But the face wasn't blank at all, it was simply that Tyson couldn't read it, and the man gave nothing away to the ocean lest it pounce on his vulnerability.

The old man pulled back on the throttle, which consisted of a looped piece of string connected to the carburettor, and the boat glided slowly to a stop, rocking gently with the soft swell. He climbed down from his perch and began tossing the nets over the side, pausing to look at Tyson, as if to say, 'Well, you gonna help, or what?', the cigarette still dangling, his lips pursing then relaxing as he hauled the net over the side. Tyson shut off his camera and stumbled over to the old man and picked up a clump of net in his hand. Soon their movements were locked in together and the net ceased to have any weight, as if they had been doing this together for years. The last of the net went over the side followed by a series of floats of various colours and shapes, fashioned from things the man had obviously found lying around. Without looking at him the old man headed back to the engine, grabbed the long shaft and gave the string a good tug, setting the boat in motion again, making Tyson lose his balance.

They seemed to be heading for an exposed sand bar at the far end of Layan beach, near Sirinat National Park, one of Tyson's favourite places. He recalled the small river that ran between the

113

headland and a small, rocky island, and the fishing community upstream. The old man grunted and said,

"Nong farang!" *Young foreigner!*

Tyson turned just in time to see a small bottle of whisky flying through the air at him. His reflexes didn't let him down, catching it in his right hand before firing a grin at the old man. He took a swig – it was barely 6a.m., and the rough Thai whisky tore down his throat like hot tar burned through your skin. He suppressed the urge to gag and threw the bottle back, and for the first time, the fisherman broke into a grin, showing Tyson what was left of his teeth, stained brown and worn down just like the old man's face.

Tyson smiled back and then turned around, his gaze fixed on the promontory. He squinted as his eyes adjusted to the early morning glare and screwed his face up as the whisky settled in his stomach and a dirty, warm burst made its way up into his chest. In the distance he could make out the shapes of the rocks that formed the island and the familiar shape of a longhaired, stooped figure darting between them.

He smiled to himself.

The old man slowed the boat down to a crawl, a wry grin on his face. Tyson took his cue and readied himself to disembark, climbing to the edge of the boat and tucking his shirt in for some unknown reason. He checked that his camera was back in his shorts pocket and, turning to the old man, nodded and bowed to him as they approached the sand bar. The old man pulled the throttle back to idle and they floated the last twenty metres. Tyson climbed over the edge and eased himself into the water, then kicked his legs briskly so that he cleared the boat and its ominous propeller. He looked back at the fisherman, but his gaze was not returned: the old guy was already looking ahead at the narrow entrance to the river and the drinking session that would ensue. Tyson made it to the rocks and dragged himself up onto one of them, his breathing laboured from the short swim, his clothes soaked and hanging off him, when Johnny appeared from behind a rock.

"You're late! Was starting to wonder if you hadn't stood me up. Imaginative method I must say!" Johnny said, whilst waving to the old man in the boat as he negotiated the narrow river entrance.

Tyson looked up at him through the water dripping off his brow.

Johnny walked to the water's edge and started retrieving small round stones from below the water line. He looked at each one carefully, and then either discarded or kept it. Most of them he kept, making a pile next to his gnarly feet. They were worn and smooth, having been shaped by the movement of the ocean for a millennium or more. He fashioned a carry bag out of his ragged T-shirt and placed all the stones in it, stood up and faced Tyson.

"So you gonna help or what?" his blue eyes smiling, his hand holding out the bag.

Tyson pushed his wet hair off his face, got up, walked over to Johnny and silently took the bag.

They clambered over rocks heading towards the tip of the small island and Tyson could hear the faint throb of the fisherman's motor coming in waves with the wind. Johnny disappeared deftly between two large boulders and then reappeared on the other side. Tyson followed, the bag of rocks knocking against the walls of the narrow pathway, echoing out in front of him, until he was out the other side and staring at the old man's latest creation.

In front of him was a perfect spiral of rocks, about two metres in diameter at the base, the large rocks getting smaller as they rose further off the ground. The large base rocks, Tyson figured, were about as big as one man could carry, especially a wiry old guy like Johnny. It was an almost impossible feat of careful placement underpinned by some natural affinity with gravity. Tyson put the bag down carefully and stared in awe whilst circling it slowly. He reached into his pocket, pulled out his little camera and held it up to Johnny, and said,

"D'you mind?"

"Go nuts,"

Tyson began filming the sculpture in extreme close up, the texture of each rock jumping out at him and causing his mouth to open slackly and, for a short time he wondered why life was so much more interesting in macro, with no vistas to help him reference, like drifting in an ocean without a map. And then he realised that it was the only way for him, the only way he could deal with it, this mess of a life. He wondered how Johnny got through it.

Johnny had climbed up the three metre high structure and had begun carefully laying the small rocks, as if the rocks had already decided for him where to be placed.

"It's always like this for me," he said, as if hearing Tyson's thoughts, "the object always talks to me, its like entering a dream and when I wake up, it's more or less done," as he placed the last small rock on the very top of the spiral. Tyson was still filming as Johnny climbed down and stood back to take in what he had created. Tyson did one more circuit of the sculpture, and then shut off the camera. He was done too.

"You heard of a guy called Andy Goldsworthy?" Tyson inquired.

"Nope, he a friend of yours or something?"

"Nah, he's a famous sculptor, does installations out in the wilderness... stuff," looking at the spiral, "just like this."

Johnny said nothing, instead he just stared firmly into Tyson's eyes. Tyson noticed that this sculpture was without his usual message of ocean pollution and senseless death. He stared back at him and watched his mad hair blowing about in the slight breeze. He watched as a thought consumed his face.

"Sometimes Tys, there's no message at all. It's just a beautiful thing and, like all beautiful things, it won't last. The tide will swallow this one up in a matter of hours..." he grinned at Tyson, then finished with,

"A fleeting moment of beauty."

Johnny stared out at the ocean, lost in other thoughts, of other times.

Horrific times that shaped them both.

He wondered when Tyson would be ready to hear what he had to tell him.

Chapter 19

Castlemaine, Australia
2004

Tyson felt like a ghost inhabiting the life he used to have as he walked through Castlemaine. He didn't know where he was going; all he knew was that the walking felt good. He walked around the outskirts of the town as it readied itself for the opening night of the festival. He walked like a man possessed as the last of the afternoon light slunk away like a comedian whose act just died. The last vestige of who he used to be passed him by, going in the other direction, towards the bright lights and hushed expectation of the already bulging crowd.

He had a vague recollection of being booked to play tonight, but playing was the last thing on his mind. He was driven by the urge to get lost, for a while at least, get some breathing space, try and make sense of all that had happened in the last few days. His head was a mash of conflicting thoughts as he turned up View Street, heading for the bush.

One of the good aspects of Castlemaine is that it is surrounded by bush; so escaping into it is, at most, a ten-minute proposition. One hundred and fifty years ago, thousands of desperate people had dug up every inch of this area looking for gold. Some had found it, but many did not. All had left a totally decimated landscape in their wake, which years later has struggled to return to its natural state, the depleted soil only managing to support a handful of species. Consequently no one cared to live on it so it had become a 'historic reserve'. In other words, a wasteland pockmarked with mine shafts, worn away by erosion and riddled with heavy metals. Tyson had always loved the place; it made him feel strangely peaceful.

Jake McCardle, on the other hand, was feeling anything but peaceful as he took his seat, front row centre Stage 1, and checked out the scene in front of him, careful to maintain his characteristic wry grin. He could see the festival director heading towards him, pushing his trendy thick black-rimmed glasses up his nose as he scurried towards Jake McCardle, Mayor of Castlemaine and direct descendant of the first squatters to clear the land of the 'black problem' and make a claim to some of the most fertile land Australia had to offer. Michael Wethers cleared his throat, unaccustomed to having to make his presence felt at all, whilst Jake seemed more intent on making sure there were no tell tale crystals loitering on the end of his nose and staring at the ample cleavage of his companion, whose name escaped him right now.

"Ahem, Jake, how ya goin' mate?" Michael asked, failing completely in his attempt to sound 'ocker', 'true blue', 'dinky di', 'fair dinkum' or any of the other colloquialisms for 'one of the boys'. And he didn't even know it. Rather, he sounded like an American doing an Aussie accent. To be fair, it wasn't his fault, coming from the leafy eastern suburbs of Melbourne, an elite private school and then university, and of course living in Europe for fifteen years after that.

What chance did he have?

Jake was used to Michael's pathetic attempts at mateship and he just let this one go, pretending he hadn't heard.

"Michael. We all set then, are we?" pointing to the stage in front of them, a fifty metre long red carpeted performance space that 'blurred the lines between audience and performer', or so the festival program said.

Michael looked over at his 'vision' finally coming together. He could hardly wait to unleash his vision on this sleepy little town.

"Mate," Michael assured Jake, "We're as ready as we're ever gonna be, Jake. Hope you enjoy the show!" and before Jake could respond, Michael disappeared into the growing crowd, his phone attached to the side of his face again, its natural habitat during this last, mad week. Jake smiled wearily, put his Ray bans on just as the drugs began to kick in, and watched the sun disappear behind Lawson's hill.

***

Tyson had been walking aimlessly for maybe half an hour before he noticed any other signs of life. The first signs were pretty standard country fair; a parked panel van and the muffled moans of two people fucking their brains out. He could hear pumping anthem rock coming out of the car speakers as they went at it. He turned quickly off the dirt track away from the muffled moans and walked straight up over the hill to his right, the last of the daylight leaving him as he did. He blundered through the mineshaft-riddled bush without a torch or a care as to his personal safety. Finally he stopped walking and sat down on a large rock protruding out of the ground. He looked around into the near darkness and listened to the sounds of the bush. The last cries of the birds were singing the light out of existence and crickets began making the ground hum around him and his body resonate. The love of his life was dead. Gone. And Tyson was scared. Scared of what he had seen, of what it might mean to others if they knew he had been there too.

The crack of a twig breaking snapped him out of his traumatised state. He held his breath and kept totally still as a black wallaby came around from behind the rock that Tyson was leaning on, sniffing the air and ambling along with it's nose to the ground. Tyson couldn't believe it; these wallabies were notoriously shy and comprehensively petrified of humans. The only time you would see one was on the side of a highway, flattened by a truck or mangled by a car. If you were lucky you might see one a hundred metres away disappearing into low scrub, never to be seen again. But here was one right next to him. Despite his low feeling, he worked on putting out a totally peaceful, non-threatening vibe, concentrating on his breathing and not making a move.

For the minute or so that their paths crossed Tyson watched its whiskers twitching and its ears doing circuits of its head, forever conscious of the threat of predators. Sadly these take the form of humans or feral dogs, and for the wallaby, the result is the same, regardless of the predator.

And then, it was gone, and Tyson was alone again. He got up slowly up and headed off in the direction the wallaby had gone.

He stopped at the crest of the next hill after smelling the smoke from a nearby fire. He scanned the valley in front of him until he saw clumps of white smoke against the black sky. From a fire. He decided to head down to check it out. As he got closer he could hear someone whistling, snatches of a tune going up with the smoke, and for a moment Tyson thought he was tripping. He stopped about fifteen metres from the little humpy to take it all in.

It was a ruin of an old miner's hut, with crumbling stonewalls, a tarpaulin stretched across some of it as a roof, and some rusty corrugated iron over the rest. Flickering candlelight shone through the window. Tyson could see the shadow of a man dancing inside, his arms flying about, throwing dramatic shadows up onto the dimly lit walls. The whistling came at him again, obviously a tune of the man's own making as he couldn't recognise it, despite his encyclopaedic memory for melodies. Then suddenly the man appeared in the window, dead still, staring out into the blackness, staring right at Tyson. What Tyson saw made him nearly collapse in relief.

A very familiar man, totally bald, naked, with wild, yet somehow calm, blue eyes.

It was Johnny Barker; an old mate of Tyson's that he thought had gone back to the Melbourne madhouse of construction jobs, and endless beer-soaked conversations to cope with it all. He watched the face break into a smile.

It was Johnny all right.

Johnny came outside, striding over to Tyson wearing only an oversized pair of boots and that big smile. He hugged him, brother style and, instead of the obligatory back slap men use to diffuse the moment, rubbed Tyson's back slow and deep, holding the hug for a good twenty seconds.

"Mate," he said finally, "heard about Suzie, I'm sorry my friend, truly sorry. C'mon in out of the cold!"

Tyson just stood there, willing a smile to break through his dead stare.

"Thanks mate. Could do with a friend right now."

They walked over towards the crumbling stone structure to the entrance, which was a door-sized hole where a wall might have been at some other time.

"Well Tys, welcome to my little hideout. You're my first visitor and I've been coming here on and off for ten years. So I am honoured to have you here!" slapping Tyson on the back and pushing him forward into the room as he did so.

Inside there was large open fire and a bed roughly constructed out of scavenged timber, one chair and a bookshelf overflowing with books. Once Tyson's eyes adjusted he stood with his back to the fire and looked more closely. Piles upon piles of books became visible to him. It seemed like every bit of available space was taken up with books.

"Cuppa mate?" Johnny inquired redundantly, the kettle already in his hand, being put on the hook and swung over the fire.

"Yeah, ta," Tyson replied, also redundantly. "Take a seat Tys, take a load off and tell me how the fuck you ended up here. Gees, mate, I'm surprised you didn't come a cropper down a mineshaft, this area is full of them!"

Tyson gave him a quick rundown of the events of the last few days, starting with Suzie's last day and everything that had ensued since. Within a minute the floodgates had opened up on him and he was sobbing like a man who has kept a horrible secret and finally let it go. He struggled to breathe between sobs. Johnny handed him his cuppa and stood with his naked back to the fire, a mug in one hand, and a book in the other, his unlaced boots a strange counterpoint to his nakedness. Tyson stared past him at the fire for quite some time before Johnny spoke.

"It seems, Tys, that you have landed with both feet squarely in the shit. Sorry to be blunt mate and I know you loved that girl but she came with... aah... baggage let's say. Everybody knew it except you mate, you being blinded by her not insignificant charms. If those murderers saw you, then you are, as the poets say, fucked. If they didn't, then it's only a matter of time before someone makes a connection to you. That little world of Doug's is pretty fuckin' bent mate and you wouldn't believe the kind of shit they're into. Just ask Jake."

Tyson stared at the fire and watched as Johnny took a sip of his tea, and then tossed his book onto the bed in the corner of the room. He tried not to notice Johnny's penis wobble from side to side with the exertion, to no avail.

'Um, Johnny? Any chance you could chuck a pair of pants on, it's like looking at a ventriloquists dummy that's wildly out of sync with the voice, know what I mean?"

Johnny looked at him with a deadly serious expression for a moment, and then broke into a huge smile that made his eyes shine insanely.

"Sorry Tys, no can do. It's one of my rules for up here in the bush, totally naked. Naked so I can take in all this amazing wisdom that I find in these books. I am naked before the greats of philosophy, the greats of literature. I am naked before nature. I am, in the ultimate and purest sense... naked. Count yourself lucky I haven't asked you to follow suit, my dear, confused friend!"

"Is that what you do up here, read books, is that it?"

"IS THAT IT? Isn't that enough? I walk though the bush and meditate on my good fortune and I sit on that bed reading all this stuff around me. At the moment it's Greek mythology. I hear the slither and wonder why an Eastern Brown snake decided to move in with me last week. He sleeps under the bed whilst I read and dream and slowly shed my skin and renew myself again, so I can walk back down that hill and delve back into humanity, delve into what we have called 'life'. Is that not enough?"

Tyson has been watching the flames dance behind Johnny's back all this time, contorting and changing shape as Johnny spoke, as if they were a visual platform for his brain's meanderings. He saw fluid female shapes transform into large fish, sharp, pointed swords, billowing sails and fruit laden trees rising up in the flames and then dissolving just as quickly.

He looked nervously over towards the bed. Johnny noticed him looking.

"Don't worry mate, if he didn't like you he would've bitten you already!"

"Oh that's a relief..." Tyson sighed, thankful that the second most deadly snake in the world liked him.

"In the state I'm in I figured he might've danced with the flames before pouncing on me!"

"Only the good ones make it this far, Tys, and one thing you've gotta remember mate, no matter what happens, I've got your back. And unlike most people, my word means something. Now, why don't you lie down over there and I'll tell you a little story," pointing to the bed with the snake sleeping under it.

But of course Tyson knew there was nothing little about Johnny's stories, nothing little at all.

Chapter 20

Phuket, Thailand
2014

Even Gaew's standard scowl couldn't bring Tyson down tonight. He peeled his wet clothes off immediately after he closed the front door and let them fall to the floor in a sodden heap. Not even the shiver that ran through him could dampen his spirit, nor could the chill that accompanied it. The long walk from Layan beach had been filled with bursts of thunder and sheets of rain and he had retained his smile all the way. Just as he did now, standing naked in front of the clothed and scowling Gaew, a towel in one hand, her other hand embedded, permanently it seemed, into her protruding hip.

"Bpai nai?" *Where you go?* she asked, and even Gaew sensed the impotence poised above the words, her scowl turning to a defeated pout before he had even given her his stock answer.

"Thee nee lae thee nan." *Here and there.*

Now that they were done with the formalities she held the towel out toward him and looked off across the room, feigning disinterest, but Tyson could see the glint in her eye no matter how hard she tried to disguise it. He padded towards her, his wet feet precariously close to going out from under him on the shiny tiles and just as he reached out to grab the towel, she pulled it away from him, the tiniest of smiles teasing the corners of her full lips. She licked them, knowing he was looking there, sensing an opportunity to extract some attention from him.

Tyson's senses were tingling but not just from the attractive woman standing in front of him. He was still resonating from seeing Johnny again and the rocks, hours later, kilometres away. Johnny had re awakened a part of him that had been asleep for a long time. So long that Tyson had forgotten how good that surge of creative adrenalin felt, how free it made him feel. He had chased that vibe for years with his music.

Gaew let her smile spread across her pouting lips as Tyson made another lunge at the towel, this time connecting momentarily before she flicked it playfully away from him, drawing him closer to her. Now he was smiling too, happy to be drawn towards her sultry charm. She flicked the towel at him again and this time his reflexes obeyed his wandering intentions and, with a firm grasp, pulled her to him, her head rolling back exposing her supple neck for him, like a dog submitting to a greater foe. He stopped millimetres away from her bulging neck and blew a steady surge of air across it, making her gasp and a causing a rash of goose bumps to rise up to meet him. He sniffed her being, sucking a large intake of her into his lungs before blowing it out again, his lips almost touching now, and for him it seemed more more powerful than if he had actually made contact. Instead there was this charged moment as he watched her lips part and listened to the small gasp of air being sucked in as her free hand left her hip and finally landed on his, slowly sliding down and around. He could feel the slight drag of sharpened fingernails on his skin, a reminder of the sleeping tiger within...

***

Tyson slipped quietly out of bed whilst Gaew slept soundly, glancing at the Buddhist tattoos between her shoulder blades and the long silky black hair cascading down around them as he did. He smiled to himself, reflecting on how long it had been since he actually felt good about himself, good about this strange relationship, good about waking up in this bed and hearing the clangs and hums of the Patong streets below. He stood naked in front of the window looking down at the street absentmindedly, lost in an ocean of thoughts, miles away from this grubby reality he called home. His thoughts came in short bursts and all thrown together as usual so he struggled to make sense of any of it. He bounced from memories of gigs he had done, to the sound of his bare feet landing in wet sand, to his beloved Suzie throwing her head back in ecstasy, to the seductive curl of a perfect wave, a lonely dance that only he could see before it smashed itself onto an empty beach. He saw his long lost Lulu in her last happy moments, spinning around and around on the playground equipment in Victory Park all those years ago. He blinked and a tear arrived with the thought that she would've been fifteen years old by now...

He stared down at the floor next to him where a copy of the 'Phuket News' lay and realised Gaew must've bought it for him, like she did most weeks. The size of the unread pile gave him an idea of how long he had been gone, how long he had wandered aimlessly, the ground moving under him as he walked, giving him the shallow feeling of going somewhere. But as Tyson was so acutely aware, he had been going nowhere fast for years.

The front-page headline suddenly came into focus on the floor next to him.

MORE BODIES FOUND AS TUNNEL CONSTRUCTION HALTS

Tyson bent down and squinted at the words underneath the headline.

> The long awaited Patong tunnel project has come to a standstill again today as another four bodies have been uncovered, just metres from last week's grisly find of two bodies. The dismembered corpses were laid out in the same way, spread out with the arms and legs placed on top of them, suggesting a pattern to the shocking discoveries.

Tyson was still looking at the paper but the words became blurry as images flooded his brain, images he thought he had shaken, images that he thought he had buried years ago, along with all that defined him. The words came into focus again and he continued reading.

> Pornsat Pungtick, head of TTC Construction Company, has stated that work will cease until the bodies have been removed and the area given the all clear by the authorities. The mayor of Patong, Pornsat's brother, Kunlik Pungtick, issued a statement yesterday... "We are shocked at

the discovery and pledge all our resources to getting to the bottom of this," he was quoted as saying before leaving on Tuesday for a conference in Penang. The bodies have not been identified as yet.

Tyson looked up from the paper and stared vacantly out at the busy street below him. He looked down again. It wasn't the shock of the grisly discovery; hell, nearly everyday a body was found in a shallow grave in a banana plantation, or shoved into a rubbish bin, or found floating off the coast somewhere. On an island with so much money coming in, with so many services offered to the hungry tourist, there was always going to be a body count. Someone who got in the way, or saw something they shouldn't, or had served their purpose. Life was cheap here and Tyson had seen it all over the years. But it wasn't that. Something about it jogged his memory. He just couldn't put his finger on it.

***

The waft of cheap perfume hit Johnny way before he could hear the cat-like squeals of the massage girls. The sickly sweet, thick scent gave him a headache almost straight away, but he maintained a smirk through his beard as he walked on by.

"Masssssage mister?" one of them screeched at him, whilst another, a ladyboy, stood up and thrust her fake tits out and rubbed a languid hand down a long leg.

"Helllllo, want massage sexy man?"

"Aah, Patong," Johnny muttered to himself, as he continued down Nanai Alley toward the internet cafe, letting the screeches and wayward hands slip off him like friends after a divorce. Things must be slow, he thought, if they are looking at me as a potential customer. He looked down through his matted grey hair and beard at his torn and dirty clothes and laughed.

Of all the streets in this city of woe, he liked this one the most. It had a village atmosphere to it, and he like the way it wound around and over the hills like an old track might have, looking for the easiest path possible. But he knew that there was no easy path in this city. He walked past shop after shop hastily constructed to pounce on the tourist dollar: whether it was a massage shop, a motorbike hire shop, a restaurant, a laundry, a travel agent, a cafe, a dress shop full of LBD's and stiletto heels, it didn't matter. They were all here, on top of each other with their needy hands out, and an eye out for the loose change that might slip out of your pocket whilst you were retrieving your smartphone to see what the forums had to say about it all.

Eventually he made it to the internet cafe, strolled in and sat down at the nearest computer. He looked across at the guy behind the counter, who acknowledged his presence by activating the computer in front of Johnny without changing the dulled gaze Johnny figured he saved for his beloved screen.

He was happy he had found this relic from another time. These shops were everywhere a few short years ago, but nowadays it was getting harder and harder to find one.

He opened the browser and typed in his user name whilst trying to remember his password. Like everyone else, he remembered it as soon as he stopped thinking about it and let his well-trained fingers do the talking. A few moments later he was looking at his inbox and clicking on the most recent email. It was the one he was hoping would be there.

He pushed the hair off his face and hit 'reply'.

'G'day Suthers, Glad to find your email waiting for me and to hear that things are falling into place at your end. It'll be good to see my old mate Dougy again, that's for sure! All good here. Tyson's a fucking mess, but we knew that already, hey? Tell Jake I need to talk with him.

See you soon.'

Johnny closed that window and opened another, this time hacking into a financial institution via a proxy server. He punched in the passwords he had extracted from Doug's computer and got to work.

Chapter 21

Castlemaine, Australia
2004

"Mummy said that your girlfriend is dead now, Daddy," Lulu said matter-of-factly as she careered backwards on the playground swings, her hair falling over her face as she went.

Tyson looked at the ground and said nothing.

"And that means you and Mummy can get back together again, doesn't it Daddy?"

At this he looked up at her in a way that tried to say 'stop', but it seemed to encourage her instead.

"And then we will be a family again!"

Tyson stared numbly at the ground.

"And you will be able to play with me every day, Daddy, and that would be totally awesome!" her last two words going up in inflection like an excited teenager.

But she's only 5 years old, Tyson reminded himself. The last thing he wanted to do was fall apart and scare his little girl.

"Not going to happen, sweetheart, I'm sorry to say," is all he could muster, using all of his will to keep his tone even, at the least.

Lulu continued swinging as if the conversation depended on it, thrusting her legs out to propel her higher with each swing. Tyson could hear the steel squeaking under the strain of her thrusts as he raised his heavy head up and looked at her.

"Daddy's not feeling well darling, maybe we should drop you home now."

With that, Lulu stopped swinging and let herself slow down. Tyson noticed how her white blond hair seemed to catch the slightest of breezes as she finally came to a stop. She hadn't said anything, but now she had stopped she looked up at him with wounded eyes and whispered,

"Alright, Daddy."

Later, just as he was pulling up at Lulu's house his phone rang, the caller-ID telling him it was Suthers.

"Hey Suthers," he said flatly as he came to a stop in the driveway.

"Hey Tys, where the fuck did you get to? Haven't seen you for a while, you alright?" Tyson could hear another hamburger being demolished, Suthers' voice thick with mouthfuls of it.

"Yeah I guess so," he said just as Lulu leapt out of the car and ran into her mother's waiting arms. Maggie was standing at the top of the driveway, looking perturbed.

"Look mate, gotta go, I'll call ya later," his voice trailing off as he made eye contact with Maggie.

"TYS! TYS! Don't forget about the gig tonight at the Bridge, hey? See you there!"

Remembering at last, "Yeah, OK Suthers," and with that he hung up.

As he walked towards Lulu and Maggie he concentrated on scraping some of the heaviness off his soul so that his 'hello' sounds light and easy but when he saw Maggie all he could squeeze out was a very clipped,

"Hi," as the unpleasantness of their demise as a couple reared its ugly head.

She returned the clipped 'hi' with the same shut down tone.

"Tys, we need to talk. Lulu, why don't you go inside and watch some TV?"

"YIPPEE!! Thanks Mum," and then, holding her hand over her mouth conspiratorially, she whispered to Tys,

"She doesn't let me watch TV much, Daddy, 'specially not 'Home and Away' and 'Neighbours'. She says it will rot my brain, will it rot my brain, Daddy?"

Not waiting for an answer, Lulu ran off squealing in delight. As soon as they heard the door swing shut behind her, Maggie launched into it.

"Sorry about your girlfriend, Tys, that must be hard."

"Yeah, it's not great," staring out at the suburban street.

"Listen Tys, what's going on? I noticed two men sitting in a car, just over there," pointing across the street. "They seemed to be watching us all day and they didn't look like Mormons, if you get my drift."

She turned back to face him.

"Don't know," he said faintly.

"Are you into something bad, Tys? Because if you are, I don't know if I want you around my daughter."

Tyson hated it when she used that term, as it basically cancelled him out as a parent.

"Don't worry, I'll ask around, it's probably nothing," he responded, but even to him he sounded unsure, "Look, I've gotta go. Got a gig at the Bridge. I'll talk to you later," adding a weak smile as a goodbye.

"Tys, they scared me, they're not from around here. They looked like thugs..."

***

Jake McCardle was nursing a scotch at the bar when Tyson walked through the door of the Bridge Hotel. He gave Tyson a wink and an uncharacteristically weak grin as Tyson made his way to the stage and the hairy, rotund shape of Suthers. His eyes were darting around the room, unable to fix on Suthers' face even though words seemed to be coming out of it. Tyson couldn't hear them. Tyson couldn't hear anything, except the screams of the man as he was fed into the meat grinder.

It was all coming back to him in a rush.

He could see Suzie's cheeky grin and he could hear the click-clack of her heels as she ran along the empty corridor. He could see the thugs holding that man's torso upright whilst Doug turned the machine on and he could see the blood splatter hit one of the thug's faces and the way he winced when it landed.

He let his instrument case and shoulder bag fall to the floor between them and it was then that he heard Suthers' voice fading up, like a tech was riding faders in some kind of bio-box in the sky.

"CAN YOU HEAR ME TYS? ARE YOU OK?"

"Yeah mate, what were you saying?"

Suthers raiseed his eyebrows and Tyson couldn't help but notice how long they were, like cat whiskers set in the wrong place.

"Mate, are you OK? I mean, what's happening is pretty fucking full on. Where were you last night?"

Tyson looked at Suthers and realised he may be his only true friend right now.

"Oh you know, just wanderin' around, man. Ended up at Johnny Barker's hut."

As he said this, another horrific image flashed through his mind, this time it was the blood running along the tiled floor and into the drain.

He blinked a few times and stared at Suthers.

He tried to remember how far back they went, how long they have been in each others' lives. He remembered their early years, young boys with a pocketful of ideas and no fear. He remembered Suthers' teenage attempts at a beard, remembered him leaning over a bench with a soldering iron in his hand and Alan Watts' *The Taboo Against Knowing Who You Really Are*' lying open on a table next to him. He remembered those first gigs, both of them so new to it and struggling to see past the egos they had created. He remembered endless raves long into the night traversing all kinds of subjects. He remembered Suthers' passion for the community, the radio station he started almost single-handedly and the hours he poured into it. He tried to calculate how many greasy hamburgers and how many chiko rolls had been consumed in that time. Enough to kill an elephant, he was sure. Yep, Suthers was a good one. One of his few real friends.

"Just *wandering* around, were you? Suthers inquired sarcastically. "Well it would've been good if you'd *wandered* into the Albion last night, 'cause that way we would've had a full band!"

Tyson looked at Suthers apologetically.

"Sorry mate, I'm a bit messy right now."

Jake was draining another tumbler of scotch when Tyson looked again in his direction. Jake gave him another weak grin and motioned for Tyson to join him, which he did, giving Suthers a raised eyebrow as he leaves.

"Fancy a production meeting, mate?" Jake inquired, already feeling the effects of his scotches.

"Of course Jake, I'm a muso," Tyson replied lightly. No sooner had they made it into the beer garden Jake produced a fat joint from his Zegna jacket and fumbled through his pockets for his Zippo lighter, which of course complimented the colour of his suit.

He lit up the monster joint and took a long, theatrical drag on it, pinching the filter between thumb and forefinger and wincing as he held the smoke deep in his lungs, before expelling it long and loud. Tyson watched Jake with curiosity as he took a few more short sucks and then passed it to him like he was passing contraband in a prison, the joint concealed in the palm of his hand.

"Sorry about Suzie," he said.

"Cheers," Tyson said half-heartedly and stared out at the beer garden, which had a scattering of regular drunks and a couple of festival crew barely visible in their black clothes in one corner, leaning into each other and talking excitedly. Tyson sucked on the joint several times before pulling it into his lungs, hoping like hell that the rush might jam up the flood of fear and grief eating away at him. As he expelled the smoke his body instantly relaxed and he felt the knots in his shoulder lose some of their tightness. The background music of the beer garden seemed to rise up in level for him and he felt his leg tapping away at the beat instinctively. He passed the joint back to Jake and asked,

"So Jake, good to see you mate, how's it all goin' for ya, the festival and all?"

Jake seemed to suck half the joint into his lungs in one long pull before expelling, again long and theatrical. He grinned at Tyson and said,

"I've had better times."

"Really? I thought you'd be peaking, cocktail parties everywhere, young women everywhere. What's the problem?"

Jake passed the remainder of the joint to Tyson, this time a little more cavalierly. Tyson took another hit of THC; enjoying the layer of relief it was giving him.

"Listen mate," Jake motioned him closer, his tone becoming conspiratorial, "there's a lot of shit going on right now, a lot of bad shit. And we've all got to be careful we don't end up in it, know what I mean Tys? How long have we known each other? Twenty years?"

"Yeah, at least," Tyson conceded.

"Well, believe me when I say that these are dangerous times we are living in, that you are living in, my friend. You see Tys, they know you were there."

Tyson stared in complete shock at Jake.

"But how did you..." Tyson started, but is cut off by Jake's raised hand.

"Never mind about that, Tys. There's a lot I know. Look, it's no accident I was sitting at the bar tonight and it's no accident we are out here smoking this joint. I've come here to warn you that these guys will stop at nothing to make sure you aren't a problem anymore. So what I suggest is that you go 'on tour' for a while, Tys, just disappear up the coast or something. Get lost in Melbourne. Whatever, just go mate! And as soon as you can, before those thugs you saw the other night pay *you* a visit."

Tyson, suddenly sober again despite the joint in his hand, took a sharp breath.

"They already have, Jake. Maggie said she saw them across the street staring up at her house. Shit!"

"Yeah, no shit, mate. I wouldn't be hanging around here for long, and as for this gig, I'd suggest bailing on it Tys, you might not get the audience you want, if you get my drift."

Tyson's momentary high had quickly turned to paranoia as he scanned the beer garden again, looking for a rear exit, for a way out of this mess. He felt Jake's hand on his shoulder and heard his voice saying,

"Do it, just go! I'll cover your tracks and Tys, throw your phone away, they'll trace you through it otherwise, OK?"

But Tyson had already left, his mind having floated toward the exit and the animated techs, his body struggling to catch up. He turned back to thank Jake, his eyes darting right, then left, but it was too late. Jake had already disappeared back into the bar.

Chapter 22

Phuket, Thailand
2014

Tyson wasn't sure whether it was the sound of the dog licking his ear or the feel of it that actually pulled him out of his dream state, but either way he was awake now, staring through bleary eyes at the owner of the tongue. The thump, thump, thump of the dog's tail reassured him that he was not being basted for a future meal and the stupid smile and happy eyes suggested that he would not be searching out a rabies shot as soon as he could. All in all it was a good start for him. He had had much, much worse.

He looked at the dog for some time, noticing the baggy over-abundant skin and fur that wobbled with every tail wag. He noticed the way the skin drooped around the dog's eyes, giving it a sad look, a soulful counterpoint to the happy wobbling flesh all over him. He smiled back at the dog, which produced an increase in the speed of the wagging tail and encouraged the drool collecting around its mouth to drop to the floor. Tyson reached out a hand gingerly, an offering that was accepted excitedly with several layers of fresh drool being placed there. He patted the dog a few times, noticing the ticks that dangled and shook with each tail wobble. They were quite large, having obviously gorged themselves for hours on the happy creature shaking beside him. He patted the dog a few more times before reaching over and pulling off the first tick, crushing it under his hand, dark blood spraying out onto the concrete floor.

Tyson sat up and took in his surroundings for a few moments before resuming his task. All around him there were people sleeping, some curled up, others splayed out, some flat on their backs, and others on their stomachs with hats pulled over their faces. There were maybe thirty people, some snoring intermittently, others deadly silent. In the distance he could hear the thwacking sound of concrete pillars being driven into the ground and hammer drills persuading concrete to move out of the way. Judging from the strong sea breeze he figured they were quite high up, and near the beach. He took time to watch the construction workers around him and time to marvel at their ability to sleep on a hard concrete floor in the middle of a construction site, and remain oblivious to it all.

They appeared to be on the ninth or tenth floor of some half built resort overlooking the ocean somewhere on the west coast of the island. There were more floors above them and a huge opening right in front where the breeze blew through with the swiftness of a pickpocket. Tyson looked back down at the dog who was sitting patiently waiting for him to resume the tick murdering; a happy, soulful look in his bloodshot eyes. Tyson felt for his Shakuhachi and was relieved when his fingers encountered its felt bag slung across his shoulder. He pulled it out and placed it next to him whilst watching the dog sniff the air and turn its head sideways, as if trying to understand a difficult concept, or simply wondering why nothing edible came out of his pocket.

Tyson resumed removing the ticks from his companion until he had most of the big ones off and had flattened them under his fist. He found himself getting a perverse pleasure from the sound of the tick's shells breaking. The loose skin on the dog's head formed a big frown above his eyes, which prompted Tyson to give him a name.

"Think I'll call you 'Frowny', that OK fella?"

The tail wagging gained momentum and thudded happily on the ground, giving Tyson his answer. He continued slowly removing the ticks until they were surrounded by fist shaped blood spatters around broken black shells and by the effortless, simple joy he extracted from the task.

A few of the nearest Myanmar workers stirred from time to time. One of them opened an eye, looked at the strange white man and the ugly dog being groomed, and promptly closed it again, thinking nothing of the image before him. Tyson took in the whole scene of a room full of Myanmar workers, finding himself struck by how surreal it looked: the mess of construction all round them, contrasting with their choreographed slumber. With the fist shaped splatters in the foreground and the dense jungle of the mountain being hacked away at in the background, it was quite an image.

He imagined Lulu as he reached down to pick up his flute; she was smiling up at him with a face full of chips. He sat with his eyes closed for a while, urging the sadness of this memory to be replaced with something else, anything else. He unwrapped the flute carefully, cradled it in his arms, then he just gazed down at it for a while, this old friend of his, left discarded in a corner for so many years. And then his eyes smiled, they smiled with so much feeling, with so much intensity of emotion that even Frowny felt it, loping over, sliding his wrinkly head under Tyson's arm and looking up at him with those bloodshot eyes.

Tyson closed his eyes and saw his little girl tilting her head to the side in rapt concentration with a precocious finger on her chin in mock contemplation as he played traditional shakuhachi for her, filling her head with questions that didn't have answers, filling her with a sense that the less you look, the more you will see, until her default response was to take the piss. But just enough so that he still knew she was into it. And now he could see the brightness in her eyes like torches at night. He used them to show him where to go.

He put the Shakuhachi to his lips and it was a full minute before he blew the first few long notes. They rose up out of him with a fluidity that betrayed his love and mastery of the instrument, and even surprised him. An instant later and he was back inside of it, watching his thoughts given audible shape, letting each one reverberate through the concrete chamber he was in, before adding another and soon enough he was jamming with the space. There was nothing frenetic about it at all, the improvisations occurring almost naturally and in his music he somehow captured the room's essence and was playing it back to it, to everyone in it. It was a divine collaboration and before too long he could hear the snorts and sniffles of people waking up and then a minute or so later, silence again. Even Frowny's tail had stopped beating on the floor.

He travelled through a series of riffs full of high notes before sliding down into a bass line that seemed to make the floor resonate. Again he closed his eyes and now Lulu was dancing with a scarf in the wind, sliding it slowly through her hands, letting the light catch it and doing the postures the Yoga dance teacher had spent years showing her. He could see her face so clearly now it almost hurt, his closed eyes forming a smile edged with tears as he continued to play.

What else could he do?

He opened his eyes and, like many times before, found himself staring at a sea of stunned faces. But these ones were covered in ochre swirls, their eyes lost in the ancient sounds he was evoking. He could feel Frowny slumped sleepily in his lap whilst he finished off with riffs so soft and sweet you could barely hear them, but you could hear the woody timbre of the instrument coming to the fore as he blew *through* the mouthpiece, an out of tune discordance that just seemed right to him.

There was a short silence, thick with bewilderment, followed by appreciative smiles and nods in his direction.

Tyson moved the flute down away from his mouth and back into his lap, which encouraged Frowny to flick his tongue at it playfully, as if thanking him too. He smiled back at the painted Myanmar faces, a smile that showed more contentment than he had felt in years and even though it was only a fleeting moment, he relished it, siphoning all that he could from it. He took a deep breath and bowed his head in gratitude to the crowd, who were gathering their hats and gloves and slowly making their way back to the toil that brought them here, complete with a perpetual mouthful of concrete dust that no amount of whisky could quench, back to the job that kept them chained to the wheel of exploitation. The wrenched back that would never come good, the toe ripped open and turned into a crater with daily doses of spilt lime, the bleary eyes as another bottle of Red Bull was tossed to the ground to join the growing pile.

Tyson put his shakuhachi back in its felt bag, and looked around for his hat and sunglasses, finding neither. Frowny looked up at him and rested his ugly head heavier into Tyson's lap, as if to say, *"No, not going anywhere without me,"* his bloodshot eyes pleading with Tyson to consider a travelling partner.

"C'mon Frowny, gotta go mate. Gotta see a man about a dog..." he paused, a smile creeping across his face, "And soon you might even get my jokes. Let's go then. *Bpai!*" at which Frowny leapt out of his slumped state and stood next to Tyson, his tail a spastic metronome, his wobbly skin like the shimmer of a belly dancer. Tyson stood up with some difficulty, leaning on Frowny on the way up.

Another day had begun and Tyson, for the first time in years, greeted it with something approaching excitement.

"C'mon buddy, lets go to the beach!"

Tyson had lived for ten years in the pumping black heart of Phuket, which turned out to be a great place to get lost.

Patong crept up on you like a thief in the night. It was that one drink too many, it was the careless lunge at the ridiculously rigid breast, it was the dead, dark eyes whilst the mouth was moaning, it was the screeching tone of the massage girls, it was the slip slop of a solitary mop in an empty bar in a dead end street.

Patong was your self-esteem floating on a belly of lies and deceit, of one-dimensional moments being bumped into on crowded streets, tripped over by drunks, and hammered beyond recognition by relentless shots. It was the eardrum bursting from too much bad music coming out of plastic tweeters and people shouting at you to be heard. It was the quiet moment just before you begin pissing when you hear the sound of footsteps, slow and sure. It was the years of living etched into your face in a matter of hours.

Frowny seemed to agree with Tyson, dodging endless legs with a snarl as they made their way through the Friday night crowd on Bangla Road. It was almost as bad as ploughing through a football crowd on their way to the gladiatorial arena, except these ones were coming at them from both directions, all with that fixed and similar sense of purpose. But here everyone was fixed on getting lost for a night, getting numbed out to it all. Bangla Road was not a happy place for the sober; there was way too much ugliness to see with the naked eye.

Hundreds of bars lined the street, all with pretty Thai girls in tight skirts and heels holding drinks special boards and staring blankly at the moving human feast. 'Priscilla' style ladyboys pranced theatrically up the street in long gowns, flashing their plastic tits at anyone who caught their eye for a brief moment whilst ping pong show touts and guys with monkeys on little chains vied for your attention and a hundred sound systems spilled sodden dance tunes out onto the worn pavement at your feet. Neon lights flashed on and off and moving lights ballyhooed the street, bathing the entire Bangla Road circus in a surreal array of colour.

Tyson had somehow become immune to it after all this time; he had managed to let the slime just wash over him like a tepid bath in second hand water. Frowny was, however, bristling at the onslaught and kept his lumpy face inches from

Tyson's tired legs at all times. Tyson focussed on the T-shirts and singlets with various 'clever' messages spread across them. Beer T-shirts, 'No Money No Honey', 'No I don't want a Massage, Tuk-Tuk, New Suit or Elephant Ride', all the testimonies to the mad grab for the tourist dollar that people bought to mark their holiday. Tyson grabbed random phrases or words and made street poetry out of them to amuse himself. That way he could rap all the way to Gaew's and not get gutted by it all. He had been here wandering around for over ten years and the more he despised it the more it endeared itself to him. It was the serrated double-edged sword of his life and he had been teetering on it for so long he didn't know any other way.

Eventually the crowd thinned out as they made their way up Pisitkoranee Road towards Gaew, her warm bed and permanent scowl. He wondered what she would make of his new friend. As they neared the apartment a couple of soi dogs woke from their slumber and put their noses in the air, picking up Frowny's scent, a snarl forming on their mouths before they had even opened their eyes. Frowny braced himself for the onslaught; puffing out his chest and making the fur around his neck stand up. He stood his ground as they lunged at him, the anger in them driven by the desperation of the streets they called home. Frowny seemed to wait until the last moment before moving out of the way, as a diseased set of jaws sought out his neck. Tyson watched as the first dog scrambled and skidded to a stop a few metres behind them. The second dog lunged and Frowny managed to baulk, then lunge back at it as it flew past him, pinning the mangy dog to the ground with his massive jaws. This gave the first dog the opportunity to go for Frowny's exposed belly, but

Tyson's foot convinced him otherwise, landing squarely and with full force on the dog's neck, the loud howl from his mouth persuading him to reconsider his options. Frowny released the second dog from his hold and Tyson's right leg again persuaded him to leave them alone. Frowny let out a muffled growl and looked up at Tyson in a brotherly moment of gratitude as they continued on up the street.

Gaew was watching from the balcony as Tyson and Frowny disentangled themselves from the soi dogs, a frown forming on her forehead to compete with the permanently raised eyebrow. Muttering to herself, she made her way to the front door and waited. A mischievous smile started up on her face but she stifled it as she heard the heavy footsteps on the stairs.

Chapter 23

Castlemaine, Australia
2004

Doug Farris leaned back in his heavily reinforced chair and blew a luxurious amount of smoke out into the empty room. He chewed playfully on the cigar butt whilst glancing at the girl chained to the floor underneath his huge antique mahogany desk. He liked the way the dog collar around her neck bit into her skin like it was almost too tight, like she might asphyxiate at any moment. Maybe she would. His eyes glistened at the thought as he unzipped his fly and dropped his cock out inches from the terrified girl's face. As a result of Doug's enormous gut he hasn't seen his cock in years, but plenty of girls like this had. He grunted at her, as if to say, 'don't make me ask' so she dutifully took his cock into her mouth and hoped that the tears flowing down her cheeks didn't upset him.

Doug's phone rang, causing him to sit upright, almost making the girl gag, and she didn't want to do that again. Last time it resulted in a savage beating and every cock in the room to be repeatedly thrust in her mouth until she learnt to suppress the gag reflex and replace it with a muffled moan, which seemed to get a better result, if only for a short time.

Doug answered the phone and looked out over his pig factory. A series of grunts indicated that he was not overly chuffed with what he was hearing.

"What the fuck?" he shouts, finally forming words, "What d'ya mean you don't know where he is. He's a fuckin' muso, he's either asleep or at a bar! I mean, for fuck's sake, how hard can it be, ya dipstick?"

The girl could hear the voice on the other end of the line and feel Doug's pathetic attempt at a hard on going down. She tightened her grip in case she gets blamed for it, adding a hand to the task to guarantee success.

"Oh you fuckin idiot! Even I know he split up with Maggie years ago. He's not gonna turn up there unless he has no other choice, and even then..."

Doug listened some more, sucked on his cigar and stared out the window at nothing in particular, whilst his latest victim worked on his cock like her life depended on it, and maybe it did.

"If I feel your teeth one more time, your life won't be worth living, sweetheart!"

She quickly retracted her teeth from proximity to his cock and thought,

It's not worth living now, what's the difference?

She used what was left of her resolve to resist biting the fucking thing off and spitting it onto the floor at his feet.

"I don't care if the town is full of musos at the moment, just fucking find him or else I'll feed *you* into the grinder, you stupid fuck!"

Doug stubbed out his cigar angrily and watched the red ambers fly off it, covering the girl straining on her collar who winced as the first of them hit her smooth, young skin.

***

Out on the street a couple of performers are dazzling the crowd with their antics. They had rigged a tightrope between two power poles and were taking turns balancing and then falling off into the other's arms. Jake grinned weakly as collective gasps came from the children watching and every now and then a passer by tapped him on the shoulder and his trademark winning smile came back and he was Jake again, everybody's mate, the life of the party, the man you can trust.

If there was an embodiment of the political animal, then Jake was it. For years nothing had stuck to Jake, he was moving too fast most of the time and when he wasn't, there was always someone to wear it for him, someone to distract attention, someone to take the fall.

He stared at the two performers as if they were using his life as a base for their art, but as Jake realised uncharacteristically, this is merely his rampaging ego overriding him again. He watched as one of them dressed in a heavily padded suit attempted to clamber up onto the wire with help from the other one, a wiry looking guy with a Mohawk and ear stretchers the size of dinner plates. The fat man fell repeatedly, squashing the Mohawk guy several times before he gave up and hung under the wire, a flabbergasted expression plastered on his face. As he lay there like a beached whale, basking in the laughter of the crowd, the Mohawk guy had surreptitiously climbed up onto the wire and was pretending to nearly fall whilst holding a finger to his lips, encouraging the crowd's complicity. A few of the children giggled as he crept like a cartoon burglar across the tightrope, towards the 'beached whale'.

Jake thought about Tyson and wondered whether he made it out alive, whether Doug's henchmen have found him or worse, whether they were picking through his friends and family like obsessive diners at an all you can eat buffet, gorging themselves on entrees in place of the main course. He liked Tyson, there was something about the guy that made Jake think he had missed out on something. There was something about the way he could hone in on core human emotions in his playing that put Jake regularly in a state of awe, and that was something that didn't come easy to Jake. Tyson had a way of taking Jake out of himself, like he had found a key to unlock the ego shroud that covered him. It made him feel like he was on the edge of something, something unattainable, something... bigger.

The Mohawk guy was now balancing precariously above the beached whale, whose legs and arms were flailing pointlessly either side of his bloated torso.

If he could've made little pig noises, Jake thinks, *then it would be perfect.*

The Mohawk guy was losing his balance, and of course the fat man was feigning ignorance of the performance happening above his head. A little boy in the crowd yelled,

"WATCH OUT!"

The bloated one lifted his head up, as if woken from a deep sleep.

"W... What did you say?"

A chorus of children chimed in,

"WATCH OUT!" but it was too late, of course, and a collective gasp rippled through the crowd as the Mohawk guy leapt off the tightrope and landed dead centre of the beached whale's stomach, bouncing back up and landing perfectly on the tightrope again. Some of the children were shrieking and some were laughing in excitement as the mohawked gymnast jumped down again and again, varying the landing posture each time. Sometimes he pin dropped onto his partner, other times he lay on his side with a finger poised on his chin as if he was thinking about something else altogether. The parents were laughing now too as he bounced up and down on the floundering, bloated man on the ground. They were both pulling hilarious faces at each other as if caught up in something neither of them had any control over anymore, the momentum itself propelling the act. If they were magicians this would've been the part where they held up their hands and exclaimed, 'nothing up my sleeves', but of course there was no point. They already had the crowd in the palm of their hands and they knew it.

Except for Jake.

Jake stood motionless and watched the act like he was watching incriminating evidence at his own murder trial, his face paralysed by an inner torment that he hadn't even begun to take the lid off yet.

Chapter 24

Phuket, Thailand
2014

The stairs to Gaew's were a battle for Tyson, his legs straining as if it was the first time he had climbed them. Each tiled step was a huge effort, and as he climbed the stairs seemed to stretch out in front of him. This was worse than a hundred Indian tailors lined up on Thanon Nanai. Worse than a dozen bloated female faces screeching 'Mass...aaage!' in unison. Worse than ten bleary eyed tuk-tuk drivers jiggling the change in their pockets. There was a rubbery feel to everything, like he was in a dream that wasn't his, like an unwanted guest at a wedding, like the pothole in the road when you're looking the other way.

He could hear Frowny's tail thumping on the other side of the door as he fumbled with his keys. Eventually, after what felt like hours of bouncing off the walls in a rubber room, he found the right one and cautiously unlocked the door. Frowny leapt on him, all floppy gums and wet tongue and heavy leaning on Tyson's legs. The greeting, unlike his regular experience, was warm and happy, the dog genuinely excited to see him. No bullshit façade here, no game playing. So different from Gaew, so vastly different that he dropped to his knees to give Frowny the opportunity to cover the top half of him in slobber as well. He was rolling on the floor laughing when he heard the bedroom door open. Frowny immediately retreated behind Tyson in anticipation.

If only Tyson had that instinct.

Gaew threw a book first, a decent sized book that skidded past Tyson and hit the front door. The next thing was a glass ball with a snow scene inside it, the snow looking very agitated as it was held above her head and launched with fierce accuracy at Tyson. He rolled just in time and then heard the yelp from Frowny as the glass ball took his legs out from under him.

She was warming up now.

He could see her black eyes and pouting lips and hear her heavy breathing as she wiped her hands on the little singlet and pyjama shorts she was wearing. Tyson noticed a glint in her eye and the beginning of excitement pleading with her lips to part.

Tyson ventured a smile at her, at which of course she sneered and turned her nose up at him.

"Morning sweetheart, how'd you sleep?" he said, a rubbery sarcasm encasing the words.

He didn't expect an answer.

She turned her back on him and began searching the bedroom for more weapons. Tyson seized the opportunity and crept up behind her. He was a foot away when she felt his hot breath on her neck, making the fine hair stand up and goose bumps rise up beneath them. He slid his arms around her and pulled her into him and he could feel the rigid flesh relax under his touch. She bared her neck to him and he kissed it, softly at first, then full and strong as he heard the first gasp escape her lips.

He reached out with his right leg and pushed the door shut behind them.

***

Tyson plugged the mini USB lead into the camera and waited for the computer to load the images. Frowny was sleeping happily in his lap, Gaew was in the kitchen cooking up a post coital breakfast Thai style, and Tyson sat there and let the short wave of happiness in. It wasn't long before he was caught in the memories of when he was always happy, and the crushing reality of when his world went to black. And when he had started running...

The mouse hovered over the folder that he hardly ever opened. It hovered there, like it had a thousand times before, as the sweat started up on his brow and the howling void winked at him. This time he double clicked and watched as the screen was filled with Lulu's five-year-old face walking towards the camera, a finger to her lips, whispering,

"You mustn't tell Mum, OK Dad?"

Tyson gulped down phlegm as he mouthed the words,

"OK sweetheart," a second before they came out of the speakers. The double tracking effect was like a knife in his gut. He felt his happiness drift away like a dead leaf in the wind.

He watched her skip across to the swings and sit herself down on the moulded plastic seat, wrapping her arms around the chain at each end of it.

"Can you give me a push, Daddy?"

The camera moved closer to her and now he could see his own arms holding on to the seat, pushing her. Once, twice, three times, then he pulled back and out of the shot as she kicked her legs and pulled with her arms to go higher. He could hear her excited squeals and the squeak, squeak of the swings as she strained to go higher than before.

Higher than she ever had.

"I'm gonna… go… higher… than… the clouds… this time… Daddy!" she gasped.

Tyson blinked and deposited the tears he had been fighting onto Frowny's lined head, making his ears twitch expectantly, as if waiting for a few more drops to confirm rain. The sound of the swing and Lulu's squeals filled the room as Gaew walked in with a couple of bowls of rice soup, saying,

"Why you do this to yourself, hey Ty-son?"

What could he say? Because he had to? They were all he had left and he felt that if he didn't do this, the memories would die like a butterfly on Bangla. Squashed under a cheap high heel like so many cigarette butts. Cheated out of him by a clever tout, leaving him truly, comprehensively lost forever. A shadow of a shadow of his former self.

Finally he said softly,

"Because I miss her."

He turned off the video, his fleeting happiness going back into the bowels of the machine as he took a tentative spoonful of soup, testing the temperature with his lips, and looked over at Gaew.

"Ok, maai?" she asked, between slurps.

"Aroi maak, baby." *Delicious.*

"Not soup, you!"

He turned back to the screen and clicked on the new files he shot last night and said,

"I'll be right, I s'pose."

"Arai na?" *What?*

But he had already switched off from her as he became immersed in the images of the ladyboys. He watched the camera cavorting around poles and chairs, swirling around fat drunk men pretending they had 'accidentally' ended up on Soi Paradise. His face glazed over as the camera mimicked the grinding of the dancing bodies. Cheesy Thai dance tunes blasted into the room, sending the sleepy morning vibe straight back to 2a.m.

"Who are they, your friends? Boyfriends, huh?" as she peered over his shoulder and bit his neck playfully. Even though it seemed playful, Tyson could sense another dose of crazy Gaew coming his way so he sat dead still, thinking of a way to diffuse it.

"Nah, I left the camera with them for the night, thought it might be fun."

"You didn't let them suck your cock?" the playful tone completely gone now and the slurping of the soup saying more than the silence around it.

He turned off the volume and listened to the silence as it took a hold of the room...

***

"Are you there, mate?"

"Yeah, I'm here but I can't see you."

"Click the little camera icon at the bottom of the screen."

"Where... oh right, got it."

160

Johnny could now see Jake and the first thing he noticed was the grey, receding hair and the slightly worried look on Jake's face.

"Long time no see Jake, how ya been?"

"Oh, you know, can't complain mate,' as he looked distractedly over his shoulder at the slim, young tanned thing strutting past him.

The image, as was fairly common with skype connections, was pixelated and kept freezing for seconds at a time.

"Where are you?"

"Somewhere..." as the signal froze, adding a poignancy to the moment that wasn't meant to be there.

Johnny pondered this for the few seconds it took for the signal to come good.

He was smiling when he said,

"Things haven't changed much for you, then. So, Jake, did everything go to plan?"

Jake took a good long pull on the massive joint that was passed over his shoulder by the girl and replied,

"Yeah mate, all good. Dougy jumped at the prospect of a free holiday, I mean, who wouldn't? Even rich cunts love a freebee mate. In fact, even more so."

"So why aren't you coming to see the show, Jake, I thought you'd love to see your old mate go down? What, you too busy being a fucking politician to take a week off?"

Jake stared at the screen just as it froze again, which left the half expelled plume of smoke stranded in mid air in front of his face, conveniently masking his paper-thin bravado and the hunted look that had torn a jagged path through his otherwise handsome countenance.

Johnny could see what the years had done though, despite the haze.

Just as Jake was about to deliver his clever retort the screen went to black, the weak signal finally dying, leaving him feeling strangely unsatisfied by the exchange, a feeling that seemed to pervade everything in his life these days. He turned around and stared out at the vista before his eyes, noticing how the tiny curve of the young things breasts seemed to fit perfectly into the dull, flat horizon stretched out in front of him. He wondered where he was, but it didn't really matter anymore.

Very little did.

Chapter 25

Castlemaine, Australia
2004

It was early morning when Tyson found himself crawling through his bedroom window, his legs still outside, hanging like a pair of jeans left out to dry. He battled to get himself up and over the windowsill and eventually made it. His head was pounding from the blood rush and his fingertips were tingling as he surveyed his room for thugs but found the room empty and in its normal state.

Like a bomb had hit it.

Tyson had waited until the neighbours had taken their dog for its morning walk before coming out from behind the shrubbery in their backyard, his bed for the night. Luckily for him the dog slept inside and was let out into the front yard for its morning piss. He had crouched there shivering for hours waiting for first light, making sure the coast was clear, praying that they weren't in his room already, waiting for him.

And now he was here, in his room, watching a barrage of scattered thoughts pierce through any rationality he had retained, like a pin to a balloon, leaving him numb and panic-stricken at the same time.

He didn't have much time: he could feel it. He could feel the weight of events pressing down on him, pushing the air out of his lungs, making his legs quiver in anticipation of a last-minute need to run. He searched the floor frantically for things he might need at Johnny's hut but his mind was blank, so the searching wasn't much more than a nervous gesture. He didn't need anything that was on the floor, what he needed was in his computer. He tapped the top of the table and waited for his computer to start up, a process that always seemed painfully long, and especially so now, with so little time left.

Tyson froze when he heard someone knocking on the front door.

Suthers, meanwhile, stirred from the noise, quickly rolled over and pulled more blankets over his body, going with the idea that the noise would go away. Another knock, this time hard and loud enough to rattle the door on it's hinges, loud enough to really piss Suthers off, loud enough for his first words for the day to be,

"FUCK OFF!"

Suthers' bedroom was closest to the front door and there was no way he was getting any more sleep if this shit kept up.

"THIS IS THE POLICE! OPEN UP!"

"Oh, for fuck's sake!," Suthers moaned to himself, emerging reluctantly from his warm cocoon, an expression of disgust furrowing his brow to go with the sour, stale taste in his mouth, a combination of cigarettes, whisky and fried food.

He was not a happy camper.

Tyson's eyes were bulging out of his skull as he waited for the insipid 'start up' music to stop and his desktop icons to emerge from the code racing across the screen. Finally the wait was over and the mouse scurried across to the top left hand corner of the screen to the 'raw footage' folder sitting there.

Suthers opened the door and a blast of sunlight turned his irises to tiny pins and formed a scowl on his scraggy face.

"Morning Suthers, Tyson around, is he?" the constable asked.

"Giiday Rick, to what do we owe this pleasure? You're not gonna bust me for pot again are you 'cause it's getting' pretty boring! It better be good, what the fuck are you doin' up at this hour anyway?"

"Relax Suthers, we're not here for you. Don't you listen? We're here for Tyson."

"Oh right, I'll check if he's home. Wait here… what's it about anyway?" feigning ignorance.

"Just some routine questions we need to ask him."

"Famous last words…" Suthers muttered as he padded off down the hallway.

Tyson had heard the muffled authoritative voices and, after realising through his haze that thugs don't knock on the door, let his heartbeat go down a few notches. He inserted the thumb drive and waited what felt like the few years it took before it appeared on the screen, then dragged the folder across to it just as Suthers came through the door.

"Um, Tys? There seems to be some cops at the door that want to talk to you. Man, you look like shit!"

"Yeah, slept rough. Tell 'em I'll be out in a minute."

"Okey doke," Suthers shut the door again just as Tyson was removing the thumb drive and putting it down his pants, next to his left testicle. He stood up, waited for the head rush to subside, then ambled towards the front door.

"Hey Rick, what's up?" Tyson asked sleepily, as if he just woke up.

"Tyson, there's a few questions we'd like to ask you down at the station regarding Suzie Farris's death. Shouldn't take long."

Tyson peered past the two cops out at the street, looking for any strange cars or strange people, and finds neither.

"OK then. What, now?"

"Yeah mate, now."

***

Maggie's head hit the wall with such force that the clean dishes jumped out of the dish rack and scattered in pieces all over the kitchen floor. Lulu was huddled down in the corner crying as the man screamed at her Mum.

"Just tell us where he is then we'll go away *sweetheart*," Nigel said, the last word laced with menace.

Sobbing, "I... don't... know. He doesn't live here anymore!"

Brian slammed her in the kidneys, taking her breath away and delivering her swiftly to the edge of consciousness.

"That's not what we wanna hear, darling. Now this will all be over when you give us his address. C'mon, you're saying you don't know where the father of your child lives? Pull the other one, Maggie, it plays 'jingle bells'!"

Between gasps she implored,

"I don't know. He always comes here, you fucking prick!"

This time the thug kicked her in the ribs and Lulu could hear the cracking sound through her constant wailing. Nigel pulled her up off the ground and held her up by the shoulders, shaking her with enough force to dislocate her left shoulder. Maggie didn't feel it though, she didn't feel anything now as she drifted perilously close to unconsciousness, her last thoughts of Lulu race across her memory like a bad nursery rhyme. Suddenly she snapped out of it.

"Go fuck yourself, shit for brains!" and that was the last thing she remembered.

But it wasn't the last thing Lulu remembered.

The last things Lulu remembered were the sound of her Mum's head hitting the edge of the kitchen bench, and the way her body slumped silently to the floor, and the way the blood filled with bubbles ran out of the side of her mouth.

Lulu screamed until the men left.

***

Tyson was scratching at his dirty hair when he felt the presence of Detective Max Bryant making his way around the desk to his well-worn chair and then watched as he sat down on it. He was still scratching when Max fired off the first question.

"So Tyson, you were Suzie's boyfriend, right?

"We were close, yes."

"I am sorry for your loss," he said with as much feel as a surgeon on crystal meth. Tyson looked blankly at him.

"So Tys, may I call you Tys?"

"Everybody else does, go nuts" Tyson answered, grinning weakly at the Detective as he looked at the receding hairline and the face displaying years of wading through the mire of people's lives.

"Ok, Tys, now we've got the niceties out of the way, let's get down to it, shall we?"

Tyson figures this didn't require an answer.

"So where were you on the night of the murder, mate?"

"With my best mate Suthers at home smoking bongs," he lied, adding a look of incredulity for good measure, "Why, d'ya think I did it?"

Detective Max Bryant looked blankly at Tyson for a few moments before breaking into a smirk.

"Just routine inquiries, no need to get defensive, yet. Can this Suthers verify your story?"

"Of course, 'cause it's the truth Detective." Another blank look.

"Do you know of anyone who may have had cause to hurt her, Tys?"

Tyson thought of the thugs and Doug and what they saw that night, her last night.

"No."

The detective looked at Tyson for quite some time before reaching into his pocket.

"Well, if you can think of anything that may help our inquiries, please give me a call," handing Tyson a business card with the police logo and his name and number on it.

"Will do," Tyson replied carefully.

"That'll be all for now, thanks for your time Tys."

"No worries," Tyson said vacantly, getting up from his chair. He gave the Detective half a smile, turned and has his hand on the doorknob when the Detective said,

"Oh, and Tyson? It would be good if you stay in the area and make yourself available if we need to talk again, OK mate?"

"No worries," looking at the card, "Max."

Out on the street Tyson let the stress out in short, quick breaths. He looked around furtively whilst trying to put a cigarette to his lips but failed, his hand shaking too much even for this regular habit. His brain was churning and powered by his growing paranoia.

What the fuck was happening?

His life had been tipped on its edge and everything he knew was busy sliding off into the blackness.

Just then, his phone rang, so he rummaged through his pockets until he felt it vibrating in his grasp, pulled it out and looked at the screen.

Lulu's Mum. Shit.

As he answered all he could hear was the sobbing and hysterical crying of his little girl.

"DADDY, DADDY!" she screamed.

"What's the matter Lulu?' trying to disguise his panic. She sniffed wet snot back down her throat and says,

"Daddy, some men came... Mummy's not moving, they hurt her, blood came out of her mouth, I'm scared Daddy, come get me!"

Tyson couldn't believe his ears and before he had time to realise what a bad idea it was he heard himself saying,

"Shit! Lulu, are you alright? I'm coming now darling!" as he started running off down the street.

"Stay where you are sweetie, OK? Can you do that for Daddy?"

"OK Daddy, but hurry!"

Tyson hung up, his mind a mess of conflicting emotions cutting and scarring each other on their way to the forefront of his thoughts, only to be squashed by another, and another until he felt them seeping out of his body and forming a wet sludge on the ground as he ran. He stopped running suddenly, realising he was walking straight into a trap. He stood there, torn apart, wanting to get to his daughter and also nailed to the ground with fear.

He pulled his phone out and called Suthers.

***

"You fuckin' what? I said rough her up, not kill her, you moron. Aah for fuck's sake!" Doug screamed through the phone at Nigel.

"Mr Farris, it was an accident, she hit her head on the kitchen bench on the way down," Nigel implores.

"A FUCKING ACCIDENT? Maybe you should *accidently* fall into the grinder, hey moron? Maybe I should *accidently* feed you to my dogs, hey moron?"

Doug paused, his mind on other things all of a sudden.

"Just go home and lay low 'til I call you. Can you do that d'ya reckon moron?" and slammed the phone down, his knee knocking the girl under the table.

But Doug Farris could not hear her sobs

Chapter 26

Phuket, Thailand
2014

Johnny was standing above Tyson when he woke. He was silhouetted by the rising sun sitting low on the horizon so all Tyson saw was a hairy mass billowing in the morning breeze. He could smell stale seawater and damp fur and realised that Frowny was curled up next to him, snoring happily, enjoying the rare comfort of a friendly and warm human being. Tyson blinked and adjusted his eyes to the high contrast, and felt a smile spread across his face.

"Morning," he squeezed out.

"Bet you're wondering where you are, am I right?" Johnny teased.

"You've nailed it, yep," dragging his aching body into an upright position, using Frowny's ample bulk as leverage. He looked around at their surroundings. A long beach fringed with distant hills and directly above them, a huge Tamarind tree.

"Is this Karon beach by any chance?"

"This time *you've* nailed it!!" Johnny replied playfully.

"You hungry?"

Tyson had to check his stomach first, feeling for that empty, gnawing sensation and finding it.

"Yeah, I am."

At that Johnny rummaged through his pockets, producing a small bag of what look like tiny dried fish.

"*Bplaa waan*. Dig in, friend!"

Tyson took the bag, reached inside, pulled out a couple of the tiny fish and popped them in his mouth. At first the taste was strange to him, expecting, as he was, a salty fish taste, like an anchovy. The sweetness worked its way past his surprise and filled his mouth with saliva and he gulped the first lot down, heading back to the bag for more of the tangy, sweet sensations.

"Wow, these are great," as he bit down on another handful. Frowny, looking more animated and awake than Tyson could recall, sat straight up behind him, placing his heavy jaw on Tyson's right shoulder, and gave him the bloodshot eyes full of desire. Tyson felt Frowny's drool hit his chest before succumbing and passing one of the fish in his direction, which he gulped down with gusto, not even giving himself time to taste it.

"Finish them off Tys, I've already eaten."

"You sure?" Tyson asked as he filled his mouth with more of the lovely sweet fish.

"Yep, besides, you're going to need the energy."

"Oh yeah, why is that?"

Johnny smiled at him, his eyes glistening with intention.

"Tyson, it's time we go on a little trip, up the coast a ways."

"Really?" Tyson's voice now that of an excited eight-year-old, about to climb the back fence into the abandoned block.

"There's something I want to show you. But first, will you play a tune for an old friend?"

"Of course, Johnny."

Tyson produced his shakuhachi just as Johnny closed his eyes. A serene stillness settled over them both as the first notes became audible.

Tyson let the melody surge up with the wind and wrap itself around Johnny as he drifted towards sleep, adding vibrato as the sound faded, making it seem as if the wind had sliced it up and carried it off towards the surrounding hills. He watched the air being drawn into Johnny's lungs in long, deep pulls.

Johnny held each breath for a while before letting it back out again, long and slow. Each cycle pulled him deeper into the meditative state, deeper into the stillness and within minutes he was drifting above Tyson, floating on the beautiful sounds emanating from the troubled man and his flute. He listened to his own soul gently moaning, partly from joy, and partly from the release from the prison that was his body slumped limply below him. He became the wind dancing with the music; he became the gentle swell throbbing on the horizon; he became the delicate branches of the smallest trees as they bent to the wind's will. He watched as Tyson laid the bed for him to lie in, the gentle screaming becoming a cry of pure elation as the awareness hit him of how rare this moment was, filling his being with a warmth that was almost too much to bear.

Suddenly Tyson found himself blowing a series of riffs that hit him hard. The sounds were sharp and full, their dynamic range pushing at the boundaries of what was known, stretching his emotions across them like a medieval rack, tugging and pulling at him , putting him through excruciating pain until, at last, he found a way back out. His phrasing was testimony to his years of practise, and his natural feel masked the struggle to get there.

He hadn't played like this for years, he had been so divorced from his heart that he didn't imagine ever being able to do this again, to feel the universal pulse and play along with it.

Then suddenly he saw his daughter Lulu with a look of fear on her face as she watched her mum getting bludgeoned to death. He felt the deep emptiness that had taken Lulu's place after she died, after he disappeared from the scene. Before he became a notch on Doug's oversized belt, before the music dried up in him.

It had been ten years and he still hadn't got over her death and sometimes he thought he never would. It was in everything he did, from his stumbling gait to the solitude that found him amongst the crowded, dirty Patong streets, to the lost wanderings and random blackouts. He was a prisoner of his grief and no one, least of all him, could set him free.

It was these small moments of grace that gave him the hope that one day he would break free of the mourning state and really start to live again. When Lulu had died, he had died too, and this numbed body that he inhabited was the slow torture he felt he deserved.

He wondered if he would ever get to rest.

Underpinning these thoughts was the woody low tones of his beloved shakuhachi, his only friend up until now. Without it he would have drifted into the easy escape of booze and drugs, both readily available on every street corner in Patong. But something always pulled him back from the most widely used exit strategy, something urged him on and he could glimpse it, if he was lucky, inside these notes, inside the air he pushed down this flute's worn shaft. And luck didn't come easy to Tyson.

Or so he thought.

Johnny saw Tyson's thoughts as energy being released back into the universe. It was almost as if he could feel the energy shooting off around him as he bounced on the shakuhachi's pulse, tumbling around like a child in a jumping castle. He could feel their sharp edges tear through him and he tried with all his might to buffer them before they disappeared. For he knew, more than he knew anything else, that the energy you released could keep coming back to you, could haunt you and bewilder you for an eternity.

Tyson was ready. Johnny could feel it. And just in time, too.

Chapter 27

Castlemaine, Australia
2004

Tyson stumbled through the sparse undergrowth like he was blind, tripping over jagged pieces of quartz and snagging himself on stunted, deformed bushes, his old man's pants a torn ragged concern after only a few minutes. He glanced at the phone in his hand, willing it to ring. He knew roughly where he was and he blundered along without the ability to anticipate what was in front of him, on one level having completely lost his bearings. Part of him was hovering above himself, another part of him squashed under his shoe as he walked.

The land around him consisted of small yet steep hills, one after the other, and a scattering of eucalypts struggling through the rocky clay bed that was their home. He heard the sound of water rushing over rocks and realised he wasn't far from the water race that went straight past Johnny's hut.

If only his phone would ring.

He made it to the top of the hill and stopped, so short of breath he felt like he might pass out at any moment. He watched the water rushing down the hill next to him and around the one he is standing on, and briefly contemplated the 150 year old feat of engineering that delivered water from fifty kilometres away to the hungry quartz-crushing machines. He could see the marks of the picks that men had held in their gnarly hands all those years ago. Years before backhoes, years before the combustion engine, years before Tyson's life as he knew it collapsed in a bloody heap around him.

From his vantage point he could see a chunk of the town below him. He could hear the various sound systems blaring away into the central Victorian morning, coming together to create a kind of mad modern symphony of festival activity. Normally he would be right into the festival and all it brought with it, but this time he couldn't give a fuck.

C'mon Suthers, call me.

His concept of time was shaky at best. He couldn't remember if it had been an hour or three since he had called Suthers. It seemed like a week. Each step he took froze time, until it seemed like it took him a small lifetime to reach the top of the hill. He was floating above time and yet he was also immersed in every millisecond. Nothing made sense anymore.

Then his phone rang.

In his haste to answer it, the phone slipped from his grasp, narrowly missing the ledge of the water race. He retrieved it, not even looking at the caller-ID as he put it to his ear.

"Suthers?"

"Yeah mate, it's me. Where the fuck are you?"

"Never mind. Have you got Lulu?"

"Yeah mate, just dropped her at your Mum's. She's pretty shaken up, man. I mean, fuck, she just saw her Mum get killed in front of her."

Tyson could hear Suthers sucking on a cigarette as he talked. He pictured the horrific scene that had just punctured his little girl's innocence.

Tyson sighed with relief. "Thanks Suthers, you're a gem. Is she OK?"

"Dunno mate, she didn't say a word on the way over, hard to tell."

"Did anyone follow you?"

"Nope, I would've known, given your Mum lives in the middle of the bush down a long narrow dirt road. Would've seen the dust flying up I reckon. No mate, all good. Called the ambos on the way outta town. They'd be well and truly at Maggie's by now."

Tyson thought of Maggie, his mouth suddenly going dry as he stifled the feeling of nausea gurgling away deep down inside his stomach.

Lulu's mum is dead because of me.

He managed to get the phone out of the way as days of fear and stress and guilt pour out of him, in the form of thick vomit.

"Y'alright Tys? I mean, fuck, this is intense stuff, man. I'd be a fucking mess if it were me. Shit, I am a mess, can't stop eating and smoking."

Spitting the last of the vomit out Tyson replied,

"No mate, I'm not, I'm a fucking spun unit... but I'm alive and Lulu is safe... I'm going off the grid for a while Suthers. Watch out for yourself mate, they might come after you too."

"Yeah righto, I'll go visit my mates at 3CR in Melbourne for a little while. Hey Tys?"

"Yeah mate?"

"Take care of yourself, bro. Keep your head down, OK?"

"Yep, thanks again Suthers, catch ya later." and with that Tyson hung up.

He looked at the phone for a second or two before tossing it into the water race, remembering Jake's advice. Tyson watched as it was carried down the hill on a gurgling bed of rushing water, smashing against the rock walls as it went.

***

Jake's trademark smirk wasn't exposing his rugged jawline as it normally would in this situation. Normally he would have an arm flung casually on the back of the chair next to him, his legs crossed nonchalantly and have his head tilted slightly to one side as he listened to the Melbourne Chamber Orchestra play in front of the Old Gaol wall. Instead, his expression was blank, he was slumped in his chair with his hands in his lap and his thumbs were twiddling frantically. Strangely, the rusty razor wire on top of the wall seemed to have him mesmerised. He had just received a call from his mate Dave, the ambo driver, and it had drained the colour from his handsome face.

As the colour slowly returned Jake stared down at his twiddling thumbs, and to him it looked like some kind of alien wrestling match, one thumb pinning the other, one after another, for the entire performance so far.

He didn't really get this sort of music; it seemed to drain his sexual energy somehow, seemed to put him in some kind of straightjacket.

He pictured himself in Renaissance Europe, prancing about in gay clothes and trying to dance to this shit. He pictured the long drawn-out courting he would have had to endure before he got to nail the girl. How much posturing and bullshit would he have had to take? But don't go getting him wrong; he liked a chase now and then. It isn't any fun if they just fall over with their legs in the air all the time. But this music wouldn't make it very easy, that's for sure.

These musings of his were just distractions, along with the chamber music bouncing off the bloodstained walls of the Old Gaol – a surreal juxtaposition whilst the real thoughts churned away underneath. Lulu's mum had been murdered and Jake knew that Doug had to be behind it.

Doug was a bloated, bald version of the school bully and Castlemaine was his playground, and if he wasn't getting his way, then everyone would know about it. Jake knew how he worked. People would disappear, blood would flow and the killing floor would be running into the early hours of the morning. Doug wouldn't stop until all thorns were crushed under his huge frame. And then he would reappear as usual, squeaky clean.

And Jake, unaccustomed as he was to feelings of doubt, realised that this fiasco was starting to go very, very wrong; too far gone for even the great Doug Farris to survive.

***

Johnny was waiting outside for Tyson as he came over the rise and saw the broken façade and patchy roofline of the hut. Tyson half trotted, half stumbled the last fifty metres as if he was wearing shoes five sizes too big for him, slowing to a clumsy stop in front of the perpetually naked Johnny.

"Heard you coming an hour back, gees you're a noisy bastard. And I could smell the fear coming off you way before then!"

Tyson looked at his friend through a face contorted by fear and grief.

"Well, at least you haven't lost your eloquence Johnny. Mate, I need to crash here for a while."

"I know."

"What d'ya mean *you know*?" Tyson's words forming, despite his haze.

"Tapped into something years ago, mate. Sometimes I can hear the universe breathing, not just some wacked out muso trampling through the bush like a teenager on crack. Come inside, you look like shit!"

Johnny put an arm around his shoulder and led him into his strange world.

Tyson immediately slumped down on the bed whilst Johnny stoked the fire, swinging the kettle over the flames. Neither of them said anything for quite some time.

It was Johnny who eventually broke the silence.

"So I take it things have gone a little pear shaped, then?" he inquired, as he cleaned out a dirty mug with a damp cloth.

Tyson stared blankly at the fire.

"Yeah, you could say that."

There was another long silence, this time broken by the whistling kettle. Tyson watched Johnny as he reached over the flames, retrieved the kettle and carried it over to the shelf with the waiting mugs on it. He was aware of the thumb drive in his underpants and took the opportunity to surreptitiously get it out of there. He spun it around in his hands a few times, keeping an eye on Johnny whilst scanning the room for a good stash spot and also deciding whether or not to tell Johnny all about it. He looked at Johnny's back as he poured the water into the mugs and wondered what strange thought processes he might be engaged in as Tyson sat there. He decided that the less Johnny knew, the less danger he would be in. Suddenly he remembered the brown snake under the bed he was lying on. He slowly reached down and flicked the thumb drive along the floor until he heard it stop, assuming it was now resting against the snake. He didn't peer over the edge to check though, even in his bewildered state retaining the ability to know when, and when not, to test his luck.

Johnny was whistling now, watching the brown water get darker with each jiggle of the tea bag and reflecting on how murky the waters can get so quickly in life. He turned to face Tyson, a mug of tea in each hand and with his clear eyes smiling, only to discover Tyson sound asleep, curled up in the foetal position, his eyes darting back and forth beneath closed lids.

Chapter 28

Phuket, Thailand
2014

Tyson woke up abruptly thinking of Lulu and Suzie. He sat up before his head had time to adjust and the rush nearly sent him straight back into unconsciousness. For ten years he had woken like this and he realised he hadn't been much more than a rabbit trapped in the headlights, mesmerised by his own imminent demise.

Living like this had a way of marking your face like nothing else. They were the marks of unrealised potential and tragic loss. For the first few years he had tried to drink himself into oblivion, and he almost succeeded. If it wasn't for Gaew, Patong would've eaten him up and spat his bones onto the roadside for the soi dogs to fight over. Somehow he had survived up until now, often waking with a fleeting feeling of gratitude that he had been given another day. He opened his eyes and slowly let the world in.

Above him was the same tamarind tree that Johnny had meditated under whilst Tyson blew a chunk of his soul out and offered it up like a soft bed to a weary traveller. His first thought was amazement that he had managed to wake up in the same place he had passed out. And his second, that Johnny had to be close by. Both of these prized a smile out of his worn face. He had found an old friend, after so many years of being alone.

He could smell wet charcoal burning nearby and hear the sound of something being fried on top of it. And then the hunger-inducing smell of fried onions filled his nostrils and had him up on his feet in seconds. His nose led him around the other side of the huge tree where he found Johnny crouched on his haunches in front of a fire pit.

"Works every time," Johnny said, not moving his gaze from the fire and the frying onions.

"What does?"

"Onions cooking. Can wake a man up from the deepest of sleeps. Once tried to wake a man up from the dead with these little beauties but as it turned out, their powerful magic wasn't enough. 'Course I knew I was probably pushing my luck with that one!"

He turned to Tyson and gave him a big grin and a wink from one of his smoke filled eyes.

"Sit down mate, got a little treat for ya! Wait 'til you get your laughing gear around this," he said, pulling a plump white snapper out of a hessian bag next to him.

Tyson watched as Johnny laid out a banana leaf and put the snapper inside it. Out of his pocket he pulled a small tin and sprinkled the fish with salt. Out of another pocket he pulled a bunch of coriander and began breaking it up and sprinkling it on the fish.

Tyson began drooling uncontrollably. Coriander was his favourite herb and it was all he could do to stop himself reaching out and grabbing it out of Johnny's hand and stuffing it in his salivating mouth. Just the thought of it brought forth another torrent of drool. He looked around for Frowny, expecting to see him within range, but he didn't seem to be around.

"Easy fella. Let me cook it first, hey?" At which Johnny wrapped up the fish in the banana leaf, sealing it with a couple of toothpicks before placing it on the grill.

The 'grill' looked like a collection of re-bar and discarded wire he had quickly strung together, and some of the onion was slipping through the cracks. Tyson watched as Johnny picked it up and put it on top of the fish. They stared at it in silence for a few minutes.

"So I thought we were going on an adventure Johnny? What happened?"

Johnny's eyes smiled underneath his long grey hair.

"Yeah, well, someone went and put me in a trance with his bamboo flute and next thing I knew it was morning!"

"Aah, happens every time!"

They both laughed.

"Fuck, I'm glad you found me Johnny."

"Me too." A look of worry fell over Johnny's face, which he disguised just as quickly.

"I still can't believe this! I mean the last time I saw you, you were throwing me into Suthers' car."

Johnny stared at the ground, lost in thought.

"Yeah I wished I could've got there sooner mate."

"Me too."

Silence descended on them as the coriander laden fish cooked its way closer to their stomachs. Tyson felt stunned and groggy with the effort of a man trying to finally wake up, to come to terms with a long buried past full of pain.

Finally Johnny spoke.

"We'll head off after brekkie, OK?"

Tyson wondered for a moment if he had in fact lost the plot completely now, that this was a dream so vivid it had convinced him that it was his waking reality. It couldn't be true, he just didn't have this kind of luck. He shook his head back and forth and looked at Johnny. Something in Johnny's expression told Tyson to shelve his worries for now.

"When can we eat this thing anyway?" he asked whilst mopping the drool off his chin with his sleeve.

A few minutes later Johnny took the toothpicks out of the banana leaf and laid it over the dying fire. The aroma of the coriander-laden fish almost knocked Tyson off his feet. He hardly ever had an appetite and when he did it was a perfunctory thing, a need that had to be satisfied so he could go on. But now his senses were alive in a way he thought wasn't possible, he was virtually in a state of love with this fish. It was as if he had never eaten before and this was his first meal. He couldn't wait to tuck in.

***

They hadn't gone more than 200 metres before Johnny started picking up the various junk he came across, his busy, short steps betraying his deep fascination with the drifting debris. He walked like a caricature of an old man and, even though he was old, Tyson had never seen him that way. Something about his eyes said he would be young forever. He was one of the most alive people Tyson had ever met; he lived in the jungle and roamed the territory around him for artistic inspiration. How could he not be?

Tyson saw a cluster of translucent cigarette lighters wrapped in netting and covered in tiny balls of foam, and he noticed as the sun glinted off the various colours.

It gave him an idea.

He picked up the lighters, stuffed them in his pockets and began searching the sand for more. Johnny was about fifty metres away picking through a pile of fishing nets.

Tyson had often seen large piles of tangled nets up and down the west coast, deposited randomly by the turbulent monsoon swell. Some were twenty or thirty metres long, a few metres wide and a few metres high. There seemed to be more and more with each passing year.

The lighters were scattered along the high tide line and once Tyson worked this out he soon had his pockets bulging and had made a bag of sorts out of his T-shirt and half-filled that by the time he caught up with Johnny. His eyes were popping out of his skull with excitement. Johnny reached into his pocket and pulled out a plastic bag tied in a knot and handed it to Tyson, without looking up from his borderline obsessive-compulsive task of unknotting nets.

Tyson filled the bag in thirty seconds, his mind racing with the possibilities of what he could do with them and didn't even notice the second bag being held out to him.

"Looks like there's more," Johnny grunted, adding the slightest of hand gestures to indicate the as yet unexplored remainder of the beach. Tyson took the bag silently, having spotted a few more lighters before he had even moved, and hurried off towards them.

"At last," Johnny muttered to himself.

Tyson returned half an hour later carrying full bags, overflowing pockets and a grin from ear to ear. He picked up the first bag and trundled off towards the hard, wet sand exposed by the retreating tide. Tyson emptied the bags onto the sand and started sorting them by colour and cleaning them on his T-shirt. Before long he had graded them according to, not only their colour, but also by the degree the sun had faded them. He hurried across to Johnny again, eager to share his idea for the day's sculpture. He opened his mouth and was about to say something when Johnny beat him to it, this time facing him when he spoke.

"You'd be wanting this then?"

Tyson was taken aback.

"But how did you know?" taking the small roll of fishing net from his outstretched hand.

"Dunno... Just did. Now get on with it, you haven't got as much time as you think."

Tyson opened his mouth to say something again but thought better of it and headed back to his lighter array glistening in the afternoon sun. When he looked back a few minutes later Johnny had left the pile of nets and was walking along the tide line, his head bowed, his short steps transforming slowly into a trot.

Hours passed before Tyson looked up from his work, the sound of approaching footsteps snapping him out of his happy, trance-like state. He could hardly believe his eyes. Johnny was half carrying, half dragging a large bamboo frame of some sort. It was about two metres long and shaped like a fish without the tail and, from where Tyson was he looked like he was smiling.

His whole face, not just the eyes.

"Don't ask me how I know, OK?"

"OK," Tyson replied.

"Been busy I see!" Johnny proclaimed, as he looked at the vast lighter encrusted net on the sand in front of them.

Tyson had weaved the lighters through the nets and created a tapestry of colour. The grading had paid off, allowing him to create some depth so that it seemed three-dimensional. He had laid them in circles starting from the middle. There were clusters of yellow lighters at its centre leaning up against each other to form a peak and the circles of lighters slowly went through the colour spectrum as they reached the edges of the net.

Even to Johnny, a seasoned sculptor, it was a stunning piece of work.

"Nice one!" he said, "Shall we drape it over this frame I made and watch the sunset through it?"

Tyson smiled and said,

"Sounds like a plan, man," and together they picked up the now quite heavy net, Johnny tying it on to the frame with string as they went.

The effect was even more spectacular than either of them had thought. The eye literally lit up when the soft, final sunlight of the day hit it, throwing bands of coloured light off in streams behind it onto the faces of Johnny and Tyson. The huge eye stared at the horizon. To Tyson it first had an expectant yet fatalistic air to it, as if the eye was waiting for the answer to a question posed so long ago that its purpose and relevance had been lost, and now it waited and danced in the blaze of colour like a mirage on a shimmering desert highway. With every movement of the sun, the expression would change as the coloured lights flickered across their bodies, bathing them in the dappled reflection of the eye's eternal optimism.

The gaze was unmistakably hopeful, and through it Tyson felt like he could really *see* for the first time.

He sat there in silence with Johnny and watched the shifting, coloured blurs until the last of the light had left the sky.

Chapter 29

Castlemaine, Australia
2004

"Aah progress! It's a fuckin' bewdiful thing, don't ya reckon Jake?" Doug said as he looked at his bulldozers and excavators lined up behind the new cyclone fence. Jake followed his gaze from their vantage point on Lawson's Hill to the hastily constructed fence on its shoulder.

From here Jake could see for miles in every direction and he let himself get lost in it, just like he used to when he would ride his bike up here as a kid. Back then there were trees as far as you could see, scrappy regrowth forests that grew out of the mining devastation that became his childhood playground. His thoughts sped up and over the many jumps they had made out of the piles of tailings that had scarred the landscape like pimples on an adolescent face, losing himself in childhood happiness whilst standing here on the windy hill with Doug.

Doug wedged a pair of binoculars against his massive cheeks and peered through them at the horizon, making phantom chomping noises, as if willing the moment to perfection by imagining chocolate chip cookies. Jake suppressed a wince and plastered a weak smile on his face, which actually looked more like a grimace.

"Yeah, beautiful Dougy," Jake finally answered unconvincingly.

"Hey," he continued, "you remember that day at Thompson's mine, Doug? When we were kids?"

"I remember a bunch of scared little shits doin' what I told 'em, yeah."

Jake shuffled and gave up on his attempt to humanise Doug with stories of their childhood.

In the far distance Jake could see the freeway approaching. A nearby hill already had the middle of it blasted out and a bevy of Doug's yellow machines were busily moving the dirt and rock about like ants just before it rains.

"It feels like walking into the middle of the MCG the morning of the Grand Final, like, you know something big is going to happen. The scene is set. No turning back, hey Jake?" Doug suggested, his fear antenna starting to twitch with input.

Jake stared out at the hectare upon hectare of pine plantation that had replaced the bush of his youth and said nothing. Instead, he listened to the eerie silence that surrounded them, a silence that signalled the complete lack of wildlife.

Pine plantations were good at that.

"Everything OK there, Jake, you seem a bit quiet? I take it you received my, ah... contribution to your election funds?" Doug challenged between snorts.

He turned to Jake and pinned him with his mean, beady eyes. Jake, sensing this, lowered his eyes to the ground just in time, before replying,

"Things are getting a bit messy Dougy. I mean fuck, two bodies already and I get the feeling you haven't even warmed up yet. Jesus, Doug, I went to school with Maggie for fuck's sake. She was a friend!"

"A friend was she, Jake? I think what you mean to say is that she was one of the hundreds of girls you have fucked whilst their hubbies were out or sleeping in the next room. What, you getting all, what do the kids say, 'emo' on me are ya, Jakey?"

"It's just that..." Jake hesitated.

"Just nothing, Jake. Look mate, you've got to remember what's at stake here and forget about fucking compassion, alright? We're too far down the track for that."

Before Jake could answer Doug was on him again like a ton of bricks.

"Now Jake, I know you hang around at bars and see Tyson, gees, I might even go as far to say you were mates, right?"

Jake stared out at the surrounding hills.

"Well let's just say I hope you're not holding out on me mate, 'cause that would have fairly nasty repercussions."

"What are you trying to say, Doug?" Jake said, suddenly wide-awake.

"Don't make me spell it out..." Doug replied, his tone soaked in the thick broth of his cruel intent.

The slightest glimmer emerged in Jake's faraway expression.

"Did you kill your own daughter Dougy, since we're being all honest and that?"

Doug shuffled his weight from one foot to the other, like a boxer warming up before a fight, and said nothing. He didn't need to, as Jake had already noticed the smallest quiver emanate from Doug's over indulged bottom lip.

It was all Jake needed to know.

***

Tyson weaved his way through the crowd; keeping the hat Johnny had given him down low so that it was hitting his wrap-around sunglasses. The crowd was moving slowly through a vaudeville inspired installation, a series of tents lining the walkway that was usually the link between the supermarket car park and the main street. Now it was burlesque cabaret central, a hip and culturally aware strip full of theatrically made up and exuberantly dressed touts, luring the weary yet wide-eyed spectators into their lairs with outrageous exaggerations and bold pronouncements. One performer was leaning on an old hat box and playing the ukulele like Hendrix might have, pulling riffs out of the thing that seem impossible, even to Tyson, until he noticed the lead going from the ukulele to the echo box, then feeding into a small set of speakers hidden behind two Asian umbrellas. The performer was rapping about the crowd going past but most of them seemed ignorant to the parody. The guy kept adding more riffs to the sound, building a funky stop-start rhythm that almost had Tyson's feet tapping as he shuffled past. He looked up at the guy and realised it was Simon Larkin, an old mate of his from his inner city days. He remembered they had jammed and partied through a drizzly Melbourne winter when they were students. Luckily, when their eyes met for an instant he didn't seem to recognise Tyson.

Why would he recognise me? Tyson thought. *For fuck's sake, I'm not the same person I was a week ago, let alone a few years ago.*

The crowd was thinning now, being slowly seduced into the various tents by their dramatic theatrical offerings. As Tyson walked by, he received a smattering of all of them, and the effect was startling. It was as if each separate performance came together to form some kind of modern montage of excess, a twisted barrage of musical/ burlesque theatre crossed with a 19th century snake-oil salesman, all in the context of an image saturated post-modern world. This combination was cool and knowing and in his face, and he couldn't help but imagine the Rogers and Hammerstein treatment over the top of it all, maybe in this case slowed right down so it sounded like one big hallucination.

In his pocket were his shakuhachi and the passport Johnny suggested he go back for, despite the danger, and now in the safety of the crowd, Tyson was glad that he did. He had a feeling this town was done with him and that he may not ever be back. And as Johnny said, he'd be as good as fucked without the passport.

He had almost made it to the supermarket car park when the two thugs saw him. The first Tyson knew of it was the sudden and hurried movement of the crowd as Nigel and Brian barrelled their way through, subtle as two bricks. He moved quickly out of the crowd and behind a row of tents up against the old market building, giving himself a clear path to the street. He pushed his sunglasses down the bridge of his nose so he could see the ropes and stakes sticking out of the ground, and then ran like hell. When he hit the pavement he noticed a wall of spectators facing the street, watching some kind of procession. He broke through the crowd and huddled down so Doug's boys couldn't see him. In front of him a procession of hot rods were cruising past.

Before Castlemaine was a 'Vibrant Arts Community' it was the 'Hot Rod Capital of Australia'. The fading signs on the highway coming into town were testimony to the hundreds of '34 roadsters sitting in garages. Tyson remembered hearing 'chopped big block' many times over the years before he knew what it meant. And now they were all in front of him, lowered '34 roadsters with chopped roofs and exposed 454 Chevy motors glistening in the sun.

Tyson could hear a commotion behind him and figured the men were just behind him. He crouched down further so that he was level with the row of children, their eyes wide with anticipation as they were showered in sweets thrown from the hot-rods. He watched as the sweets fell into the gutter and were shovelled up by hungry hands to waiting mouths. To him, the falling sweets had no sound. What he *did* hear clearly was the revving of fifty V8's on the street in front of him, and that was when he felt the time was right to make his move.

He slowly stood up and casually walked into the middle of the procession, timing it so he squeezed between two hot-rods, ducking under the flying sweets as he did so. As one of the hot rods motors past him he walked with it, eventually climbing onto the long step on its side, then crouched down. The driver leaned down and asked,

"You right there mate?" behind strip sunglasses and 1950's rocker hair.

"Can I get a ride to the end of the street by any chance? I seem to have two mafia guys chasing me and I don't think they want to wish me a happy birthday!" Tyson replied, trying to appeal to the guy's laconic nature. Inside his heart was pounding and his head raced with thoughts of escape.

The rocker looked over both shoulders.

"No worries mate."

Tyson caught his breath and looked back in the direction of Doug's thugs, hoping they hadn't made it across the street, which would give him a bit of a head start. They hadn't. He stared up the street, willing the hot-rod to go faster than the walking pace it was doing.

Fuck, he thought, *I'm in a chase that's slower than walking pace and the only thing moving faster than the procession had weapons and bad tattoos about their Mums or some long lost girlfriend.*

Finally the hot-rod reached the end of the street and was executing the wide U-turn that would send them back down the other side to the sugar-stoned children. He decided to make his move.

"Thanks for the ride," he said as he leapt off.

"Too easy mate," the rocker replied as Tyson stumbled over the temporary barrier, looking over his shoulder for the tell-tale signs that he had been spotted. He saw the thugs stop suddenly upon seeing Tyson, then heave their collective bulk forward into a run, spraying people off to the sides as they went. Tyson bolted around the corner and sprinted up Hargreaves Street.

The street was virtually empty and he covered a lot of ground quickly. He had to get off this street before Doug's boys made it to the corner, where they would have a clear shot at the running musician with the terror in his eyes. Ahead of him there was a small sandwich board with 'Fringe Junkyard Percussion Jam' scrawled across it and an arrow pointing down a laneway. He took the left, rushing down an old set of stone stairs to a basement below the corner building. The stairs finished in a mound of dirt about one foot high. When he came to a stop on it he looked around, panting and wheezing. There were about a dozen people smiling at him with a look of expectation on their faces.

"Hi," one of them said,

"And welcome! Everyone who stands on the mound has to say something about themselves. Anything: your thoughts, dreams, fears, desires, whatever you like!"

Tyson tried to catch his breath and listened for the tell-tale thud of heavy feet on stone stairs, but he could only hear the slightly annoying voice of the woman in front of him.

"So, what have you got for us, friend? Whenever you're ready!" furrowing her brow with compassion, wearing the smile of someone who just stepped out of an ashram. That faraway, blissed out vibe.

Tyson wasn't in the mood.

"Aah… um… have you ever felt like, I don't know, like there's a dark presence chasing you and you've just gotta hide somewhere? 'Cause that's how I feel right now."

He stepped down off the mound.

"Come jam with us brother," one of them said.

"Come hide in our cave," another said, giggling.

"Choose your weapon of mass percussion," another one chortled.

Aah Jesus, he muttered to himself, as they led him into 'the percussion space'.

Tyson ducked under various steel objects that were hanging from rope, dodged several upturned steel rubbish bins and car wheel rims, and hurried to the other side of the room, as far away from the doorway as possible. Someone had started bashing the various objects at random and the others joined in and within seconds Tyson's top end hearing had shut down as the clanging filled the damp room to capacity. Eventually a lost, wandering rhythm began to emerge out of the primal therapy chaos. Tyson picked up a stick and kept time with the guy hitting the plastic drum and realised right then that no one was coming down here to look for him. For all intents and purposes it appeared to be some kind of feral torture chamber. He recalled the slogan from his favourite tobacco.

'*Not everyone can drum.*'

And for once, it was a good thing.

Chapter 30

Phuket, Thailand
2014

Gaew wasn't sure how much more of this she could take. Two days and nights of whining and whimpering were just about enough for her. Every so often Frowny would stop, get up from his vigil at the door and trot over to her, his tail wagging with a pleading look in his eyes. She would ignore him and keep him happy with titbits of food and the occasional friendly slap of his chunky backside. Distractions were all they were.

She played absentmindedly with her long, black hair and chewed her bottom lip and watched Frowny go through his 'let me go' routine, a shimmering, slightly retarded looking half-dance, half-trot set of moves accompanied by a flailing tongue and a tail that threatened to sweep the coffee table clean of its contents at any moment.

Tyson had said he'd back 'in a few days', a term she had grown to hate just as much as his general lack of interest in her. She couldn't understand why, though. She was young, still had a tight body and a variety of pouty looks that usually made men melt, but Tyson seemed almost immune to her charms. Every time she went out shopping she was aware of the eyes watching her tight arse bouncing under her dress. She could almost feel the hungry hands as they covered her body with their film of desperation, mixing it with the stinking bravado that came from a few bucks in their pockets and the awareness that most women here could be bought for the price of a packet of cigarettes in any other country.

It was fine. She knew she was hot.

It wasn't that. She'd never had to be the one doing the chasing before and at first it was kind of exciting, a new game to play. She remembered their early days when she was oddly turned-on by this twist in her fortunes. She imagined herself as a cat, prowling around him naked as he lay there with that faraway look in his eyes. She would flick her nipples occasionally and watch for his reaction, the lack of which would drive her to a state of frustration in the blink of an eye and the game would go up a few notches as her long nails sought out his flesh. And he would just lie there and take it, which would incite her more. Orgasms were never far away after that and for someone who had largely switched off her desires, she never ceased to be amazed at how he could keep her on the boil by hardly doing anything. In fact, the less he did, the more it did to her.

And it drove her crazy.

Her teeth let go of her bottom lip when she felt the blood mixing with her saliva and she sucked it down her throat with something approaching relish, drawing air into her mouth through the smallest of gaps.

Frowny made one last attempt to convince her to let him go by launching his lumpy body off the ground as she climbed out of her sad eroticism and tried to avoid copping the full load of Frowny's bulk. To no avail as it turned out, as Frowny landed in her lap with a thud, looking up at her with his frown turned up to full. Gaew couldn't help but laugh at him and raise her hand in playful combat, a move she had practiced growing up, which was dished out to babies, dogs and chickens. With it came the mock disapproving frown and the beginning of a grin and at this Frowny knew he had finally got through to her. He sealed the deal with a couple of slobbery kisses to the face, which had her reeling and pushing him out of her lap.

He waited by the door, his gaze moving from the door to her face with increasing regularity until Gaew got up, muttering in Thai to herself, and walked towards the door. Frowny couldn't contain himself any longer and let out an excited yelp that came close to bursting Gaew's eardrums. She reached for the doorknob and turned it. Frowny put his nose into the gap, trying to make it big enough to get his body through. Gaew opened it wide and fast and said,

"Bpai loei!" *Go now!* To which Frowny replied by giving her a view of his bulky rear legs as he took off down the stairs.

Gaew stood for a minute biting her lip and running her slender hand through her long, silky hair before shutting the door with a bang. She leaned against the door and looked around the empty room.

She missed Tyson already.

***

They had walked for miles in silence, passing through Kamala, Laem Sing, Surin, Bang Tao and Nai Thon beaches as well as the rocky cliffs between without even a slowing of the pace. Tyson walked a few metres behind Johnny and watched the mad movement and the wild grey hair and marvelled at his luck in being here. Every now and then Johnny would pause mid step as a piece of ocean debris caught his eye.

And so it goes, Tyson mused. He smiled to himself.

And then he understood. The debris of humanity was a source of wisdom for Johnny and a way to get more inside the moment. To transform rubbish into beauty was his way to make sense of it all. A way to breathe, a way to feel connected whilst remaining immersed in his self-imposed solitude.

Tyson's thoughts started tumbling over each other and he struggled to slow them down as usual. He had so many questions for Johnny, so many loose threads to pull at. With these thoughts came a light-headedness that made him feel like he was floating. A tune came into his head and he listened, drawing his focus there until he was riding the wave again, re-inventing the riff over and over, like a kind of mental workout, without the steroids and the mirrors. It made him feel good, giving him a sense of direction that he otherwise lacked completely, and for years he didn't even have that, having lost his feel inside one of the early blackouts years ago.

It had been days since his last blackout and as he walked behind Johnny he felt the fog slowly lifting around him at last. His being was becoming sensitized again: food had flavour, the sand beneath his feet a comforting texture, the wind blowing off the ocean filled with the scent of fish and burning diesel. And the colours... wow! It was like someone had pulled a veil of post-coital bliss over the world around him. Everything looked like it could be written about or turned into a melody that cut to the core of human experience. And there was something light coming off Johnny that he couldn't put his finger on; some kind of larger understanding and at the same time, the wisdom of not knowing anything at all.

He felt for his camera as they rounded the point that would lead them to Nai Yang beach. They didn't round the point though; rather, they made off towards the rocky outcrop that was the very tip of the point, which Tyson quickly worked out would become an island with the rising tide. He switched on the camera as they waded through the rock pools, both holding their few belongings above their heads as they went.

He set the camera down on a ledge of rock behind them as they both sat and looked out at the ocean. Neither of them had uttered a word for hours and Tyson began to realise there was a certain calmness in silence, something words couldn't capture; something, in fact, that words often destroyed in their ham-fisted exuberance. It was such a shame and intensely ironic, Tyson thought, that communication was often thwarted by words.

It was Johnny who broke it.

"Your legs sore?"

"Not sure, I'll let you know when the feeling comes back!"

Johnny's eyes squinted into a grin.

"Reckon we might camp here tonight, OK?"

"Fine by me."

"There's a spot in there under that bank of trees," Johnny muttered, pointing a lazy finger in the general direction.

And then the silence again.

They both watched the horizon and the gentle mid-season swell spreading itself over the rocks.

"Not far to go now, mate," Johnny's accent slipping back into broad Aussie.

"So, are you going to let me know where we are going or what, mate?" Tyson asked playfully.

Johnny waited a while before replying,

"You'll know soon enough, my dear friend."

Chapter 31

Castlemaine, Australia
2004

Johnny wasn't there when Tyson finally made it back to the hut.

Probably a good thing, he thought, but he wasn't really sure why. He listened to his heart thudding in the empty room and the unmistakable slither of Johnny's friend, the brown snake, repositioning itself under the bed as if Tyson wasn't even there. He was too tired to be frightened of the snake and its deadly venom, too wrung out to be able to take on any new threat. All he could manage was a vague irked sensation and a weak one at that. He pictured the thumb drive under there guarded by the snake.

It was his only bargaining tool, if he needed it.

He leaned against the rough stone mantelpiece staring into a fire that wasn't even lit and came to the conclusion that the thumb drive full of images themselves weren't enough. Not enough to stop Doug torturing the whereabouts of the thumb drive out of him. For a moment his mind went back to the night that started all this mess, the sound of flesh being ground and bones crushed, the whir of the motor the only constant and out of which the man's guttural screams rose with a demented, gruesome time signature.

Even death had a melody.

Tyson knew exactly what Doug could do. And that he was no match for him.

He continued staring at the non-existent fire for a while before he saw himself leaning there, lost in thought, again feeling like a spectator in his own life. It reminded him of the times he had left his body whilst playing music. Except this time, there was no music. This time it was the brutal, expressionistic howls of a man's wild imaginings, his knuckle clenching fear, his paralysis of grief, and he watched his thoughts race through his head like masked assassins, murdering his sanity piece by piece.

Get a grip, he told himself, *you're losing it, man. Think! Think!*

And the more he tried, the more slippery the options become: vague, translucent shapes that lurked just out of his reach.

He snapped out of his haze with the idea of putting the kettle on, which meant starting a fire, which meant collecting wood, which meant going outside, which of course meant he was shitting himself. He pulled back the grey blanket that was serving as a door and peeked through it, before peeling through soundlessly.

Or so he thought.

The last of the sun was burning a crimson hole through the surrounding hills as he knelt down to pick up some dry leaves and twigs. He shoved them into his pocket and continued creeping through the silent bush. Not even the sound of birds giving their last calls of gratitude to the sun gave him peace. No sign that everything was going to be OK, just another day in the forest.

In fact it was eerily silent.

He heard footsteps a few seconds before he saw someone coming over the hill, silhouetted by the sun and resembling a shadow puppet in some sad show. These few seconds were a lifetime for Tyson. Frozen mid–crouch he noticed that his pounding heartbeat matched the man's purposeful steps, the thumping doubling in intensity with every step closer.

He hopes like hell it was Johnny.

As the figure came down the small hill towards him out of the searing crimson sunset, Tyson could see that he was holding something in his right hand, and he was holding it high up in front of him. At first Tyson thinks the man was waving at him and he had to stifle a return wave in case it wasn't Johnny. Or maybe Tyson was lost in the middle of a blackout again, or maybe in the grip of another hallucination.

How could he tell?

As the man got closer he realised that he wasn't waving at all.

He was reading.

He was holding a book out in front of him and reading as the light began to fail behind him and his legs negotiated the steep, rocky path without his conscious input. Tyson stood up and marvelled at the image in front of him. You don't often see a guy walking through the bush reading a book. Not often at all. Amidst his turmoil Tyson couldn't help but squeeze out a broad smile. He could feel Johnny's energy lightening his load, even as he approached.

***

Jake snorted the last of the coke off the girl's back just as she came, her thrusts guaranteeing the coke delivery to his hungry pleasure receptors. He threw his head back, gasped at the air and waited for the raw, hungry sense of power to wash over him. His massive whisky intake was slowing it down and for a while he hung between euphoria and nausea, which he disguised with a few more thrusts into the girl he had impaled on his ridiculously hard cock.

What was her name again? He asked himself, and then decided it probably doesn't matter. *Paris? Brittany? Barbie? Whatever! Means, that's what I'll call her. A means to an end.*

Fuck, he loved that first rush of a big line of coke, he loved how the ideas flowed like a swollen river, how he seemed to catch a glimpse of the way things really were and could nail the thought in a few well-chosen words.

Problem was, no one was listening now.

There was only Jake and his own rampaging ego to be dazzled by his brilliance. The girl didn't count and besides, she had just been fucked by the mighty Jake McCardle and, as experience had taught him, she'd be lucky to be able to string a sentence together after a pounding like that.

In her normal state she'd be lucky to string a sentence together. Jake smirked to himself.

He pulled out and walked around the room in a big circle, like a victory lap, as the girl slumped herself down on the chaise lounge she had been bent over whilst Jake was giving her the Mayoral treatment. It took him a while to get his bearings, to work out where the fuck he was, and for that matter, what day it was. He was in a large room filled with antique furniture, the ceilings were high and there were paintings and sculptures everywhere. There were overstuffed chairs and walnut coffee tables, Persian rugs and bookshelves brimming with well-worn books, delicate art deco vases of impossible porcelain women holding onto lamp bases with their long, slender arms. Red velvet curtains with gold trim over the arched mahogany doorway, which led to who knows where. If it wasn't for the crude 'tramp stamp' tattoo just above Means' arse then he might've thought he had travelled back to the 1920's and F. Scott Fitzgerald was about to stroll in with two glasses and a bottle of *Dom Perignon*.

He took it all in on fast-forward and still had time to give each painting a brisk critique on the way through. He was on fire tonight, the clarity of his insights sharp to the touch. He looked down and realised his hard-on wasn't going to go down for hours and if he kept on being so brilliant, it may become a permanent thing. He entertained the urge to roll Means over and pound her some more but realised in an instant that she was the only thing in the room that wasn't beautiful, even though she had the body, the lips, and the bone structure to say that she was. A studied wistfulness overcame him, which he countered with another two lines, one for each nostril, off the small, round table next to the chaise lounge and the sleeping girl.

His nose was an inflamed, bulbous portal to another world and he snorted with all his might as the portal slowly closed down in protest to the battering it had received so far. He blocked one nostril and heaved air in through the other until he felt the lump of coke-filled snot fly down his throat, almost making him gag. But Jake McCardle didn't gag. Jake McCardle could handle anything. He reached across to the nearly empty bottle of whisky and took a manly swig with musical theatre overstatement, as if the more he hammed it up the more authentic it would feel.

But Jake was wrong.

His stomach rumbled as the coke-filled snot mixed with the hard ball of doubt that had been sitting there for days. He stood there in silence, his body humming like a racing car at idle, and waited...

When he came to, he had his head in his hands, his hard-on was a distant memory and his eyes were filled with the image of Means' naked body in front of him. He took her in and it was as if she was in macro and he could see every blemish, every bruise, every lump the tattoo gun had hit on its way to creating the most unremarkable tattoo he had ever seen. Every rise and fall of her body, which hours ago he had worshipped like she was a goddess, looked pale, saggy and well used. He pulled focus to the whole room and remembered where he was. Upstairs at the Imperial Hotel. He could hear the boom of a big sound system through the floor and walls, and then he remembered how he got here: lots of drinks at the bar whilst listening to a great funk outfit that drifted into frenetic ska when the mood took them. The drinks and the coke made every girl look hot and available. Jake was a bit miffed that he had only snared the one.

Must be off my game.

The doubt climbed out of his belly, fuelled by the coke, swept over him like a rising full moon tide. Suddenly his thoughts were racing again, but this time there was no hard-on to accompany them. He wondered where Tyson was, and how he could possibly deliver him to Doug without letting him get too hurt, because deep down, he was fond of Tys.

And slightly envious too.

Tyson had always seemed so much freer than Jake, much happier, much more willing to go with the flow. And the music! He could pull a feeling out of nowhere and turn it into the most heart wrenching solo Jake had ever heard. Sure Jake had plaques around town with his name on them, but what had he left as his legacy? A bunch of stuff borne out of family money, family business connections and his eye for a dodgy and lucrative deal. Even now, the older of his constituents still referred to him as Evan's boy, little Jake. He bristled at the thought.

He quickly returned his attention to picturing Tyson's friends, in an effort to narrow down the options.

Suzie was dead. Suthers had not been seen for two days. Who else?

Like Jake, Tyson had lots of people that called him a friend but weren't much more than barflies and band groupies. Not even half a friend, Jake mused and for a moment got lost in the glare of his clever insight, but only for a moment, since it was the uncharacteristic doubt and fear driving him now.

Where would I go if I were Tys?

Then he had it. He'd go bush, that's what Tyson would do. Grab a few things and get lost in the hills.

But where?

He resisted the urge to snort the last of the coke to deliver the truth to him, opting instead to ride out the wave without it, in case it sent him back to hard-on world instead.

Who lives where no one else would?

He pictured a man walking towards him wearing an old man's hat and tracksuit pants reading a book.

He couldn't press speed dial number two, Doug's number, faster than if he had the winning numbers of the Saturday night *TattsLotto* and was calling to claim his prize.

Jake had just hit the jackpot.

He felt his erection rising with each un-answered ring.

***

Johnny sipped his tea and nodded whilst Tyson blurted out days of confusion, fear and grief into the room. His words echoed up the fireplace and were swallowed by the orange flames. Johnny just stared at his tea with a knowing smile on his face. Finally he said,

"Sounds like the walls are closing in on you Tys. Is Lulu safe?"

"Yep, she's at my Mum's, Suthers took her there."

"Does anyone else know where ya Mum lives Tys?"

"Don't think so."

Johnny kicked at the fire with his unlaced boot, sending sparks out onto the floor at their feet.

"Mmmmm," he pondered.

It was quite some time before either of them spoke. It was Tyson who broke the silence.

"So what should I do? Turn myself in to the cops? Disappear? What?" exasperation contorting his face into a caricature of confusion.

"Well, seems to me that your video is the key to you staying alive and also the thing that might get you killed. Where'd you say you stashed it?"

"I didn't," Tyson replied, trying hard not to look at the spot. "Better you don't know mate, for your own sake."

"Do you think so, Tys, I mean, does anyone else know?"

"Nope."

"Have you considered the fact that if they do find you, and I am assuming they will, then you've got nothing? Show's over mate, minus a few of your toenails and maybe a finger or two. They'll torture it out of you and you'll cave in like a tent in the wind. No offence mate, you're an artist, just saying..."

"You're right Johnny. Ok, I'll tell you then, but please don't go there unless you have to. Everyone who gets involved with me ends up dead."

Johnny laughed when Tyson told him, the first time Tyson could recall a full-bodied laugh coming out of the guy, ever.

"Well, as it turns out, I'm about the only one who could go there and survive. Ha! Clever! And besides, I'm already involved."

Johnny eyed off the bed, his eyes darting from side to side, as all the options have their moment on his stage, the stage lights fading on each one as they were discarded in turn. Finally Johnny said,

"I've got a mate who can get you out of the country, 'cept he's in Darwin. Got a prawn trawler. Yep, that's the ticket! They'll be watching the airports so we can't go there."

"Fuck!" Tyson exclaimed, "Do you reckon Doug's reach is that long?"

"Not Doug, mate, the cops. Seems you're the prime suspect in your girlfriend's murder!"

"W... What?"

"That's the problem with you artist types, so disconnected from reality," and slapped him on the leg, smiling.

"Let's get you the fuck out of this country, hey? But first, one more cuppa and a goodnight's sleep."

Johnny rubbed his hands together. He seemed to be enjoying himself.

Chapter 32

Phuket, Thailand
2014

Tyson and Johnny were sitting under a stand of huge *dton soon* trees as the morning sun burst through them, sending dappled light to the forest floor. The trees reminded Tyson of the She-oaks in Castlemaine, but five times the size, big enough to have that ancient feel to them. He had woken early after an oddly deep and trouble-free sleep but not before Johnny, who had been sitting in front of Tyson calmly gathering the energy around him and becoming it. Wherever he was, whether it was at his jungle tree house or in an enclave between rocks on a beach somewhere, Johnny always greeted the day like this.

Tyson, meanwhile, was busy welcoming the wave of gratitude that was hitting him like the swollen beach break that filled his eyes with blue blurs of wonder.

Not far away he could see half a dozen Thai fishermen tending to a boat up on blocks, hand-rolled cigarettes dangling from their lips and looks of concentration on their faces. The slight breeze enabled him to catch snippets of their conversation and he just imagined the rest. He immersed himself in their world, he felt the sinewy old muscles and the habitual squint that shielded their eyes from the glare of an ocean that wasn't even there right now and yet was a presence from which they could never escape. And nor did they want to. They could read the ocean the same way others read a road map. It was their food source, their mistress and their greatest foe, it was their life. It was fickle and volatile one moment and beautifully clear and serene the next, abundant or destitute on the whim of the wind. Everywhere around him was living proof that music was in everything people did. Most had just simply forgotten the melody, like he had. And then all you heard were the notes, random sounds without a context, floating meaninglessly away on the breeze like the old men's voices.

Johnny was still meditating on how to prepare Tyson for what was to come. He watched his thoughts give the stillness a reason to be, and smiled, knowing right then that the time was right. He could sense Tyson waiting and Johnny was hoping that the more he intimated, rather than stated, the more Tyson would build the story himself. Fill in the blanks that trauma had swept away years ago with the urgency and desperation of a thief on ice.

He had almost got there by himself, Johnny realised. It was now a matter of how to wade through the mud together, how to dredge the past and not drown in it. And after that, how to get him ready for what was to come, just a few kilometres up the beach.

He came slowly out of his meditation, opened his eyes and stared out at Nai Yang reef a few hundred metres offshore. He watched a couple of surfers go down either side of the same wave and execute large, sweeping bottom turns, then launch themselves back up the wall that threatened to dump them onto the reef at any moment. He watched as they added their own individual moves to the wave's hollow-bodied howl, one of them flying over the lip into mid-air before landing miraculously back down on the sliding musical wall below him.

"Now that was fuckin' bewdiful!" Johnny's voice a gravelly bed for his Bogan sarcasm. If he could've mustered a thick ball of phlegm and spat it onto the ground, he would've. He always enjoyed taking the piss out of himself after meditating, it levelled him back out in some way.

And he so rarely had an audience.

The slight breeze gave the tops of the old trees a voice; a low whooshing sound that seemed to spread a layer of calm over everything.

"D'you remember much, Tys, about the old days in Castlemaine?"

Tyson looked at him for a moment, then away at the Thai fisherman as they tended to an old boat.

"Not alot mate, and I don't think I want to. I lost everything mate, what is there to remember except loss?"

"I guess you have a point. If I were you, I would've done the same, run away and never looked over my shoulder. The thing is, Tys, alot of shit went down after you left."

"I'm sure it did Johnny, but I don't really give a shit. I can't go there mate, there's too much hurt there for me. Everything I loved, everything I was got bludgeoned out of existence in a matter of days. I'm still reeling Johnny, and the years haven't made it easier. Every night I fall asleep petrified that my blackouts ARE the reality and this is all just a distraction to stop me blowing my head off. It's not easy, mate, getting through each day being me."

Johnny looked at Tyson, torn between compassion and the need to set things right, and now he wasn't sure which way to go. He stared out at the two surfers again, hoping that the lines they carved in the waves would give him back the direction that the years of planning had promised him they would but had now left him rudderless. Now he was unsure how to do it, how to unravel the man in front of him so that he had the chance to live again. Years of reflection, of meditation and he was fumbling the ball mere moments before the final siren.

"I know mate, I've been watching you tearing yourself apart for the last three years."

"Wh...What? What do you mean?"

"I've been waiting for you to be ready."

"Ready for what?" Tyson's vulnerability now infecting his words, leaving them raw and reverberant and they both watched them spread themselves out over the soft grass all around them.

"Ready for you to meet yourself again."

Chapter 33

Castlemaine, Australia
2004

Tyson and Lulu are running through long grass and laughing hysterically as the dried seedpods spray off into the air around them, landing in their hair, on their arms and spearing into their socks as they run. Lulu's excited shrieks fill the gully with the simple joy of a child and the birds seem to like it, joining in with return screeches that almost seem to be mocking her.

What do they know that we don't? What strange mating ritual are they involving us in? What proprietorial instincts are they re-enacting as we tear through here without a care in the world?

He stops running, stands still and listens to his heart pounding in his chest and watches the long grass being pushed over as Lulu zigzags through it. It is early and the morning dew has yet to be relinquished by the already scorching sun. An hour or two of stillness left before the hot, north wind comes in and air-dries everything in its path.

He loved this time of the day more than any other. For him, was usually after an all-nighter, after a gig where the buzz of the moment refused to go away that he found himself staring at an alien sunrise.

But this time he is clear and sober and it is even better, here with his little girl.

Shit, he thinks, just being around Lulu's spirit, her zest for the next moment and what it might bring is enough to give me a reason.

He watches as she continues darting through the grass, drawing his focus to the seeds flying above her head, which are given flight for a moment or two as she jogs through them, and then he watches them fall to the ground.

Maybe that's what the birds are going on about. We are trampling their food source, ransacking their supermarket!

Suddenly the seeds aren't flying about anymore, Lulu having come to a complete standstill.

"DADDY! DADDY! COME QUICK!"

Tyson woke in a sweat, sat bolt upright in bed and peered into the semi-darkness of the hut. He was short of breath and there was a heavy pain in his chest. He blinked several times as his surroundings came into focus.

"DADDY! DADDY! HELP ME!"

This time there was no excitement in her voice, instead it was thick with fear, and Tyson hoped like hell he was still dreaming.

In a car not far away Doug Farris sat smoking his trademark cigar, a look of spiteful triumph on his face. He listened to the tape playing at full blast through the car stereo and looked at his watch, mindful of his press conference later in the day. He hoped that this wouldn't take much longer.

"DADDY! THE MEN TOOK ME FROM GRAN'S. I'M SCARED DADDY!"

At this Tyson leapt out of bed and started for the door, convinced now that this was not a dream.

This was a fucking nightmare.

"DADDY! HELP ME!" she screamed, as he burst through the grey curtained doorway and straight into the waiting, heavily ringed fist of Nigel, Doug's number one 'assistant'.

That's all he knew for a while.

When he came to the first thing he could see was the ground moving under him and Nigel's thick legs as they carried him away from the hut. He squirmed, realising that his hands and feet have been bound, and his groans of anguish are barely audible due to the gaffer tape over his mouth. They seemed to go back down into his diaphragm and kind of disappear.

"Easy, little guy!" Nigel growled, "keep that squirming up and I'll punch a rib into your lungs to make it REAL fun for ya!"

Tyson stopped squirming on Nigel's advice and tried to get a handle on the fucked-up situation he found himself in as Lulu's voice echoed through the gully again.

"DADDY! THE MEN TOOK ME FROM GRAN'S. I'M SCARED DADDY!" the sound of her voice getting louder as they approached the top of the hill.

They have my little girl, his realisation accompanied by a dull blow of helplessness; making his whole body shudder and a stream of tears pour down his face.

From the opposite hill, about a kilometre away, Johnny watched them take Tyson away and cursed himself for not getting back to the hut in time. He had thought they had more time, but Doug's tenacity had robbed them of their morning escape. He had felt something ominous the previous night as they sipped tea but he hadn't acted on it, careful as he was to examine all the angles before committing. This time he was wrong. And now he had to make it right.

And quickly, before Doug unleashed himself on Tyson.

Chapter 34

Phuket, Thailand
2014

"I've been lost for far too long, Johnny."

"Yeah mate, I know."

They stared out at the swollen ocean slumping onto the beach, the low hiss reminding Tyson of a Tom Waits song where the cymbal runs cascaded over the walking bass line and Tom growled in off-beat counterpoint.

"How did you find me?"

"Well it wasn't easy, Tys. Took me years. Of course I meandered off here and there. Ended up meditating in the Himalayas for two years and that's when I discovered that, in order to find you, I had to stop looking, and just follow my nose."

In the distance they could hear the sound of dogs fighting and they both turned to look. As usual it was a group of dogs against one, sand flying up in all directions as the pack circled the loner, and Tyson reflected on the brutal nature of the world around him.

"I still can't believe this, know what I mean? Fuck, I've had so many blackouts I can barely distinguish between my reality and my dreams anymore and I'm gettin' worried that this is all some fuckin' trick I'm playing on myself. It's too good to be true, mate. You're too good to be true!"

"Maybe try trusting yourself for a change Tys."

"That's a pretty dodgy proposition at the best of times, but at least I know that. But it's a start, right?"

"Shit, Tys, the young man I remember was pretty switched on and he played music like someone who had tapped into the 'pulse of the universe', as the monks I hung out with used to say."

"Yeah, that was a long time ago, Johnny. Losing Suzie, and then Lulu, well it broke me, man. Everyone has a breaking point and that was mine. I'm a shadow of that guy you remember..."

He stared back at the dogfight and noticed a standoff occurring, the one dog snarling and crouching whilst six circled him and it was then he heard a familiar bark emerge from the fracas. Could it be? So far from home?

He called out Frowny's name loudly and saw the lone dog's ears prick up and twist in their direction. This gave one of the other dogs the opportunity to latch onto Frowny's throat and drag him to the ground and before he knew what was happening Tyson was running flat out straight at them. He picked up a stick on the way and readied himself for the six rabid mouths and six pairs of hungry, bloodshot eyes. About ten metres away he picked up another piece of wood, simultaneously launching the first stick at the dog mauling Frowny, producing a yelp from the mauler and startled looks from the others. He ran towards them with his arms raised high, changing the lump of wood to his right hand as he did so. This distraction worked and as the wood came down on one of the dog's rumps, the others scattered. Tyson growled and yelled,

"FUCK OFF!" whilst swinging the wood back and forth, eyeing any dog off that looked at him. Then he stopped swinging and looked down at Frowny, and he couldn't believe his eyes. The dogs had torn into him, ripping his throat and leaving one of his ears hanging by some loose skin. His right rear leg had a large gash that ran the length of it. Despite his wounds, Frowny looked up at Tyson and smiled at him with those slightly maddened eyes, a smile of pure love mixed with the relief that it was over.

The fight *and* his search.

Tyson picked his furry friend up in his arms and carried him back to Johnny, reassuring him as they went.

As he was putting Frowny down on the grass, Johnny said,

"Not a shadow of your former self, hey?" beneath a smirk as he dragged his old bag over and fished through it for supplies, wearing a grin that made his beard look like it had pitched a tent over his mouth.

The two men worked for over an hour together, silently sewing up and disinfecting Frowny's wounds, and it was about half way in that Tyson started to feel something different, almost alien to him. He could feel a warm flood rising up from his gut, and he was turning to jelly in its wake. A smile worked its way across his mouth until it had overtaken his whole face, making his eyes shine like silvery water spread thin across white sand. It was around this point that the tears started.

"Why do we bleed, Daddy?' he heard Lulu asking between sobs, as the hairy torso of Frowny

turned into the smooth, white leg of his little girl, a trickle of blood running down her shin from the graze on her knee.

"Umm, I don't know, love, we just do," he remembered saying, and now, under the *dton soon* trees; he wished he could've given a better answer.

"Well, why do we feel pain, Daddy? I mean, why does it hurt so much when I fall over?"

"I guess, sweetheart that if we didn't feel pain, we would never know we'd been hurt, would we?"

"But why? What's the point if we have to feel so much pain?"

He wanted to tell her that there was no point, no point at all, and that was the beauty of it, but he knew a five year old would never understand, no matter how well he explained it.

"Mate, I finished sewing his leg up five minutes ago, you can let go now!" Johnny's characteristic wry grin spreading his lips wide.

The sobs came in on Tyson in big, rolling waves, making his body shake. They came from a place he had locked down ten years ago and now they were out, he felt that they might never stop.

And then the words came, but there was nothing graceful about them at all.

"Mm... my Lulu... could've saved.... if... I... if only..."

He wailed like an Italian mama at her son's grave, the sobbing and the wailing taking a suffocating hold on him. And yet, as he ploughed through his deeply buried anguish, lightness slowly took its place. Later he would refer to it as the day he finally let love back in, but immersed in it as he was, all he could think of was how it felt like he was drowning. The tightness around his shoulders, which had held him so rigidly on his path of destruction, was loosening as this strange, warm pulse worked its way through him.

Johnny stared at his friend, and he too got lost in the horrific events in Castlemaine ten years ago but smiled with the realisation that, for Tyson, his nightmare was coming to an end.

"Tys, there's something I've got to tell you. I've wanted to tell you so many times over this past few weeks, but the time just hasn't been right. You weren't ready mate, and I hope that you can understand why I didn't tell you straight away."

Tyson was still immersed in his ten-year-old grief, and the words coming out of Johnny's mouth weren't much more than background noise. He patted his furry companion absentmindedly as Frowny slept off his wounds on Tyson's lap. He looked up through a veil of tears at his old friend, a friend he thought he had lost, like everything else in his life that mattered.

"Tys. TYS! Listen to me, friend!"

Tyson blinked away tears and dragged some phlegm back down into his lungs.

"Tys, Lulu is alive, my dear friend, and we are on our way to see her."

Everything around Tyson began to spin.

Chapter 35

Castlemaine, Australia

Tyson hit the concrete floor with a loud thwack and even though the impact split his cheek open, it was the sound that seemed to really hurt. He felt for the trickle of blood running down his face and found a strange comfort in the salty taste of it on his tongue. The kick that broke his ribs seemed a distant thing to him, like someone tapping him on the shoulder, as he drifted in and out of consciousness. Nigel rolled him over onto his back and slammed his shoe down on Tyson's crotch, and if he wasn't pinned to the ground by Brian, Doug's 'Number Two', he might have doubled over in pain. He might've even told them to go fuck themselves if he had the presence of mind, but he didn't.

All he could think of was Lulu, his little girl, and the screams of fear that woke him. Brian was stretching Tyson's arms out above his head and he could hear the tell-tale click of handcuffs snapping shut around his wrists. He almost laughed out loud but caught it just in time. He needed to find a place to hide his fear, and fast. These guys would smell it coming off him. His breathing was raspy and heavy and accompanied by sharp stabs of pain from the shattered ribs pressing into him. He stared at the look of delirious pleasure on Nigel's face and used it to keep him strong.

"Is that the look you have when you're fucking your girlfriend, Nige, 'cause I'm starting to get hard," he offered through a mouthful of blood, giving him the bloody grin for good measure.

Nigel considered his options for a moment and Tyson watched his grin turn to a confused, sort of glazed look, before he chose option one, slamming his fist into Tyson's face, squashing his nose flat and spraying blood onto Nigel's recently laundered shirt.

"Aw FUCK!" Nigel exclaimed, his attempts to wipe the blood just spreading it around more. Tyson's body lay limply on the floor, but he did not scream in pain.

"You little cunt!" Nigel yelled, before using Tyson's busted ribs as leverage to stand up. Smiling through bloodied teeth Tyson half groaned, half whispered,

"Probably better if you don't think, Nige, like, you know, it's not your strongest trait, is it?"

Another kick to the groin, this time with full force. Tyson writhed on the floor silently, opting not to open his mouth for a while. Next thing he knew they were dragging him along the floor and he could hear the clanging of thick chains. They pulled him up by his arms and hooked him up to the chains, pulling them tight so his feet just touch the ground. It felt like his ribs were going to break open and spill his guts onto the floor in front of him, and the excruciating pain of it robbed him of his next line.

"No hard feelings, hey Tys? Just doing my job mate, nothin' personal."

Nigel was inches from Tyson's face and all Tyson could manage was a weak nod as he slipped out of consciousness again to where he was running through the long grass with Lulu again. He could even smell the fresh morning dew rising up around them. This time she was running towards him, her arms outstretched with a massive grin on her face. He smiled back at her and watched the tall brown stalks fall down under her tiny feet.

He became aware of another sound, not one that you would find in a paddock of long grass. This one was of trolley wheels rolling over a flat floor, the momentum creating a low hum shared by all four wheels.

Doug was whistling as he came into the room pushing the TV trolley, a hard feat for a man dragging 200 plus kilos of excess fat with him. The tune was familiar to Tyson and after a few bars he realised it was 'Son of a Preacher Man', one of Suzie's favourite songs. He attributed the fucked up timing of it to Doug's laboured breathing.

He pushed the trolley into place facing Tyson and if it wasn't for Doug's morbid obesity Tyson might have noticed his small, plump hands leaning on his knees for support as he attempted to pull some air back into his spent lungs. To Tyson he just looked like a huge ball of human waste. Tyson took a shallow breath and winced.

"G'day Doug, you're looking good! You lost weight or somethin'?" his gravelly whisper getting a liquid sound to it.

Doug smiled at Tyson then nodded at Nigel, who completed the transaction with a fist to Tyson's stomach. Tyson's reflex vomit landed in a lump on the floor in front of them all.

"Now, let me see," Doug pondered, "aaah yes, that was what I was humming when I squeezed the life out of your *whore* of a girlfriend with my own hands!" holding them up as if to testify to the veracity of his comments.

Tyson's eyes go wide with hatred.

"She turned a pretty shade of blue, don't ya reckon Nige?"

"Yeah, real pretty," Nigel agreed. They both snickered at that.

Tyson writhed in his shackles.

"You killed your own daughter?" Tyson asked, incredulous, letting the last of the vomit slide off his chin onto his T-shirt.

"Yep," Doug says matter-of-factly. "Of course we didn't feed her into the meat grinder. That would've been going too far, you know what I mean Tys? I mean, she was my only daughter, after all."

Again, more snickers.

Nigel walked over to the trolley with the TV on it, unconsciously dropping his tongue out the side of his mouth as he held the plugs and connectors in his thick hand, the blank look on his face his default expression when faced with the inexplicable, which was all too often.

"Anyway, enough of the past. Let's talk about your future, hey Tys? You're a slimy bastard, aren't ya mate? Took us a few days to track you down, you little fucker. Oh yeah, sorry 'bout the ex Tys, Nige just doesn't know his own strength, I'm sure you understand."

With some effort Doug extracted a cigar from his pocket, bit the end off and lit it, completing the ritual by spitting the piece onto the floor and then blowing the spent smoke into Tyson's face. Tyson collected the snot and blood in his throat and spat it straight into Doug's face.

Doug reeled back, wiping the gunk off his face with his fat hand as he did, a look of genuine shock on his face.

"Fuck, didn't expect that from a lazy, hippy, commie, muso like you. Gees, who would've thought a couple of old mates like us would end up like this?

Tyson just stared at him.

"Well, looks like we should fast track this a bit then. Cut the bullshit. Where's the tape Tys?"

"What have you done with Lulu? What tape?"

"Nige, need you over here!"

Nigel put the bewildering leads back on the trolley, lumbered over to Tyson and planted a fist into his soft belly, following it with a cheekbone-crushing blow to his face. Tyson's eyes rolled back in his head, his body becoming another whole rubbery reality as it shut out the pain to keep him alive.

"Easy, Nige, we don't wanna knock the cunt out," Doug wheezes through a wall of diseased throat and lung.

"We've got a bit more talking to do first. Is there a chance you might be able to get that TV working sometime this century, Nige? I mean, I don't want to pressure you or anything," Doug's sarcastic tone betraying his growing impatience.

Nigel resumed the battle between his diminishing logic and his steroid-filled animal instincts, the latter winning as usual. He fumbled with the connectors until he had managed to insert the yellow, red and white plugs into the yellow, red and white sockets on the TV and suppressed the urge to celebrate. Finally the power lead found its way to the socket and the screen came to life.

Tyson lifted his head up off his chest and forced his eyes open just as Doug placed his considerable girth between him and the screen.

"To answer your question Tys, Lulu is safe for now and, how do I put this delicately?" pondering the options for a moment before saying,

"Right, got it. If you don't hand over the tape we'll feed her into the grinder, mate, it's that simple."
A surge of hatred filled Tyson's body as he struggled against his shackles.

"What bloody tape? What are you on about Doug? Besides..."

Doug held his hand up in front of Tyson's face, stopping him mid-lie.

"C'mon Tys, that's not how this game goes, you know that, or do I have to show you a couple of family snaps of Suzie's last day on earth to get you going? Nah, I've got a better idea."

Doug stepped aside to reveal the TV. Through his bleary eyes he saw Lulu's screaming tear filled face, but he couldn't hear her screams. She was tied up to something, just like him. He writhed hard in his restraints as the tears that threatened to give him away burst forth and rolled down his cheeks.

"Bit of volume would be handy, Nige," Doug snorted.

Tyson's sanity finally slipped from his tenuous grasp when he heard Lulu's terrified screams. They cut through him like the worst feedback squeal imaginable. He watched in horror as his little girl screamed for her life, calling his name, over and over, and pleaded with him to save her.

"DADDY! DADDY! I'M SCARED HELP ME!!"

"LULU!!" Tyson screamed back, a howl of pure terror following the scream like a mugger follows a drunken punter down a dark street, the shadows absorbing his ominous intent. Tyson turned to Doug and stared at him pleadingly,

"Let her go, you bastard!" dribble and blood running down to join the tears.

"Well, Tys, that's kind of up to you, mate."

He pulled a two-way radio out of his pocket and muttered something into it.

Tyson heard the sound of a large machine starting up and it was a few delirious moments before he made the connection to that fateful night with Suzie and the meat grinder that reduced a man to mince in a matter of minutes. He became paralysed by the images of his little girl being untied and led off screen towards the grinder, her screams the only sound Tyson could hear now.

The only sounds that mattered.

Doug's voice was a background blur that mixed with the sound of the machine.

"Like I said Tys, up to you how this ends up. Tell me where that fucking tape is and I'll let your Lulu go. It's that simple. Isn't it funny how things can end up reduced to a fairly simple choice?"

Doug expelled more smoke from his heaving lungs and grinned at Tyson the way a car salesman grinned at you just before you shake his hand.

"Now, we know that you were there that night and my *inquiries* around town told me that you don't go anywhere without that fucking little camera of yours, so I put two and two together and came up with you. So, what's it going to be, Tys? We can do her slowly, one limb at a time, or go the whole hog and start with her pretty little face? What'll get me the best result, I wonder?"

Tyson used the last of his strength to spit again at Doug's face, but this time he missed and it hit the floor, and just lay there along with everything else.

"Go fuck yourself Doug!" Tyson's last glimmer of bravado sounded weak, even to him.

Doug laughed loudly at this pathetic display, building up to a belly laugh that threatened to shake the room off its foundations and rob him of the precious air his bloated body needed. So he capped it, which turned his face a bright red. He regained his breath, lifted the two-way to his face and looked at Tyson.

"Your funeral mate, or should I say, Lulu's funeral... and all the blood that will flow will be on Daddy's hands. What a shame..." and with that he delivered the order that dragged the colour from Tyson's battered face.

"NOOOOO! LULU!!" he yelled with all of his dwindling strength, his voice a crackly mess of fear and hatred and love, the love for his little girl, the only good thing left in his life. No haunting melodies left for him to dream up, no calm, easy moments of post-coital bliss as the sun burst through the window, no cruisey vibe left for him to ride. Everything he was had been extinguished; reduced to this moment. He knew what he had to do, perhaps for the first time ever.

"It's at Johnny's hut under the bed. Now let her go!"

Doug looked at him like a proud father would his child and said,

"Now that's more like it Tys. Only problem is how do I know if you're telling the truth?"

"For fuck's sake Doug, are you even human? All I've got left is truth, you fuckin' cunt! Now let her go!!"

"I guess you've got a point there."

He stared at Tyson for a full minute before continuing,

"Only problem is, I'm a sadistic bastard."

The last thing Tyson remembered is the horrified scream of his beloved daughter, and the spray of blood that filled the TV screen in front of him.

There was nothing left for him now.

Chapter 36

Phuket, Thailand
2014

Tyson tried to get a grip on himself as Johnny's words echoed through his head over and over, like a damaged CD looping itself helplessly between glitches. Nothing could've prepared him for this, nothing could've softened the blow that hit his exhausted body with enough force to make his legs buckle, and he stumbled towards Johnny with an arm out for support.

His thoughts were a hastily constructed montage of his last days in Castlemaine, mixed with random and grotesque imagery of the mad Patong nights that had successfully kept him distracted for so many years. Images of dodgy young men with monkeys perched on their shoulders, ladyboys with impossible legs and dream-like fake tits, tuk-tuk drivers with hooded eyes like lizards, pole dancing young girls from *Esaan* with their dead-eyed stare and shorts so short they hid nothing. Tattooed East Londoners with crass gold bracelets, fast speedboats and even faster tongues. Street vendors with faces so lined they looked like a dry creek bed in the desert, worn out Ping-Pong show girls trying to feed their grandchildren on tips from drunk tourists who *still couldn't believe she had a live turtle up there*. Interspersed with these were the bloodied memories drenched with fear that had sprung out of one mad night in an empty pig factory in Castlemaine, and the love he held for Suzie, a ghost that had travelled three steps behind him wherever he had been since.

Lulu was alive.

He snapped out of his stupor long enough to throw a half-hearted punch at Johnny's face, who caught it in his left hand, inches before it hit its target.

"Figured you might do that. Fair enough, too."

"You fucker, Johnny, why didn't you tell me until now?" a look of disbelief stuck to his face like Mormons to a doorstep.

"I couldn't mate, you weren't ready for it until now, and just in the nick of time too. C'mon, let's walk and I'll fill you in on the way."

"Do I have a choice?"

Johnny ignored the question and picked up his eclectic pile of belongings and stuffed them in his bag. Frowny saw the movement and wagged his tail once before letting it fall to the ground.

"But I saw her... I saw them killing her!"

"Just a bit of theatre to get you to talk mate, and it worked. C'mon, let's go."

Johnny walked off towards the beach. Frowny dragged his injured body up off the ground and limped towards Tyson, shaking his ears from side to side as he adjusted to the stitches and bandages that were holding him together. They both stumbled off and followed Johnny. Tyson caught up to him, his mind racing with questions.

"But how...?"

"Do I know that she's alive? I just do."

"So what, Doug kidnapped her?"

"No mate, Doug adopted her."

Tyson let the words flow over him like a turgid river, hoping that eventually he would be washed up on the bank and it would all make sense. The years of denial, the years of drowning in sorrow, the years of bewildering blackouts, the sadness of a forgotten flute in a lonely room as the car headlights beat on the window-pane and the doof-doof seeped in through the walls, like background music in his own personal asylum.

Johnny stopped every now and then to inspect various pieces of debris lying on the high tide line, even though the last thing on his mind was turning it into some mad sculpture. He just couldn't help himself.

He maintained a steady pace throughout, his busy, short-stepped walk propelling him forward with great ease, to a reunion he had waited ten years to manifest.

Tyson's mind was miles away, having drifted off to the sound of a swing set swinging emptily in a black void, the image pregnant with time lost, time stolen from him by a fat man with a cigar and a penchant for sadistic sexual acts.

Shit!

It hit him like a bolt of lightning.

"Oh, fuck Johnny, he didn't..."

"Abuse her like he did Suzie? Nah, not yet. He saves them until they are fifteen."

Johnny stopped and watched Tyson's distress dissipate like a gently retreating breeze, his brow furrowing as he tried to do the math.

"What's the date?"

"Tenth of Feb, Tys."

Tyson took this in by nodding his head repeatedly and looking at a spot of sand two feet in front of him.

"It's her birthday tomorrow, mate," he added redundantly, since Tyson was already awash in memories filled with birthday cakes with candles reluctant to go out, excited faces covered in chocolate, frilly dresses stained with the day's excesses, sugar comas in the early evening and the squeals of joy that resonated all through his lost years. Every missed birthday had hurled him deeper into his lost state. He waited for her birthday every year with utter trepidation, teetering on the edge of losing it all and admitting himself to the nearest asylum that offered shock treatment. Even the madness of Patong was a thin veil over his rapidly encroaching breakdown and he knew it. He had lit a candle every year for ten years, not knowing if he was courting madness or healing himself.

"If we keep walking, we'll be there before nightfall. Your head must be spinning off its dial at all this!" Johnny quipped, trying to drag Tyson back to the land of the living.

"You're not wrong," and then, after a long silence,

"I just can't believe that she is alive mate... after all these years of stumbling around Patong getting lost and watching everyone else grinding out a life, knowing mine had been extinguished that night, years ago. I wallowed in my grief for so long it consumed everything... my career and anyone that came too close... it ate away at any interest I had in anything, especially my music... I... Suzie was dead, and I watched my little girl get murdered right in front of me. Man, don't you see, it was the end for me, there was nothing left."

He paused to take a breath.

"And now, in the last twelve hours I have been told that not only is she alive, but she's staying on this island for fuck's sake, and we are now off to rescue her! Excuse me if I seem a little deranged, but this has pretty much knocked my whole dismal world apart and, you know, it's really fucking me up Johnny. And all of this: my fucked up lost life, because of Doug fucking Farris! FUCK! WHY?"

Blood coursed through his body with the momentum of a freight train.

"Who knows why anything happens? Maybe you were just in the wrong place at the wrong time. Tys, none of this was your fault, you've got to remember that. Doug's one demented prick, and you just got in his way. Your whole family did. But it's OK now, mate, because now we are going to get in Doug's face. It's no accident he is staying here with Lulu and his debauched friends, Tys. I have been orchestrating this get together for years mate, and now, my friend, we get to give Lulu back to her Dad!"

The tears didn't floor him this time; rather they filled him with a fierce determination. He felt the aches and lethargy of his body disappear and his pace quicken, driven by a new energy, a fixed intensity that seeped out of the pores of his skin to match the tears.

Tyson was walking towards a future that wasn't even possible twelve hours ago, and he felt more alive than he could ever recall.

He stared up at the beach ahead of them and watched the sun turn the horizon into a shimmering mirage, and he realised how much he liked it like that.

Chapter 37

Castlemaine, Australia
2004

Johnny burst into the room, his eyes wide in anticipation. What he didn't anticipate was the slipperiness of the bacon factory's floor and before he knew it he was flat on his back and staring into the beady eyes of Nigel. He thrust his right leg up into Nigel's crotch just as Nigel's first punch landed on his chin.

Johnny had never heard a man scream as high as Nigel, nor had he felt such a heavy weight land on him when Nigel slumped down with the blow. He used most of his strength to heave Nigel off him and the rest of it to roll away from Brian's patent leather clad shoe as it made its way towards Johnny's face.

Then he was up on his feet and analysing Brian's lumbering movement like everything had gone into slow-mo, and he had all the time in the world. The first punch Brian threw came at Johnny like an old lady in a Zimmer frame, he ducked under it easily and landed one on Brian's muscular neck, momentarily halving the blood supply to his largely redundant brain and making his thick legs buckle under him. Another blow to the back of the neck sent Brian to nigh-nigh land.

Johnny got up from his half-crouch and eyed off the ridiculously obese frame of Doug. He noticed a bead of sweat attempting to run down Doug's rotund face as Nigel stirred on the floor behind him. He took two measured steps backwards and on the third delivered a punishing blow just above Nigel's right shoulder blade, hitting a pressure point and rendering him unconscious in an instant. Doug took this opportunity to scurry out of the open door. Well, as much as a hugely obese man can scurry. Johnny yelled after him,

"We're not done here yet, *MATE!*" then turned around to face Tyson.

The man he used to know was not there anymore. Instead there was a shell hanging by a thick chain, the kind used to secure bulldozers onto low loaders. Tyson's eyes stared blankly at the floor where a steady stream of blood was landing with alarming regularity.

Johnny hurried across to Nigel and went through his pockets, searching for the keys to the handcuffs, but only found a half-eaten Snickers bar and a business card for a nightclub in Bendigo. He rushed across to Brian's inert form and quickly found what he was looking for, and as he headed back across to Tyson he raised a hand in preparation for the slap that he hoped will rouse Tyson from his daze long enough to get him out of here.

"C'mon Tys, snap out of it! We haven't got much time!" he shouted as the slap landed on Tyson's chin. Tyson's gaze shifted slowly upwards until he was looking at Johnny. Johnny smiled encouragingly as he went in for the hug but not out of brotherly love, more out of a need to shoulder Tyson's weight as he slipped the key into the padlock and Tyson slumped heavily onto Johnny's shoulder. Within seconds he was heading out the door with Tyson over his shoulder, who was leaving a trail of blood all over the back of his shirt.

"Lulu, Johnny, they've got Lulu," Tyson wailed, depositing more slobber and saliva on top of the blood.

"I know mate, I'll go after her after I've gotten you out of here!"

"It's too late, they killed her, right in front of me." Tyson went quiet then, sinking back into the near catatonic state again.

"SHIT!"

Johnny erupted into a quick jog as they approached the large EXIT sign at the end of the corridor.

Suthers reached over and flung open the door of his battered van when he saw Johnny crash through the entrance to DF Bacon and jog towards him. He had Tyson's slumped body over one shoulder and a hand out if front of him as a counterweight. The car rocked as Johnny lets his load go onto the front seat next to Suthers.

"Holy shit! What did they do to him?" he asked, his mouth agape.

"Not much compared to what they were going to," Johnny replied, whilst heaving much needed air into his lungs.

Suthers had his hanky out and was soaking up some of the blood when he asked,

"So what's the plan? You haven't told me where I'm taking him yet."

Johnny fished through his pockets and produced a crumpled piece of paper and handed it to Suthers.

"All the info you need is here. Did you grab the rest of his stuff?

Suthers studied the paper.

"Um... yeah, some of it. Johnny, why does this address say Darwin? That's, like, 4000k's from here!"

"Well, you better get a move on then," taking one last look at the semi-conscious Tyson before saying,

"Now get the fuck outa here!" and with that Johnny turned and headed back into the factory.

"Buckle up, mate," Suthers said to Tyson, whilst reaching across and securing his seatbelt for him. He looked over his shoulder at the few belongings he had gathered for Tyson.

"We've got a long way to go!"

Back inside the factory, Doug Farris made his way along the dimly lit corridor, wheezing and panting like he had just run a marathon. He turned back to stare belligerently at the stairway that nearly did him in, and if he wasn't dangerously short of breath he would've scowled and maybe blew smoke in the stairway's face but, alas, his body was barely capable of moving the massive chest to get some air in.

He dragged his hugely obese body along the wall and tilted his fat head forward to create some momentum as he slid his way towards the only other room with light pouring through the open door. He nearly blacked out as his chubby hand made contact with the doorframe. He rested there for a minute, before heaving his massive frame through the doorway and into the room where Lulu lay, curled up on the floor, crying.

He cleared his throat loudly, as if his presence wasn't enough to make Guido and Joe straighten up and wait for their next order.

"Nice job boys. Looked very realistic on the screen."

He paused, not for dramatic effect, but for the simple need to breathe. He stared at the meat grinder with someone's leg hanging out of the top of it before saying,

"OK, things haven't exactly gone to plan, boys. What I need you to do is stop the guy who will be coming through that door in a minute, and Lulu and I will exit this way," pointing past the meat grinder perched above the conveyer belt to the double doors beyond.

"Um, OK boss, but what about...?" Guido started.

Cutting him off with a raised hand, Doug said,

"It's better when you don't talk!"

Doug walked over to Lulu, who hadn't moved the whole time. He turned to the boys.

"Now go, dickheads!" and with that he picked Lulu up and tucked her under his arm. She screamed in such terror that it made Doug cringe, and he gripped her tiny five-year-old body tighter in case she wriggled away.

"Now, now, little one, struggling will only make everything harder for you," as he heaved his bulk towards the exit door. His tone was alarmingly tender. He thought of Suzie for the first time in days, remembering that she, too, struggled at the beginning.

Behind him, Doug could hear Guido or Joe flying across the floor and screaming in Italian, just as he pushed himself and Lulu through the doorway and into another corridor.

He looked down at Lulu. She was staring blankly ahead.

"This time Daddy's not going to make any mistakes, right sweetheart?"

Chapter 38

Phuket, Thailand
2014

Johnny straightened up and slowed his busy walk whilst Tyson's heart began to thump in his chest, drowning out the low hiss of the breaking waves.

"Not far now, Tys, it's just up ahead. See that big silver whale sticking up out of the roof of that resort? That's where we're going mate. That's where Lulu is."

The reality of seeing Lulu after all this time took on a surreal edge as Tyson stared in a vacant way at the huge whale's tail coming out of the roof. It looked like the silver whale was executing a dive and the rest of its body has merged into the bowels of the elliptically shaped building, a strange sight indeed on this long expanse of deserted beach. The *dton soon* trees lined the sand like a guard of honour. It was the most untouched part of the island and the tail stood out like dog's balls.

And yet somehow it worked.

"Took us ten years to get here, but we made it," Johnny continued, "there were times, mate, when I wasn't sure if everything was going to line up right. Organising to get Dougy out of his little fiefdom of Castlemaine was the hardest. So many things that could've gone wrong along the way..."

A look of quiet satisfaction crept across Johnny's face as he stopped and stared at the funky looking resort ahead. The roofs of the four buildings were made of fish scale-shaped wooden shingles that seemed to wrap themselves around the buildings, stopping a foot before the ground, making each one look like a huge, brown toadstool. Infinity pools seemed to be everywhere, surrounding each structure, lapping at their doorways, caressing the timber decking in a velvety, liquid hug. Furniture that crossed the line between sculpture and function was scattered around like forgotten guests at a cocktail party, absentmindedly stirring their drinks and staring into space. The place had a vaguely lost feel to it, like it was in the wrong place, in the wrong country.

"Better not get much closer right now. We'll wait for the cover of darkness before making our move."

"And what is our move, Johnny, outside of bursting in there and rescuing my daughter?" Tyson's urge to pounce staining his voice like ink on paper.

"Everything has to be done right, Tys. I've been planning this moment for years, hoping that I didn't have to drag you back to Castlemaine to do it, hoping that you hadn't done yourself in in some way, hoping that Doug would survive his life of excess long enough to deliver justice to the fat prick. It has been my sole overriding focus, and now we are here I have to admit I've got butterflies dancing inside of me. C'mon, I'll fill you in."

Tyson didn't move for a while, even though Johnny and Frowny both set off towards the cover of the surrounding jungle. He just stood there, looking out at the resort, still trying to digest that his daughter was not more than a hundred metres from him. He wondered what she looked like now, whether she still kicked her legs when she was excited, whether she would remember him at all.

He made his way over to Johnny and Frowny.

Johnny's lips were moving but Tyson wasn't listening, every now and then a key word punched through his racing thoughts and he would snap out of it, giving Frowny a pat before drifting off again.

"TYS! TYS! Come back buddy, try and stay focussed."

"I am focused, Johnny. On Lulu."

"Look mate, there's a lot I haven't told you yet. Like how I followed Doug around for years after that night, and how I had to stifle my urge to kill the fucker several times for what he had done because I knew it made no sense to do anything until you were ready. I watched Lulu like I would my own daughter as she grew up in Doug's demented world of privilege. I watched the sadness on her face slowly shift to anger and then to a resolve I didn't think was possible in someone of that age. She's a tough one, your daughter. But I had to bide my time. And then I finally tracked you down three years ago, only to find you just as lost as before, just as useless. And all the while, holding this little gem in my old hands," turning the thumb drive over and over between his thumb and forefinger.

Tyson roused himself out of his haze and looked up.

"What the... You got it before Doug's boys?"

251

"Yep, and I've been hangin' onto it all this time, re-burning it every two years and of course making plenty of backup copies!" a look of expectation on his face now.

"And tonight Tys, we're finally gonna take that fat fucker down for all he has done!"

Tyson had completely forgotten about the tape.

"What're we gonna do, blackmail him?"

"No, much better than that, mate, much better."

Johnny closed his eyes and there was silence between them for quite some time.

"You still got that Shakuhachi with you?"

"Yeah, why?"

"Could you play something?"

Tyson reached into his bag and produced the flute, wrapped up in its felt cover.

He unwrapped it and brought it to his lips, his eyes still fixed on the oddly shaped resort that housed his little girl.

He started with some low woody notes that seemed to vibrate through his entire body and, outside of a suggestion or two of where it might go, stayed with the low drone for quite a long time, until Johnny had closed his eyes again and was drifting on the aural cloud pulsing through his body.

Tyson began to lose himself in the music and as he did the music got bolder, more precise in its direction, until he began to feel that the music was playing him. He laid down a melody on top of the drone that wasn't just sweet, it was sublime. It was like all the gigs he had done had led him to this, this moment, this melody. And all the sorrow of the last ten years was being blown away on the gusts of wind.

Inside the resort, in her room, Lulu sat cross-legged on her bed listening to music on her headphones, the white plugs that marked her generation jammed in each ear, indicating to anyone nearby that the world around her was not getting in right now. She was, however, updating her current status to 'bored in paradise' and 'liking' the hundreds of posts waiting for her from her 'friends'. Connected and disconnected at the same time, she sat and stared out through the bi-fold glass doors at the palm trees and turquoise water and absentmindedly played with her long blond hair, wishing she was somewhere else. Somewhere, you know, cool and that.

Tyson started in on a tune that he hadn't been able to bring himself to play for years, a tune that had given him and Lulu a lot of happiness back when that was a daily option. Before their world was blown apart and the spectre of greed and hate and loss and grief took its place.

A lightness grabbed a hold of him. He was playing for his girl again, and as he played he focussed all his energy on her beautiful face, to the point where he could hear her five-year-old laughter again and see her legs swinging excitedly, like it was yesterday.

Lulu looked up from her iPhone to see an ATV bike tearing across the sand in front of the resort, with a vaguely hot guy with long blond hair riding on it. She flicked a headphone out and listened to the bike ripping into the sand whilst checking out the tanned specimen straddling the hot motor.

"He...llo there!" she said to the room, and for a moment imagined jumping on the back of the ATV and riding towards the horizon with her hot surfer

253

boy. She resumed twiddling her hair, curling it around her finger then letting it go and waiting for it to spring back, full of life.

It was then that she heard it, rising up in level as the ATV disappeared from view, the soft tones coming in waves with the wind. She sat upright and pulled out the other headphone and listened to the oddly familiar tune. Suddenly she was sent back into her childhood, swinging higher and higher on the swing set and her Dad watching happily, without a thought to the potential of her to fall.

She got up from the bed and went through the doorway onto the timber deck in front of her own personal infinity pool and stared out at the beach, straining her ears to the earthy sounds of the shakuhachi, and held by the sensation that this felt so much more real than before. She peered into the haze and was the five-year-old girl again, waiting for her dad to come home.

How could it be? Her Dad was dead and so was her Mum. Everything she ever loved was dead. And yet this seemed so real to her.

The breeze stopped suddenly and she was left with the silence that makes music so powerful. She let her doubts take a hold of the stillness and she was just about to go back inside when a burst of exquisite music rose up with the wind and caressed her eardrums. She turned around, looking into the vastness, pleading with the emptiness that it was real, that what she was hearing was not the work of her active imagination.

She listened, smiling until it was gone, just like it had come to her, on a gust of wind. And she was left standing there, stunned and bewildered, full of hope and longing, however flimsy the connection.

She had never stopped hoping.

***

Nightfall couldn't come soon enough for Tyson. After he had stopped playing he had watched Johnny meditate and then he willed the sun out of the sky, all the while grasping his flute in his hand like his life depended on it.

Johnny opened his eyes wide, unaware that over an hour had passed. Tyson was staring at him as full consciousness returned.

"Aah, that's better," Johnny whispered, the words dripping with the caramelised wisdom of utter calm. He stood up and stretched his body out, bending his back on itself until his head was nearly upside down and resting on his shoulder blades. He pulled his head slowly back up, and said,

"Well, better get into it then!" rubbing his hands together,

"Now Tys, I need you to keep your shit together, just keep your head down and follow my lead."

He looked down at Tyson and noticed the whites of his knuckles around the flute and his jaw rhythmically grinding his teeth away.

"Better still, just stay a few steps behind me. This'll probably get rough until it doesn't, OK mate?"

"OK, Johnny, whatever you say, it's your gig."

"It's not my gig, mate, it's yours. I'm just here to... uh... what do they call it? Facilitate, that's it. Now c'mon, let's go get your daughter and nail this prick to the wall."

They crept silently towards the resort; Johnny, Tyson and Frowny. Somehow the dog had sensed some action and no way was he going to miss it. They approached diagonally from their hideout and made it to the side of one of the toadstool buildings without any security lights going on or sleepy security guards asking them, 'bpai nai?' *where you go?*

So far, so good.

They slid their bodies along the rough shingle roofing and shuffled their feet silently through the sand until they came to a small flight of stairs. They climbed them slowly, Frowny at the rear out of some sort of deference. Any other time and he would've been the first up, with his nose to the ground and his tail thumping.

They crossed the vast expanse of timber decking in darkness, staying close to a curved wall that masked a Jacuzzi sitting amongst lush tropical plants, one of many. When they got to the corner they could hear muffled voices and the unmistakable laugh of Doug Farris, which put a smile on Johnny's face and a look of fear on Tyson's. A chill ripped through him, then evacuated his body just as fast in the form of a cold sweat that made him shiver. Johnny crouched down to peer around the corner, then pulled back and whispered to Tys,

"OK, they're all in there, Tys, now we're going to just sit tight for a little while and suss out the situation."

This time they both peered around the corner, and it took a few long seconds before Tyson made any sense of what he was looking at.

The men were in a large room sitting on a blue leather couch shaped like an octopus and looking up at Doug, who was helping himself from a bar that seemed to disappear into the wall when he was done with it. The walls were decorated with thousands of what looked like bowls and plates of various sizes, all with the same blue design on white ceramic. There was an oval shaped mirror dead centre of the two opposing walls, giving the illusion of an endless space with Doug Farris at its centre. The men were listening to Doug's grand statements, whatever they were, and nodding their heads whilst sipping at their scotches.

"Can't hear 'em Tys, let's get closer. Probably be better to leave the dog here. Can you make him stay?"

Tyson looked down at Frowny, who seemed to have understood and had already slumped his injured body down onto the timber decking, letting out a deep, pointed sigh whilst looking up with those sad eyes at Tyson.

The two men tiptoed towards the room that held their nemesis with a stealth fuelled by their simmering vengeance. From this position they could hear clearly through a crack in the huge bi-fold glass doors, and after a few sentences, Tyson wished that they couldn't.

"Well gents, the time has come to initiate a new member into our club, and I can't think of a better room to do it in. Christ, it looks like the set of a porn movie!" Doug snorted at the men, which resulted in a cacophony of muttering and glass clinking. He looked up at the shards of mirror stuck together as a light fitting and stood right under it. Due to the cake like wedges of glass, as he walked under it his reflection disappeared, then reappeared as he moved his massive bulk across the room.

Tyson looked at the man who stole his life and saw that the years had left their mark. He was now completely bald and his skin a ruddy pink, testimony to the near impossibility of every movement his obese body made.

"But first gentlemen, a slight diversion to whet your appetite. Please follow me to the cinema, but before we do, may I introduce you to tonight's special guest and birthday girl, the lovely Lulu."

Tyson's heart leapt out of his chest as he struggled to keep quiet.

As Doug called out her name, a side door opened and a shy, beautiful young girl shuffled into the room, looking fixedly at the polished marble floor. A series of wolf whistles and exclamations sent a shiver through her body and Johnny grabbed Tyson firmly by the shoulders to stop him running straight in there.

"Yes gents, isn't she a little beauty? I've been saving this one up for years and at the stroke of midnight we will wish her a happy fifteenth birthday, as only we can!"

At this the men erupted into applause, one of them standing up and heading towards Lulu before Doug halted him with his commanding voice.

"Now, now Jimmy, hold your horses, all in good time. Now, if you'll follow me..." as he flung open the bi-fold doors that led to the cinema.

"C'mon darling, let's watch a movie, shall we?" Doug's ingratiating tone was laced with sarcasm and Johnny had to put his hand over Tyson's mouth before a scream of anguish erupted from him. Doug's bloated hand searched out Lulu's and pulled her roughly through the door.

Tyson was a seething coiled spring of retribution.

"Quick Tys, let's go," Johnny whispered.

It was some minutes before they found the cinema amongst the myriad of doors and corridors to choose from and the men were already settled in to the hermetically sealed space. Johnny and Tyson rounded a corner just as Nigel emerged from the bio box door and entered the cinema itself through another.

"Quick, here's our chance!"

They slipped through the bio box door, Johnny reaching into his pocket and pulling out the thumb drive as he did. He walked across to the projector sitting in the middle of the room on a stand, the multi-coloured streams of light coming out of the lens turning to images as they hit the large white screen that constituted one of the walls.

"Tys, things are going to get messy from here on, so I suggest you stand behind the door before Nigel comes through it, OK? Then I want you to follow me into the cinema and get Lulu out of there whilst I create a diversion, OK?"

He didn't wait for a reply and pushed the thumb drive into one of the input ports on the side of the projector and said,

"It's party time Doug!"

Tyson backed over to behind the door as the images he filmed ten years ago flew up onto the screen and silence descended on the room full of twisted men.

Tyson couldn't help but watch the images: Suzie's stockinged legs running along empty corridors; the sound of the meat grinder and the screams of the poor man being tortured; and finally, Doug's immense bulk coming into frame and his hand reaching across to the machine's big green 'go' button. Time seemed to stand still for him, trapped unknowingly, as he had always been, in the horrific events of that night. He didn't even notice the door fly open next to him and Nigel come bursting into the room.

"G'day Nige!"

Johnny despatched Nigel to the floor before Tyson had time to register what was happening and seconds later he was following Johnny into the room where his daughter sat trembling.

Johnny was a flurry of fast moving hands and legs as he dealt out one knockout blow after another to the confused men sitting around Doug. Tyson looked around the room for Lulu, crying out her name when he saw her cowering behind a chair. Johnny knocked Doug's stupid cigar out of his hand and placed a strong hand around his neck.

"And you just stay put, you fat cunt, and shut the fuck up, OK, Dougy?"

Lulu poked her head up and looked at the man yelling her name.

It couldn't be. Doug told her he was dead, just like her Mum. No, it couldn't be!

Tyson was dropping tears all over the plush carpet when he said,

"Darling, it's Daddy, I've come to take you home."

She looked at him in disbelief, tears running down her face, her world now a blur of colour where her reality and her dreams clashed and then merged, leaving her numb. She stared at the hairy talking face claiming to be her father.

Seeing her confusion, Tyson pulled his shakuhachi out of his pocket and showed it to her.

"See, sweetheart, it's me! I thought you were..."

"Dead? I thought you were too!" her tears choking her words until to her they seemed not much more than a whisper.

"So I *did* hear you playing today. I thought I was dreaming…"

"Not a dream, darling, more like the beginning of the rest of your life," he beamed; smiling so hard it felt like his face would crack. Lulu was running towards him now and in his mind it took an hour and a half for her to reach him, and then she was in his arms again and they were both crying now and he was whispering in her ear.

"And I'm never going to stop playing for you!"

She buried her face in his chest.

"I… never… stopped… hearing your music, Daddy! Even when I thought you were dead, I never stopped… listening… whenever I got scared, your flute would soothe me, I carried you around in my head, where it was safe…" her sobs of relief echoing into his chest cavity.

Johnny took his eyes off Doug for a moment to watch an event he had been waiting to witness for what seemed a lifetime, and he allowed himself a few moments of joy before returning to the task at hand; nailing Doug to the fucking wall.

He watched these two people that had defined his life, had given him purpose, had compelled him out of his solitude in the bush, and had given him such a rich palette of experiences to fuel his soul. The feeling of happiness that swept over him was something he had only read about before in the classics; those treasures that had carried him through half a lifetime of loneliness.

Johnny turned his attention back to Doug.

"Well, Dougy, I've waited ten years for this moment, and you know what? It was worth the wait."

"Johnny Barker? That you under all that fuckin' hair?"

Johnny delivered a short, sharp jab to Doug's bloated face and a few moments later blood started to run down onto his massive expanse of white shirt.

"It's better when you don't talk, Doug. Got it?"

Doug nodded. Johnny turned to Tyson and Lulu.

"Tys, good time to go, mate. Take your lovely daughter away from this piece of shit of a human being. I won't be long, I'll meet you on the beach, OK?"

Tyson and Lulu shuffled out the door, Lulu staring up at her long lost father with a look that would melt the hardest of men.

Johnny Barker walked in a slow circle around Doug, his hands behind his back, a pensive look on his face, like he was digesting a gnarly thought, or had encountered a curious twist of logic, or maybe he was wrestling with two opposing urges, and the pacing helped him resist the urge to bludgeon Doug over a period of hours, if not days.

He cleared his cascading thoughts like a surgeon cutting out tumours, and continued,

"Now, Doug, I'm going to say this once, so you'd better pay attention. Tomorrow, at 9.30 a.m., I have arranged for your bank accounts to be emptied and you will be declaring bankruptcy thirty minutes later via your financial advisor. All your business interests will be extinguished and you will be homeless and completely broke. Nod if you understand so far..."

Doug nodded with an expression that you could fry bacon on.

"The tape you just watched is due for worldwide exposure at 10.30 a.m. If you like I can write down the link for you and you can sit back here and watch the destruction of your life from the comfort of this lovely chair, and wait for the police to arrest you..."

Doug's eyes took on an uncharacteristic look of defeat.

"And if you so much as think about retribution of any sort, I will be on you so fast you won't have time to shake your next poor victim off your pathetic cock. Nod if you understand."

Doug nodded reluctantly.

"But how..."

"How did a lonely mystic do this to you?"

He smiled at Doug.

"You will never see Tyson or Lulu again, understand? Tyson doesn't know it yet, but he is about to become a multi-millionaire!"

At this Doug's eyes bulged as he pushed dead air through his pig-like nose.

"Oh yeah, almost forgot. At the end of this tape there's a bunch of, what should I call them, happy snaps of you and your club mates at your secret club, except it wasn't so secret, thanks to your mate Jake and his loose mouth! We installed a couple of cameras eight years ago, so as you can imagine there's quite a lot of them. You can watch them now if you like, or wait 'til tomorrow and watch them with the rest of the world. As they say here Doug, 'up to you'..."

"Anyway, Dougy, been good catching up over old times, but I've gotta go now. See you in the soup," and with that Johnny backed swiftly out of the room and headed to the beach, where the rest of his life waited.

Chapter 39

Castlemaine, Australia
2004

Nigel and Brian approached the hut from the south with great caution. Nigel was still reeling from the embarrassing beating he received at the hands of a skinny book nerd, and he wasn't taking any chances this time. In his left hand he held a baton, and in his right his trusty 9mm. He looked down at the gun and reflected, as much as Nigel was capable of reflection, on how many times they had gone into battle together, how many times he had sprayed someone's brains onto the wall behind them and how many times the butt had crushed a reluctant skull.

He liked this gun, it was the closest thing he had to a friend.

The sun had been up for an hour but still hadn't flooded the gully with the golden light that turned the flowering Cootamundra wattles a bright, luminous yellow, like beacons in the middle of the vast ocean of dry, brown crackly bush. The air was crisp and the silence around them amplified their clumsy movements to the point where Nigel realised that, if Johnny was in there, then he would have known they were coming for the last ten minutes. Nigel tightened his grip on both weapons and motioned for Brian to come closer.

They were a few metres from the blanketed doorway when Nigel signalled for Brian to stop. They stood there in silence for a full minute with only the occasional screech of a bird and its laboured breathing to keep them company. Nigel signalled bouncer style that on the count of three they will burst through the doorway, Nigel first, and neutralise the inhabitants. Brian nodded eagerly.

Brian loved this shit, especially the Special Operations stuff and he could hardly wait to be let off the chain. He had opted for a simple length of iron bar as his weapon of choice.

On the count of two a magpie swooped down and attempted to peck at their heads and it scared the living daylights out of Brian, sending him headlong through the doorway screaming like a little kid. Nigel followed, wiping the disappointment off his face as he went.

The room was small and Brian didn't have time to slow down before hitting the far wall, the sound of it echoing for a few seconds and was still dissipating as Nigel reached the doorway and stood, weighing his options. He looked at Brian bent over and breathing deeply and considered putting a bullet in him right there and then, but thought better of it.

Johnny was nowhere to be seen, and if it wasn't for the hundreds of books stacked up everywhere, the hut might've appeared to be abandoned. Nigel walked across to the hearth and gingerly put his hand on the kettle. Still warm. Johnny had been here, and not too long ago. He scanned the room, willing himself into a higher state of awareness and failed, as usual. He resigned himself to finding the memory stick and getting the fuck out of there.

"Tyson said it's under the bed, Brian, and since you're already half-way there," nodding his head at the bent over bulk in front of him, "would you mind?"

Brian obeyed Nigel's request and diligently got down on all fours and peered into the darkness under the bed.

"Can't see a fuckin' thing, Nige. D'ya reckon you..."

The eastern brown snake moved so fast Nigel barely saw it striking Brian repeatedly on the face, neck and shoulders and within seconds, the attack was over, the snake retreating back to the dark recesses under the bed, a slow hiss leaving its body like a sigh of relief. Brian reeled back onto the floor, holding his face in his hands and screaming whilst Nigel snapped the safety off the 9mm and emptied the contents into the snake under the bed, using Brian's body as a buffer in case the snake wasn't satisfied yet. After a few moments he pushed the pipe in there, hooking the bullet-ridden snake on the second sweep, and flicked it over towards the door. He retrieved his flashlight from his belt and scanned the floor under the bed for the memory stick.

All this time Brian was groaning and pleading for help but Nigel already knew there's nothing he could do, the poor prick had ten minutes to live at best, and most of that he would be paralysed.

And no memory stick to be found.

"Ah fuck!" he screamed into the room, the echo reverberating out over the dry gully way before he exited through the grey-blanketed doorway and out into the harsh morning light.

Johnny watched Nigel blunder out of the hut from high up in a tree not more than twenty metres away. A sadness crept over his face to erase the laconic grin that has been there since the two men made their noisy way down into the gully. That snake was his companion: in the depths of summer he had recited entire books to his silent friend; he had sent unsuspecting mice under the bed to satisfy his hunger, and he had never felt even a glimmer of fear the entire time he had lived two feet from instant death. In some ways it had made him stronger and given him a greater insight to do with fear and how to cap it before it tore your world apart.

As Nigel walked under him, he resisted the urge to spit on his shaved head.

You'll keep, he muttered to himself, *you'll keep*.

***

Suthers hadn't stopped driving all night and they had made it as far as Red Cliffs by dawn, some five hundred kilometres north of Castlemaine. Tyson woke from his stupor as they were leaving the Roadhouse and Suthers was on his second Chiko roll. The chips and gravy would have to wait until he could put his foot down on another dead-straight stretch of road and steer with his knees. He was changing into third gear when Tyson finally spoke.

"Pull over mate, think I'm gonna spew!" Suthers careered off the road and parked in something called the 'Barclay Recreation Reserve' just as Tyson was opening the door to let the first lot go. Suthers continued feasting on his roadhouse food as if nothing was wrong, but opted to get out of the car when the stench hits him, taking his precious chips and gravy with him.

Immediately in front of him was a huge black tractor that looked a hundred years old, surrounded by well-kept garden beds full of tulips and daffodils. He walked over to the plaque at its base and started to read as Tyson continued to empty his stomach onto the roadside.

BIG LIZZIE

BIG LIZZIE AND HER REMAINING TRAILER
WERE PURCHASED BY THE PEOPLE OF
REDCLIFFS, AS A FITTING TRIBUTE TO OUR
PIONEERS, IN WHOSE MEMORY WE CELEBRATE
50 YEARS OF PROGRESS AT REDCLIFFS.

He read on as Tyson moved on to coughing accompanied by sporadic spitting. Suthers started in on the chips and gravy.

"Fuck Tys, you won't believe this!" he turned around to face Tyson, who was on his hands and knees.

"This thing was made in Melbourne and they drove it up here doing a thundering 3k's an hour and they got here over a year later! Now that's a fuckin' road trip! Then they connected huge long steel cables with hooks and loops in them and cleared the land with it! Took everything and burnt it!"

He looked around at the parched, red, dusty landscape bereft of trees, and then continued.

"Weighs forty-five tonnes and has a turning circle of sixty metres! Sixty metres mate! That's what I call pulling a 'U'-ey!"

Tyson dragged his head up out of the gutter and asked,

"Where the fuck are we?"

"Where the fuck are we, Tys? We are standing, or kneeling in your case, at the foot of greatness, no less! This magical contraption turned this whole area into an arid desert within a generation, my friend. A fucking generation! This is Big Lizzie, Tys, and we are in a place called Redcliffs, and no, I'm not sharing my chips and gravy with you!"

He shoved a forkful into his mouth to drive the point home and grinned at Tyson.

"Well, where are we going then?"

"To the hospital mate, your face is a mess!"

Tyson felt his nose and cheek for pain but he couldn't feel any. He touched his crushed cheekbone and suddenly he was back hanging off that chain in that room, watching his daughter getting killed on a TV screen. Not even his knees could hold him now as he slumped down, his chin striking the edge of the gutter on the way.

Suthers finished his chips and gravy on his way to pick up his friend.

Chapter 40

Phuket, Thailand
2014

Johnny came out of the darkness, the negligible sounds of his approach further disguised by the cool night breeze blowing back towards the now eerily empty resort. Tyson and Lulu were sitting under a palm tree, the fronds above them swaying and rubbing against the trunk, laying the soundtrack for their silent joy, when they heard Johnny's disembodied voice in the mix.

"Don't know about you guys, but I'm starving!"

They both looked out into the blackness, and it was Lulu who first saw Johnny's smiling white teeth floating in space, complete with rogue hairs blowing across them.

Tyson barely noticed Johnny, lost as he was in Lulu's eyes. He took in every small detail of her, as if focussing on her would bring back the past, make up for nearly half a lifetime lost. He watched her demure smile bounce up against her red cheeks, looked at her small slender hands grasping his, noticed the relaxed slump in her lean shoulders, and the sparkle in her eyes dancing in the pale moonlight.

Tyson's mind meandered helplessly through the fragments of memories he had retained through his lost years, like he was purging them to let her in. He saw a full, rowdy venue transform into a howling void of canned laughter with him at the centre, playing away feverishly. He could hear the sound of his trumpet bouncing around in the empty space, careering off the walls and coming back at him, all at slightly different times, creating a haunting reverb that just added insult to injury.

He saw a playground swing with no one on it, moving backwards and forwards regardless. He could hear a child's squeals of delight, rendered distant and faint by time and the tricks his mind played on him.

He could see Maggie's smile when she was holding baby Lulu in her exhausted arms, he could hear the click clack of Suzie's heels on a cold tiled floor with her cheeky over the shoulder grin. He could see Johnny Barker gesticulating in front of the fire in the hut, an infectious raw curiosity for life emanating from him in long shimmering waves that seemed to distort the very air around them.

And all the while he was staring lovingly at this dream becoming real in front of him, so entranced that he barely noticed the images that had plagued him for years dissolve and slink away into the black night around them.

Lulu looked up at Johnny as he appeared out of the darkness.

"Say goodbye to your past Tyson," Johnny quipped, as if he too could see them leaving, "and don't ask how, OK?"

Lulu jumped up, ran over and hugged Johnny. Tyson watched the tears well up in Johnny's eyes and his face break into a grin that could power a small city.

They all let the moment envelop them silently.

It was Lulu who spoke first.

"Don't know who you are, but welcome to the family, Johnny Barker."

"Uncle Johnny it is then. Let's go eat, shall we? I worked up a healthy appetite in there with my old mates. Who would've thought a bit of reminiscing would be so bloody taxing on the spirit? There's a place not far from here that's open late, run by a philosophical German electrical engineer called Hans and his wife Nui. She does the cooking, he does the drinking!"

***

They both watched Johnny devour three Thai dishes in the same way he did new ideas, with gusto and accompanied by loud intakes of air. He sat and munched and looked at Tyson and Lulu like the father neither of them had had, and again Tyson felt a wave of gratitude flood his being as he appreciated the depth of the gift Johnny had given him. The night had robbed him of his train of thought, and had in some ways broken it forever, so he sat there full of life again, and yet unable to express it. He squeezed Lulu's hand.

It was almost too much to take.

"That was, as the poets say, fucking bewdiful!" Johnny exclaimed, wiping his mouth with a napkin.

He stared back down at the virtually empty plates, tossing Frowny the leftover chicken skin and rice, which was inhaled with an accompanying soundtrack of slobber and smacking lips.

"It was like my taste buds had been deadened til now, and then this explosion of flavour hit me like some kind of culinary wet dream, and then I am gone, mate, I am drooling and my tongue is hanging out of my mouth like a public servant on psych meds. Fuck, it's good to be alive."

He looked past Tyson to the bar.

"Hey Hans, any chance you could bang out a tune for me and my friends with that dusty guitar you've got hanging on the wall?"

"Sure thing, Johnny," he said, signalling to Nui and soon enough she was coming over with three shot glasses, smiling like she knew what was about to come, and Hans was saying,

"If you want to hear my music then you will need to drink those first!" at which they all laughed.

"Do you know '*Khe San*', mate?" someone yelled from the doorway.

Tyson couldn't believe his eyes. Walking towards him, still wearing his dero coat despite the heat, was another ghost from his past. Tyson couldn't mistake Suthers' wide, mischievous grin even after ten years of not seeing him.

Suthers wrapped Tyson in a bear hug that nearly took his breath away, and as his tears flowed he could hear him saying,

"Fuck, I'm glad we found you Tys, I've fuckin' missed you, bro!"

Johnny looked at them both with a smile from ear to ear as Tyson replied,

"I'm glad I found me too."

Suthers turned to Johnny and shook his hand old school style before pulling him in for the hug.

"Looked like things worked out at your end?"

"Yeah mate, Dougy's back at the resort waiting for us. You got the footage?" referring to the CCTV footage of Doug's BDSM cellar.

"Is the pope a catholic?"

Suthers turned his attention to the wide eyed Lulu and watched her trying to make sense of the walking spectacle that was Suthers. Her gaze travelled down to his un-laced second hand army boots.

"Hey sweetheart, you probably don't remember me, since you were, like, five or something last time we met?"

"Oh, I remember you Suthers. I have this memory of being, like, stalked really obviously by you for, like, the last ten years."

"Whoops!" Suthers replied, turning to Tyson before saying,

"Just keeping an eye on my best mate's daughter the only way I could figure out. Probably should've worn a disguise."

"Or stopped eating fish'n'chips dripping with vinegar whilst you were doing it, I didn't even have to look around, I could smell you every time!"

She went over and buried herself in his chest. Tyson noticed that her arms didn't even make it part of the way around his waist. Suthers laughed so much his heart nearly stopped.

Nui made it over with a second round of drinks. The party had begun.

They all took turns dancing with Lulu, laughing and drinking until even Tyson's clunky dance moves started to look fluid and purposeful. Hans bashed out one classic rock tune after another on his old out-of-tune guitar, and even to Tyson it didn't matter.

It was the first time he had felt like dancing in years.

After Hans had worn out his repertoire, they all flopped back down in their chairs, laughing and loving and being... just plain *being*. After a while, Johnny roused himself from the drunken slump he was in, and faced Tyson and Lulu.

"Hans will put you up tonight." he said quietly.

"W... What?" the first word Tyson had uttered in a long time.

He looked quickly across to Lulu, only to discover her sound asleep.

"It's better this way, mate. You two have got a lot of catching up to do; besides, we've got a little bit of housekeeping to do with our dear old mate Dougy."

He turned to Suthers, who was busy ordering food with Nui and gestured for him to come and sit down.

"Does that guy ever stop eating? So, Tys, I figure you've got a few questions for us, then?"

"Yeah, just a few," he retorted, his understatement surrounding the words like drunks at a pub brawl.

Suthers sat down and Johnny began to fill Tyson in on what had brought them to this moment together, and all Tyson could do was grin through tears in the presence of two great friends as Johnny outlined the years of planning that went into what turned out to be a few short moments in a strange resort in a weirder country.

"So Tys, let me know when you're ready to do some gigs, I'm keen if you are." Suthers said, grinning at his old mate.

"Been a while, Suthers. Only picked up the flute a few weeks back, the rest of the ten years I just looked at it."

"Haven't worked with anyone half as good as you since," as he popped the first of a pile of spring rolls into his mouth and happily munched away.

"Me neither."

"Anyways, Tys," Johnny interrupts, "we'll have more time to talk over old times later, after the dust has settled. C'mon Suthers, we've got work to do! I'll catch up with you guys later on, down the track a bit..."

Suthers looked forlornly at his spring rolls.

"But how..." Tyson started, and then a smile crept across his drunken face, "you'll find us, right?"

Johnny smiled at Tyson, and it bored itself right down to the core of his soul. He could feel it, a pure energy, a brotherly exchange to keep them both strong.

"Don't worry mate," Johnny said as he backed away from Tyson and the sleeping Lulu, "got your back. Always will."

EPILOGUE

The Ranong pier was a hive of activity as Tyson, Lulu and Frowny boarded the boat to Myanmar. People around them were shouting in Thai and Myanmar, bags and boxes were being flung on and off the small timber fishing boat as they carefully made their way across the deck. They held each other's hands tightly, and as far as Tyson was concerned, he knew that he'd never let go. Frowny, trailing behind, followed Tyson's feet like he was in a trance.

Tyson watched a man with a handful of passports held high above his head leading around thirty people onto a very small boat. He stared at the panicked expressions on the visa runners' faces. He felt in his pockets for the card Johnny had given him before he had left them at the pier, took it out and studied it. It was a Mastercard with his name on it and, according to Johnny, he would never have to check the balance. There would always be funds available. He looked around before carefully putting it back in his pocket, and smiled as he thought of his greatest friend, the man who dedicated years of his life to reuniting Tyson with his daughter.

Johnny had given him a glimpse of what wealth really was, and he knew now, for the first time in his life, that he was *definitely* one of the lucky ones.

He and Lulu found a spot between a pile of fishing nets and some large foam floats, sat down and stared out at the chaotic business being conducted around them. The air was still and dank and smelled of gutted fish; the whole place had an air of neglect that seemed to have stuck to the sodden beams and worn out pylons. Lulu got out a brochure she had picked up at the customs checkpoint and was staring at the photos of the hundreds of temples they were about to visit when she looked up at her Dad.

"Dad, I was wondering, like, what's with the dog?"

"Frowny? He's my shadow, has been for a while now, and it looks like he's decided to stick like glue, and I kinda like it."

He looked down at his wrinkly companion.

"He might have a face only a mother could love, but his heart is huge and loyal *and* a touch crazy. He's part of the family now."

"I love our new family dad, we're all beautiful lunatics!"

She smiled up at him, and to him it felt like the most blissful thing on earth. After all these years, to be looking into the smiling face of the daughter he thought he had lost.

He could hardly believe his luck.

"Where did you go, Dad?

He knew what she meant right away.

"I just got lost, darling."

She caught a look in his eye and seemed to understand intuitively that it was better to leave the questions alone for a while. She studied the brochure again.

"You know Dad, I think I want to get lost too."

They both stared silently at each other, the feeling of love between them almost palpable to the touch. Tyson felt for the comforting shape of his shakuhachi, and found it.

"Let's go get lost then!"

He put his arm around his little girl, put a smile on his face from ear to ear, and looked out at the broken down pier as their boat pulled sluggishly away, the loud thump of the diesel engine vibrating his body as the exhaust covered the jetty in a final layer of grime.

He let the day come all the way in.

www.ingramcontent.com/pod-product-compliance
Lightning Source LLC
Chambersburg PA
CBHW031339020726
47499CB00005B/1338